"I feel like you're the only friend I have."

The warmth in her brown eyes was a magnet, drawing Josh to her, and he knew he could no more turn his back on her and walk away now than he could fly out the hospital window.

"It probably won't be long until they learn your identity. They're checking missing persons. Did the police tell you that they've put a guard outside your room?"

"Yes, they did," she said, frowning and rubbing her forehead. "I don't know what I was involved in or why I was running, or even *if* I was running."

"You may find out within a few hours. Just relax and try to heal."

"The man who ran me off the road came back, didn't he? That's who you chased, and who shot you?

"That's right. Unfortunately, I didn't catch him. If I had, we might know your identity right now."

She shivered. "I feel so incredibly alone." Her gaze focused on Josh with an intensity that made his pulse jump. "But with you here, I'm not so afraid."

Dear Reader,

As the year winds to a close, I hope you'll let Silhouette Intimate Moments bring some excitement to your holiday season. You certainly won't want to miss the latest of THE OKLAHOMA ALL-GIRL BRANDS, Maggie Shayne's *Secrets and Lies*. Think it would be fun to be queen for a day? Not for Melusine Brand, who has to impersonate a missing "princess" and evade a pack of trained killers, all the while pretending to be passionately married to the one man she can't stand—and can't help loving.

Join Justine Davis for the finale of our ROMANCING THE CROWN continuity, *The Prince's Wedding*, as the heir to the Montebellan throne takes a cowgirl—and their baby—home to meet the royal family. You'll also want to read the latest entries in two ongoing miniseries: Marie Ferrarella's *Undercover M.D.*, part of THE BACHELORS OF BLAIR MEMORIAL, and Sara Orwig's *One Tough Cowboy*, which brings STALLION PASS over from Silhouette Desire. We've also got two dynamite stand-alones: Lyn Stone's *In Harm's Way* and Jill Shalvis's *Serving Up Trouble*. In other words, you'll want all six of this month's offerings—and you'll also want to come back next month, when Silhouette Intimate Moments continues the tradition of providing you with six of the best and most exciting contemporary romances money can buy.

Happy holidays!

Leslie J. Wainger
Executive Senior Editor

Please address questions and book requests to:
Silhouette Reader Service
U.S.: 3010 Walden Ave., P.O. Box 1325, Buffalo, NY 14269
Canadian: P.O. Box 609, Fort Erie, Ont. L2A 5X3

Books by Sara Orwig

Silhouette Intimate Moments

Hide in Plain Sight #679
Galahad in Blue Jeans #971
*One Tough Cowboy #1192

Silhouette Desire

Falcon's Lair #938
The Bride's Choice #1019
A Baby for Mommy #1060
Babes in Arms #1094
Her Torrid Temporary Marriage #1125
The Consummate Cowboy #1164
The Cowboy's Seductive Proposal #1192
World's Most Eligible Texan #1346
Cowboy's Secret Child #1368
The Playboy Meets His Match #1438
Cowboy's Special Woman #1449
*Do You Take This Enemy? #1476

*Stallion Pass

SARA ORWIG

lives with her husband and children in Oklahoma. She has a patient husband who will take her on research trips anywhere, from big cities to old forts. She is an avid collector of Western history books. With a master's degree in English, Sara writes historical romance, mainstream fiction and contemporary romance. Books are beloved treasures that take Sara to magical worlds, and she loves both reading and writing them.

FOREWORD

Stallion Pass, Texas—so named according to the ancient legend in which an Apache warrior fell in love with a U.S. Cavalry captain's daughter. When the captain learned about their love, he intended to force her to wed a Cavalry officer. The warrior and the maiden planned to run away and marry. The night the warrior came to get her, the cavalry killed him. His ghost became a white stallion, forever searching for the woman he loved. Heartbroken, the maiden ran away to a convent, where on moonlight nights she could see the white stallion running wild, but she didn't know it was the ghost of her warrior. The white stallion still roams the area and, according to legend, will bring love to the person who tames him. Not far from Stallion Pass, in Piedras and Lago counties, there is a wild white stallion, running across the land owned by three Texas bachelors, Gabriel Brant, Josh Kellogg and Wyatt Sawyer. Is the white stallion of legend about to bring love into their lives?

Chapter 1

The sound began as a distant rumble. On the wooded hillside that was part of his Texas ranch, Josh Kellogg's hands stilled while he raised his head to listen. The damp, foggy February afternoon had been quiet, but now the sound in the distance was growing in volume. Deciding it was just an approaching car, Josh bent over his barbed wire fence and continued to repair what had been ripped up in a storm during the night.

He raised his head again, listening to the approaching whine grow into a roar that sounded like a car accelerating to an incredibly high speed.

Someone was in a hell of a hurry, he decided. Fog limited visibility, and he knew that a quarter of a mile to the west the road curved, so even on a clear day he wouldn't be able to see much farther. Something was wrong about this noise, however. It wasn't the usual engine rumble made by cars and pickups that traveled past his ranch.

The county road was lightly traveled, mostly by neighbors and people he knew, and Josh was certain this would be neither. He realized his guess was right when a gray sedan came around the curve, tires squealing, going off the road slightly to spew mud and gravel into the air. Immediately behind the gray car was a black one, equally powerful, and moving at an equally dangerous speed. The black four-door sedan gained on the gray car, almost touching its bumper.

"Damnation!" Josh breathed, while he watched the cars flash past as if they were on a raceway and not a curvy country road.

He knew every foot of road in this county, particularly the stretch of asphalt in front of his ranch, and he knew the next curve was too sharp for such high speeds. Concerned they wouldn't make the turn safely, he dashed up the incline.

As Josh reached the road, the lead car swung into the curve. Stunned, he watched as the second car pulled alongside, sideswiping it deliberately.

"Hey!" he yelled in an angry protest, as he raced toward them.

Above the roar of engines, metal clanged against metal. The first driver lost control. The gray car tore off the road and plowed down the ravine, churning up weeds and mud, smashing brush.

Scraping against bushes and branches, the car ran through the creek, hit a tree, rolled over once and smashed into another tree. The sound of metal crumpling mixed with the tinkle of breaking glass and the hiss of steam from the radiator. Then an ominous silence settled. The black car disappeared around the bend and into the fog.

Josh raced back to his green pickup where he snagged his cellular phone to call an ambulance and the sheriff. As he talked, he got his first aid kit and a blanket from the back. Fearing the worst, he rushed back toward the wreck.

As he neared, Josh could see that the car was crushed, the windows completely shattered. Afraid that he wouldn't find anyone alive in the wreckage, he splashed straight into Cotton Creek and waded across. A spiral of smoke rose from the front end of the vehicle, and as he approached, he smelled gasoline.

The closer he got, the stronger the stench became. If any occupants were still alive, Josh knew he had to get them out in a hurry. A red curl of flame licked up from the crumpled hood.

Stopping beside the car, Josh looked inside. A woman was flung facedown across the front seat, her long brown hair hiding her face and shoulders. The buckled roof narrowed the space above her. Jagged shards of glass covered her and the seat. One of her hands was cut and bleeding.

When he tried to open the door, nothing budged, so Josh went around to the passenger side. Reaching through the gaping window, he checked the woman's throat for a pulse.

To his relief, she felt warm to the touch and had a strong pulse. When he pushed her hair away from her face, he saw that she had a deep cut across her temple. She groaned and stirred.

Still bending, he called, "Lady, I have to get you away from this wreck. I can smell gasoline and your car is on fire."

At the sound of his voice, she raised herself up. "I need to get out," she rasped.

Suddenly, Josh found himself gazing into a pair of enormous brown eyes. For a frozen moment they stared at each other, and in that instant he nearly forgot the wreck and the danger.

Then she unfastened her seat belt and scrambled wildly away from him, twisting around and trying frantically to open the door on the driver's side.

She bent almost double to push at the door, making a futile effort to escape.

Josh leaned in and caught her jacket, yanking her toward him. Grasping her beneath her arms, he pulled her to the passenger side. "Let me get you out."

To his surprise, the woman fought him. She jerked away and twisted around to strike at him. He realized she must be in shock, possibly thought he was the man who had run her off the road.

"I want to help you," he told her forcefully, and caught her tightly beneath her arms again, hauling her across the seat and through the broken window. He hoped her clothes—a leather jacket and jeans—would protect her from the jagged glass.

When he swung her into his arms, she fought him again, and he tightened his grip. "Be still!" he snapped. "I'm trying to help you." She quieted, wrapping her arm around his neck, and gazed at him.

Once again Josh stared into eyes that were the color of sweet, dark chocolate. Even with her injuries, he knew she was one of the most beautiful women he had ever seen. His breath caught, and he gazed at her almost in wonder.

She stared back, wide-eyed, her lips slightly parted, while her arm tightened around his neck. He inhaled, and the smell of gasoline finally registered again, as did the awareness of the increasing danger.

"We've got to get away from the car," he muttered, still holding her as he grabbed up his first aid kit and folded blanket.

"My things!" she cried.

"The hell with them." Clutching her tightly, he waded back across the creek, heading west and angling up the ravine. His long legs swiftly put distance between them and the car. She was light, easy to carry, and he was intensely aware of her body pressed against his.

From the top of the slope he glanced back at the car. Flames danced from beneath the smashed hood now. As he watched, they flared and he could see a streak of fire beneath the car. He dodged behind a thick oak and sat down with the woman on his lap, trying to shield her, and bracing for a blast he was certain would happen.

As soon as he sat down, she struggled to break free. "Let go of me!" she cried.

He tightened his grip, holding her against him. This was one stubborn woman. "Stop fighting me! You'll hurt yourself. The car is going—"

There was a *whumpf* as the flames found the gasoline, and a loud blast ended the conversation. Josh leaned around the tree to look.

A fireball shot into the air, yellow and orange flames twisting high through dark green leaves and brown branches. A column of black smoke followed. The ground shook with the blast, and Josh ducked back behind the tree. After a few long seconds he leaned around again.

Bits and pieces of metal, chrome, clothing and paper money rained down. He stared at the money. Some bills fell back into the fire, but others fluttered among the trees, drifting to earth.

He released her slightly, and she raised her head to again stare at him wide-eyed, in obvious shock. "The car?" she whispered.

The wound on her temple was bleeding badly. He would have liked to carry her to his pickup, but Josh decided he'd better clean and bandage the cut on her forehead immediately.

She blinked, and startled him as she once more struggled to get away. He caught her wrists and braced her against the tree, kneeling to face her.

"I have to go!" she cried, grappling with him desperately.

"Where do you have to go?" he demanded, pushing on her shoulders to hold her down.

She gave him another startled look and grew still.

"You're in shock and you're bleeding badly. Just sit tight and let me put some pressure on that cut," he ordered, his patience gone. He scooped her up, stepped around the tree and put her down again with her back to the road. He wanted to keep an eye on the road and he wanted her out of the line of fire in case whoever had run her off the road came back.

She leaned back and watched him. Guessing she wanted to get away in case whoever was after her came back, Josh glanced toward the road.

"You're safe. Don't worry," he said, realizing in his haste to go to the aid of the crash victim, he had left his pistol in his pickup.

She merely stared at him in silence, but she was sitting still and doing what he'd told her to do. Even though her leg was bleeding, judging from the dark stain spreading along the jeans covering her thigh, her head wound needed attention first. He retrieved the brown blanket, shook it out and covered her with it, tucking it around her—and received a trusting look that made his insides tighten.

Josh opened the first aid kit and pulled out some gauze, taking out his knife to cut it. He picked up a bottle of antiseptic, then glanced at her, to find her watching him in silence. While the sedan crackled and burned, Josh heard the noise of an approaching car, then the slam of a car door.

He froze and placed his finger on the woman's lips to silence her. Seconds later he saw a dark figure emerge from the fog and hurry down the ravine toward the crash. The man was fairly nondescript in appearance—medium height and build with brown hair—nothing distinguishing that Josh could see. Whoever had run her off the road had come back.

Hot anger flashed through Josh. The man had attempted murder!

Josh leaned forward to put his mouth near her ear. "Don't move or make a sound," he commanded. "I'll be back."

In spite of the danger and his anger, Josh dimly noticed her perfume. He was aware that his lips were brushing her ear as he whispered to her.

Tearing his attention away, he turned and started running as quietly as he could. But a few seconds later the man's head whipped around in Josh's direction.

Instantly, the stranger switched course, running back up the incline to the road.

Josh stretched out his legs, racing after him and gaining. The man spun around and raised a gun.

Josh dived behind a tree as a blast shattered the quiet, whipping his hat off his head. Then he was racing after the man again.

Once again the other driver spun around to fire. As two more shots rang out, Josh jumped behind a thick tree, but before he reached cover, he felt a hot stab in his arm.

Furious and determined, he rushed forward once more, seeing the shooter top the incline, reach the road and dash for his car.

Josh pushed himself unmercifully, narrowing the distance as the man jumped into the black vehicle and started the engine.

Lunging forward, Josh landed on the trunk, but he couldn't get a grip anywhere. He slid across the smooth metal and fell to the ground.

Swearing in pain as he hit the earth on his wounded arm, Josh rolled over and stared at the license plate, memorizing the number as the car sped away.

He swore again, wishing he had stopped to grab his pistol from his pickup. Staring at the empty roadway, angry and frustrated that the man had escaped, Josh finally got to his feet.

Gray swirls of fog hovered above the land. Josh looked at his blood-covered hand and noticed his jacket sleeve was soaked, as well. He yanked off his jacket and ripped his bandanna from his neck to tie it around his arm. To his relief, it looked as if the bullet had gone through without too much damage. He pulled his jacket on again. Clamping his jaw shut when the pain rocked him, he headed back to where he'd left the woman. On his way he found his hat and jammed it back on his head.

She, as well as the blanket, was gone. At least that meant she didn't have any broken bones. Either that or she was in total shock and going on adrenaline. He scanned the woods and spotted her, making her way slowly up the slope toward the road.

Trying to ignore the pain in his arm, he went after her. When he came close, she looked around and saw him coming. Once again her eyes widened and she started to run.

"Wait a minute, lady!" he called.

He wondered if she had forgotten that he had helped her.

He caught up with her easily and tried to be gentle as he grabbed her arm. "Wait a minute. I want to help you. An ambulance is coming."

She whipped around and fought him, struggling to break free.

Ignoring the blows of her fists, Josh pulled her closer. "Shh, be still. I'm here to help," he repeated quietly.

Her fist struck his injured arm, and he swore as white-hot pain stabbed him. Tightening his grip, he held her, talking softly all the time.

"Easy, just be still. Medical help is coming. I won't harm you. Shh."

She wriggled in his arms and then quieted. While he held her, he was too aware of her soft curves, her exotic perfume, her silky hair. "Let me see about your cuts, okay? You're bleeding badly."

"Yes," she answered.

He released her slowly and looked down into her seductive brown eyes. "You're safe. I promise." Her full lips were like an invitation. "Come sit down."

When she nodded, he led her to a nearby tree, so that she could lean against it while he kept watch—even though he didn't expect her assailant to return.

Josh glanced around and realized he didn't have his medical supplies. "Look, I'll have to go back to get my first aid kit. Will you stay here and wait for me?"

She nodded. "I'll stay," she said quietly.

Wondering whether she would or not, Josh dashed back to where he had left her earlier. He was close enough to the burning wreck to see all the money lying on the ground. He hurried over to pick up a bill—for a hundred dollars, he noted. He picked up another bill—for the same amount.

He glanced in her direction and saw she was sitting and quietly waiting for him this time. He picked up a few more hundreds, gathering them within seconds. He was getting a bad feeling about this, along with eleven one-thousand dollar bills. More bills were scattered all around the wreck. He was certain a lot had to have burned in the blast. She'd been carrying an enormous amount of cash. Stuffing the bills into his pocket, he retrieved the first aid kit and went to help her.

Once there, he knelt beside her. Trying to concentrate, he drew out a gauze pad, ripped the package open and placed the gauze against her head wound. "You're cut," he said. "But the ambulance will be here soon."

"Where am I?"

"On my ranch," he answered as he worked to stop the bleeding from her temple. "You're lucky to be alive. I'm Josh Kellogg."

She was silent, and he gazed into her eyes to see her staring blankly back at him. He wondered who had tried to run her off the road and why. With her looks, it could have been a jealous husband or lover, but with so much cash, she must be involved in something worse. Glancing at her slender fingers, he noticed she didn't wear a ring on her well-manicured hands with bloodred nails.

"Where are we?" she asked.

"This is Piedras County near Stallion Pass, Texas," he replied, glancing at her long legs and then into her thickly lashed eyes again.

"Stallion Pass, Texas?" she repeated, sounding confused. Josh could see uncertainty in her eyes. "My head…"

"Hold this pad against the cut on your temple, and I'll bandage your head."

"You're a doctor?"

"No, I saw you go off the road," he said, meeting the same blank, puzzled expression. "Someone ran you off the road," he explained quietly.

"Someone ran my car off the highway?" she repeated in a questioning tone. Josh knew without doubt that she was in shock.

"What's your name?" he asked her. She frowned, staring back at him.

"My name?" She rubbed her temple. "My head hurts."

"Look, just sit still. Help is on the way." As he started to dab antiseptic on her cut, he looked closer at her hair.

"You're wearing a wig," he said in surprise.

Once again those brown eyes widened, and her hands flew up to her head. She frowned, groaning slightly as she peeled away the wig and studied it. As she did so, long, golden tendrils of her own hair cascaded over her shoulders. He stared at her, once again mesmerized by her beauty.

A beauty, cash and a would-be killer. The three added up to disaster. Josh wanted the ambulance and the sheriff to arrive so he could turn her over to them. She was trouble from her blond hair to her toes.

Trying to ignore his throbbing arm, he turned his attention back to the problem at hand. He wound gauze around her head carefully.

"You have a ranch?" she asked.

"Yep. I'm a cattleman. Where were you headed?"

She frowned again and rubbed her head.

"Give me your hands," he ordered in a no-nonsense voice, and she held them out. He cleaned the cuts on her palms, too aware of her soft skin and slender fingers. Her only jewelry was a plain watch with a leather strap, yet he recognized the expensive brand.

He worked over her swiftly, cleaning and disinfecting the cuts on her right hand and then her left, bandaging the deepest ones. As he worked, he glanced often toward the road, even though he didn't think the other driver would return.

"You must not have any broken bones."

"My head and my leg hurt," she said quietly. Josh gazed over his shoulder through the trees at the still-smoldering wreckage, marveling that she had survived at all, much less with as little damage as she appeared to have.

She had a cut on her throat and he wiped away blood. His face was only inches from hers, and when she met his eyes, he couldn't breathe or move. He was trapped for a long moment, a tingling current rippling along his nerves. Her golden hair was a sharp contrast to her dark eyes, irresistible eyes that held both mystery and invitation.

"So what's your first name?" He tried again.

"I don't know. I can't think...."

Josh noticed that her pupils were uneven, one larger than the other, and he suspected she might have a concussion.

When she winced, he said, "I'm sorry. I'm trying to avoid hurting you." Now, on top of tons of cash and the fact that someone had just tried to kill her, she couldn't or wouldn't give him her name. Plus she wore a wig, a disguise.... Josh's unhappy suspicions about her grew with every discovery, yet until the paramedics arrived, he felt a sense of responsibility for her care.

Even with the cuts and his crude bandages, he found it hard to keep from staring at her, she was so beautiful. Her skin, where it wasn't injured, was silky smooth. Her large eyes made his pulse jump whenever she glanced at him. Her rosy mouth was full and well shaped.

"I'm beginning to hurt all over and my head is pounding. My leg hurts."

"Let me move this blanket and take a look," he said, frowning. Her jeans were ripped and she had a jagged gash high on the inside of her thigh. "I'm going to cut your jeans and put disinfectant on that cut," he added. "You'll feel this one."

"All right," she said. "You told me your name. I've forgotten—"

"It's Josh. Josh Kellogg." He whipped out his knife and began cutting the blood-soaked blue denim, too aware of his fingers against her warm thigh. He glanced at her and saw she had leaned her head against the trunk of the tree and closed her eyes.

"Lady," he said, shaking her gently, and she opened her eyes to look at him. "You might have a concussion. I think you should stay awake until the medics arrive. All right?"

"I just wanted to close my eyes."

"Try to stay awake for a while." He looked into her eyes and recognized the same confused, blank stare. "Do you know where you were headed?"

"I don't know," she whispered, and frowned. "I can't think...."

Her leg, too, was silky smooth, and he was conscious of each brush of his fingers against her. The gash ran along the inside of her thigh, starting above her knee and continuing on for about six inches. "I can cut away your jeans, disinfect your wound and bandage it, which should stop the bleeding, but the gash runs high on your leg."

"Go ahead and do whatever you need to," she answered vaguely, and he wondered whether anything he was saying was registering with her.

It registered with him. He would have to get up close and personal. Josh drew a deep breath and tried to keep his attention strictly on the job, yet it was impossible to avoid being aware of her firm thigh, impossible to keep from noticing her fancy, lacy pink panties. Despite the cool February weather he was sweating.

He heard her gasp in pain. "I'm sorry. I'm trying to avoid hurting you," he said. In seconds he had her leg bandaged, and let out a sigh of relief.

He shed his denim jacket, which had grown even more soaked with blood while he worked over her injuries.

"You're hurt," she observed in a sleepy voice.

"I don't think it's bad," he said, peeling away his bloody bandanna. The bullet had gone through without hitting bone or lodging in his muscle. He poured antiseptic on the wound and gasped as it burned sharply. Then he pulled out his handkerchief to wrap it around his arm.

"I can help you," she said, reaching out to tie the handkerchief for him. He met her gaze, and in spite of the throbbing pain in his arm, he was intensely aware of her. She looked down at the handkerchief. "You're hurt worse than I am."

"No, I'm not," he replied. "Thanks." Gritting his teeth, he pulled his jacket on again. "I'm going up on the road to watch for the ambulance," he said, standing.

Her hand shot out and closed around his wrist, and the moment she touched him, it was as if he had been given an electrical shock. Her touch sent tingles through his entire body.

"Don't leave me, please!" Panic swam in her eyes, and he wanted to put his arms around her and hold her. Josh knew that protective feeling was ridiculous. She was a stranger. But her grip on his wrist was like iron, and the lady could be mule-stubborn when she wanted to be.

"I'm not going far."

She shivered. "Please."

"Look, I'll be right up there at the top of that incline. I want to make sure they can find us down here. I'd like to tie some gauze to a tree so they'll know where we are. Then I'll come right back."

"I don't want you to leave."

"I can't go if you don't turn me loose." Not without hurting you, he thought. Stubborn, stubborn. Was she accustomed to getting her way about everything? He looked at her face and decided she might be. He wiggled his hand to free it. "I promise I'll be back."

She released his wrist, and he left, scrambling up to the edge of the road. Yanking the cellular phone from his pocket, Josh punched in the numbers, telling the dispatcher to pass on the word about the gauze marker. Then he tied a long strip of it to a low-hanging branch of an oak on the roadside.

When he returned to the woman, she was watching him intently.

"See? I promised I'd be back and I am. I keep my promises," he said.

She nodded solemnly.

"Do you know who was after you?"

"After me?" she asked, frowning. "I don't know what you mean."

"Another car was right behind you. Do you remember?"

"No," she said, looking at him with round eyes.

"Do you remember your name yet?"

When she shook her head, Josh glanced over his shoulder

at the burning wreckage. Only a few small flames and wisps of black smoke rose from it now. "I'm going to look for any identification that might have survived the explosion. A lot of your clothes flew into the air. I'll be right back."

As he walked around the burning car, he picked up many more hundred-dollar bills, but he finally gave up hope of finding a purse or identification. He went back to hand her the money.

She looked at the stack of bills in her hands. "This means nothing to me."

"Most people don't carry cash like that."

Her eyes flew wide. "So what are you trying to say?"

"Tell me your name," he ordered forcefully.

She inhaled and frowned and rubbed her brow, looking away from him. "I can't remember—"

He grabbed her shoulders and yanked her around to face him. "Think. Something should come to you."

"I don't know," she said, looking even more worried.

Nodding, Josh released her, finally deciding she really didn't remember her identity.

At the whine of a siren in the distance, he stood, tucking her money beneath the blanket. "Here they come. I'll go—"

"Please, stay with me," she said, once again catching his wrist in a tight grip.

He looked at her white-knuckled fingers closed around his wrist. At her touch, his skin tingled and a protective urge welled up in him.

"I'll be here with you," he said in a gentle voice, smoothing her hair from her face. "I'll come right back. I told you, I keep my promises."

"I feel alone, except for you," she said, shivering and releasing his wrist.

Josh didn't want her relying on him. He wanted to hand her over to the professionals and tell her goodbye. He tucked the blanket closer around her. ''Help is coming right now. The medics will take you to a hospital. Now I need to go up to the road and lead them down here.''

She released her grip on his wrist, and he gave her shoulder a light squeeze before he left her. As he climbed out of the ravine, he glanced back to find her leaning around the tree, watching him solemnly. Turning, he went on to the road where he waited. In seconds the ambulance whipped around the curve into sight and slowed, cutting the siren, but leaving lights flashing.

The first medic that emerged was tall, brown-haired and freckled. He thrust out his hand. ''Ty Whitman,'' he said.

Chapter 2

"Josh Kellogg," Josh said, shaking the paramedic's hand. "She's down there," he added, pointing. "She's cut badly and doesn't remember anything before the wreck. I had to get her out of the car before it exploded."

"Okay, we'll take it from here. Looks like you got hurt, too."

"It's not too bad. Gunshot," Josh said tersely. "Take care of her first."

"We can take care of both of you," the man said. "You look like you need help badly. You've bled a lot."

The Piedras County sheriff's car was right behind them and a deputy's car behind it. Josh went ahead, leading the paramedics to the woman.

As they bent over her to talk to her, Sheriff Will Cordoba scrambled down the incline and walked over, standing behind the paramedics. His deputy nodded at Josh as he passed to look at the wrecked car.

Josh gritted his teeth at the pain that enveloped him as a

medic treated his wound. During the process, Will Cordoba approached. The sheriff was stocky, black-haired and two years older than Josh, and the two had known each other all their lives. Josh was glad to see him.

"That is one good-looking woman," the sheriff said. "What happened and what happened to you?"

"I don't think she remembers anything," Josh said, shaking hands with Will. "I think she's got a concussion."

"Is she from anywhere around here?"

"I've never seen her before. I'd remember."

"Yeah, who wouldn't?"

"Will, someone tried to kill her. A car ran her off the road."

"You saw it happen?" the sheriff demanded.

"Yep. I was mending a fence when two cars sped past. When they reached this curve, the other car sideswiped hers, and she went off the road right over there. That wreck was no accident."

"Looking at her, I'll bet a jealous husband is involved."

"There may be more to it than that," Josh said, thinking about the money she was carrying.

"What about you?"

"I pulled her out of the car," Josh began, relating everything that had happened.

"Did you shoot at him?"

"Hell no. I'd left my pistol in my pickup. I was so worried about whoever was in the crash that I just grabbed my first aid kit."

"You went after him without your pistol?"

"Yeah."

"You're lucky that shot wasn't to the right a little. You wouldn't be here to tell me about it."

"I'm all right."

"Sure. But if someone tried to kill her and you were a witness, you may be in as much danger as she is now."

"I got a license number. It was a black, four-door sedan with dark windows. The man was alone." Josh watched the sheriff jot down the plate number and call it in along with the description of the car.

"Want something for pain?" the paramedic asked Josh. He shook his head. "No, thanks."

"Let them look at that at the hospital. This is a temporary fix," the man said.

"Thanks."

Josh nodded as the paramedic moved away.

"I put her money under the blanket," Josh said, when Will had ended his phone call. "She's carrying too much cash. When the car exploded, bills flew everywhere. You'll find more. I just picked up a few of them."

Will Cordoba walked over to the paramedics, talking to them a few minutes before bending down to talk to the woman. She reached beneath the blanket and pulled out the fistful of money to hand to him.

Frowning, he counted the cash and whistled, thumbing through hundred- and thousand-dollar bills. Then he returned to Josh.

"I want to check the serial numbers on this money."

"I don't think she robbed a bank," Josh remarked dryly.

"You don't know," Will said.

"Look at her. Who would forget her?"

"Maybe, but I'm still going to check the numbers on these bills. This is a hell of a lot of money to be carrying. Nobody carries cash like this. She's mixed up in something bad right up to her big brown eyes."

"Someone wants her dead, and they may come back again to finish the job. She could have witnessed a crime, Will. Or she could have committed one."

"Yep. The ambulance will take her to a San Antonio hospital and they'll take her in. With this kind of money, she won't be indigent."

"She can't tell them about hospitalization. I'll call my doctor. He'll probably be willing to see her."

"Good. I'll have to contact the Bexar County sheriff. He may want to put a guard on her room today," Will said as he pushed back his wide-brimmed hat and rubbed his forehead.

"Until she remembers who she is or you locate her family, Will, she doesn't have anyone."

"I'll get on this right away. If she's going to a hospital, she shouldn't leave cash like this around. You want to keep it for her?"

"I'll never see her again," Josh replied emphatically. "You keep it at your office."

"Okay, if she wants me to. I'll ask her. I'll see what I can find out about her when I get back to the office."

Josh suffered a twinge of guilt when he thought how she had gripped his wrist and asked him to stay with her.

"As far as your not seeing her again, you're going to have to go to the hospital to have your wound treated, and I'll need a report from you. I'm sure the Bexar County sheriff will want a report. You'll be in that ambulance, buddy, and you'll have to stay awhile at the hospital."

"No way. I can drive myself, so I'll have a way to get home. I don't need an ambulance or a damned ambulance bill afterward."

"Your hat's got a nasty rip in it."

"A lot of things happen out here," Josh said, not caring to discuss getting shot at any longer.

"My deputy and I will go over the crash site. I'll see you in the San Antonio hospital."

"Yeah," Josh said reluctantly, leaving the sheriff and heading over to observe the paramedics. It was another fifteen minutes before they had the woman in the ambulance. After a terse argument, Josh turned to go back to his pickup. He had to go to the hospital or it would stir up a flurry, since he had a gunshot wound and had to fill out reports. But he wanted to walk away right now and never see the woman again. He had a grim foreboding that made him feel he should stay away from her. She was involved in something that was a life-and-death matter. Whatever she was running from, the whole thing reeked of illegitimacy.

Yet he couldn't keep from feeling responsible. She couldn't remember anything, a condition that should pass within the next few hours. He had seen plenty of cowboys with concussions in rodeos—he'd even had one himself—and the memory loss was temporary. Until she remembered or until a family member came looking for her, she was totally alone.

He sighed and called his family doctor. Then he climbed into his pickup to follow the ambulance into San Antonio.

After being treated in emergency, Josh was tempted to just leave and let the police hunt him down for his statement. Yet Will had helped out when Josh had had cows rustled a few years ago, and he didn't want to run out on the sheriff now. Reluctantly, he found the woman's room number.

A uniformed policeman already stood outside her door. Josh introduced himself and said that he would be in the waiting room.

Half an hour later Will appeared with a grim set to his jaw. "Since she's in this hospital and in a different county now, I've talked to the Bexar County sheriff and they've provided police protection for her. The sheriff is keeping this low-key and giving the press as little information as possible."

"That'll be safer for the woman," Josh agreed.

"I expected to find you down in the emergency waiting area. They're not supposed to give out her room number, so how'd you get it?"

Josh gave him a lopsided grin, and Will shook his head.

"I'll bet you flashed that million-dollar smile of yours and some cute little thing just gave you what you wanted."

"I wouldn't have put it that way," Josh replied with amusement, "but she was cooperative. And you think I have a million-dollar smile? I'm flattered!"

Will drew himself up. "I'm quoting Jolene," he snapped. "As far as I'm concerned, you've just got a full set of teeth, which is a plus in these parts."

Josh grinned. "Shucks. Your secretary is married."

"How you stay single, I'll never know. Women seem to melt when you walk by," the sheriff told him.

"Don't I wish," Josh replied mildly. "And with my life on the ranch, it's easy to stay single. Let's get this report done so I can go home."

"You have to wait for the Bexar sheriff. Don't skip out on him. All right now," Will said, raising a clipboard and getting out a pen.

Josh shook his head, annoyed that he would have to hang around the hospital.

"They're running a missing-person check, and so have we. So far, nothing," Will said.

"What about the car that hit her?"

"They ran the license number you got. It was a stolen vehicle, so that's a dead end. How's she doing?" Will asked, looking toward her room.

"I don't have any idea. My responsibility stopped when the paramedics took over," Josh said, feeling another guilty twinge about the woman. He'd had fuzzy moments from a concussion in a rodeo, and they weren't pleasant, but he'd been surrounded by friends who knew him well. He could imagine the worries she might have without anyone around who knew her, especially with someone wanting to kill her.

"Could you recognize the guy again?"

"Nope. He was of a medium build, shorter than I am. His head was covered with a cap, so I'm not sure about hair color, but what little I could see might have been brown. He was running and shooting, so I never did get a good look at him.''

"Okay. Tell me again, slowly, what happened from the first moment you saw them on the road.''

Josh related the incident while Will wrote it all down. As they talked, Josh saw nurses wheel the woman out of her room, and he guessed they were taking her for tests. The guard sauntered along behind them.

"Now I have to type up all this,'' Will said, putting away his pen. "You know, you might be in danger now. You're a witness and that guy doesn't know you didn't get a good look at him. You better start packing your pistol.''

"I'll be all right. I'm just a cowboy, and he's not going to worry about me.''

"Watch your back, Josh. She's carrying a lot of money. And if you spot him again, don't be the tough guy and go after him by yourself. Leave that to us.''

"Will, I'm not going to be around that woman at all.''

"Maybe not, but you're involved. And remember—stay here until the Bexar sheriff arrives. In the long run, it'll save you the hassle of having to drive back to town.''

"Yeah, yeah,'' Josh grumbled. He shook hands with Will, who turned and left. Strolling down the hall, Josh got out his cellular phone and called his stepmother to tell her where he was. When he couldn't reach her, he left a message and then called Drake Browning, his ranch foreman.

After another half hour of waiting, Josh told the guard where the sheriff could find him and went to the hospital cafeteria for the lunch that he'd missed earlier. It was late in the afternoon before he got tired of sitting in the cafeteria and went back to wait in the hall outside the woman's room. Twice he called the sheriff's office, and both times was told that the officer was on his way to the hospital.

Eventually a doctor emerged from the woman's room and crossed the hall to Josh. She extended her hand as she approached him.

"I'm Dr. Vandenberg, Tom Girard's niece. Are you Josh Kellogg?"

"Yes. Doc told me he couldn't get into the city, but he said he would call you, so thanks for taking the woman as your patient."

She smiled. "Glad to do it. My uncle spoke highly of you."

"He's been great to my family. Does your patient remember her own name yet?" he asked the tall, blond physician.

She shook her head. "No, she doesn't recall anything significant from her past. I want to be notified as soon as she remembers, and I know the sheriff does, too. You didn't know her before the wreck?"

"No, I was just a witness."

"She doesn't remember whether she has any family or not. My uncle vouched for you, so I can trust you with her. And it's nice that you're here for her because she feels very alone."

"Actually, I'm just here because I'm supposed to wait to see the Bexar County sheriff," Josh said stiffly.

"Oh? I hope you'll go see my patient. She's frightened and alone. She's talked about you quite a bit."

That wasn't what Josh wanted to hear. He glanced past the physician toward the closed door. "I can't imagine she's frightened now."

"Well, she is. Can you stay a little while with her and talk to her?" the physician asked. "It would mean a lot."

"Sure," Josh agreed with reluctance.

"Hopefully she'll have family show up soon, searching for her. From what I understand, both sheriffs are checking missing persons. And the sheriff wants a guard on her because, according to what you told him, someone ran her off the road.''

"Yes, they did. Quite deliberately.''

She nodded. "She's lucky to be alive and lucky she wasn't hurt much worse. And lucky you were there. Thanks for being a Good Samaritan.''

"Anyone would have done what I did.''

"I don't think so,'' she replied. "I heard you got shot.''

"It's nothing,'' Josh answered, wanting to end the conversation.

"Well, thanks for your help and kindness,'' she said, before walking away.

Josh watched her go and silently swore to himself. He didn't want to get pulled into knowing the mystery woman. In a few of those moments alone with her, back on his ranch, there had been a volatile chemistry between them and he didn't want to feel any such thing again—not with this woman.

Putting off going in to see her in hopes that the sheriff would come and the matter would be taken out of his hands, Josh paced restlessly to the window. His arm throbbed, and he wanted to go home. He hated hospitals, particularly this one, where his father had died. He hated being back inside it.

Josh remembered looking into her big eyes as she'd gripped his wrist. With a sigh, he decided he couldn't walk out on someone who needed help. Wondering what he was getting himself into, he knocked lightly on the door.

When she called, "Come in,'' he entered a room that had pale green walls and one beige vinyl chair. The woman was sitting up in bed. His bandage around her head had been replaced by a more professional one. She wore a pale blue hospital gown and had a white sheet across her lap. The short sleeves of the hospital gown revealed long, slender arms with well-toned muscles, as if she worked out. Even with the bandage and the hospital gown, she still stole his breath with her cascade of golden hair, big eyes and full lips. Color was returning to her skin making her cheeks rosy, and she seemed more composed.

"Thanks for staying, Mr. Kellogg," she said as he walked to the bedside to look at her.

"It's Josh. They told me you still don't remember anything."

"Only things after the wreck. Before the car accident, I'm drawing a blank. I don't remember the wreck at all. Sit down, won't you? I really appreciate what you've done."

"They expect your memory to return soon. And your family is probably searching for you now. They may even find you before your memory kicks in."

"All I know is I have something I'm running away from," she said, frowning. "And someone tried to kill me. I think I need my memory back quickly. Anyway, thanks for being here. Even though we're strangers, at the moment I feel like you're the only friend I have."

The warmth in her brown eyes was a magnet, drawing him to her, and he knew he could no more turn his back on her and walk away now than he could fly out of the hospital window.

"It probably won't be long until they learn your identity. They're checking missing persons. And as I said, I'm sure your parents or husband are looking for you."

She fluttered her hands. "I don't have a wedding ring. Maybe I'm single."

"Maybe, but the lack of a ring isn't solid proof. The Piedras County sheriff has your money, by the way. He didn't think you should have that much cash with you in the hospital. He gave me a hundred dollars to bring to you so you can buy things while you're here. If you want more, here's his phone number." Josh put a slip of paper on the table beside her bed. "Did they tell you that they've put a guard outside your room?"

"Yes, they did," she said, frowning and rubbing her forehead. "I don't know what I was involved in or why I was running or even *if* I was running."

"You may find out within a few hours. Just relax and do what your doctor says and try to heal."

He stood with his hands on his hips, and she studied his fingers. "No wedding ring. No wife at home waiting for you?"

"Nope. I'm not married. One of my stepmothers is living with me right now, and I've already called and left a message for her, telling her where I am."

"You said one of your stepmothers. How many do you have?"

"Five."

Her eyes widened. "That's a lot of stepmothers."

"My dad drew women like picnics draw flies." Josh pulled the chair near the bed, shed his denim jacket and sat down.

"And I'll bet you're just like him," she said with a smile.

"I'm not one bit like my father," Josh replied gruffly. "Now my half brothers, that's different."

"I'm sorry. I didn't mean…you're just a good-looking guy and—"

"That's okay. Forget it."

"The man who ran me off the road came back, didn't he? That's who you chased, and who shot you?" she asked quietly.

"That's right. Unfortunately, I didn't catch him."

Her eyebrows arched. "I'm glad you didn't. You might have been hurt much worse. I feel responsible that you were shot."

"You didn't have anything to do with it. That guy shot

me. I'd like to have caught him. And if I had, we might know your identity right now.''

She shivered. "I feel so incredibly alone." Her gaze came back to Josh and focused on him with an intensity that made his pulse jump. "With you here, I'm not so afraid.''

"You have a guard outside, so you don't need to be afraid at all," he replied.

Once again he was caught in her gaze, while his nerves zinged. The mood was swiftly going from two friendly strangers to a man-woman thing, and Josh couldn't seem to stop it. He was mesmerized, unable to pull his eyes away. And she wasn't doing any better. She ran her tongue across her lower lip and inhaled. With an effort he shifted, leaning forward with his elbows on his knees, and looked away.

Silence stretched and he stared at the floor, trying to let his jangled nerves calm and his body cool.

"It would be easier if you had a temporary name, something I could call you until you remember your real name," he said, knowing with every sentence he was getting more involved. "What should I call you?"

"I don't know," she answered, rubbing her forehead.

He tilted his head to study her. "Amelia, Margo, Nina, Caroline, Trixie, Becky.''

"Trixie?''

"I'm giving you the names of my mother and my stepmothers," he said, smiling at her.

She smiled in return. She was stunningly beautiful even with bruises beginning to darken. When she smiled, his breath caught and his pulse leaped into double time.

"I don't know. I don't feel like a Trixie or Nina or Amelia. I don't feel like anyone," she said, her smile vanishing. She reached over to take his wrist again. "You don't have to stay here with me. I can get along, but thank you for coming and thank you for visiting.''

The moment she touched him, the contact was as electrifying as it had been before. Without thinking, he covered her hand with his, marveling at its softness. She was getting to him, and he realized it had been a long time since he had let a woman do that.

"You're not alone. I told you I'll stay awhile longer. The sheriff said he would call if he finds out who you are or gets any leads." Josh was aware they were still holding hands, and he wondered whether she noticed. He strongly suspected she had been showered with attention from men all her life, and holding hands like this was insignificant to her. He released her hand, but wanted to reach for it again. "We need to give you a name. You want Jane Doe?"

"No, I don't."

"It would help if I could call you something," he said, thinking that stubborn will of hers was beginning to resurface. He tilted his head. "How about Amanda, Beth or Laurie?"

She smiled again. "All right. I'll be Laurie for you," she said, and the idea that the name was for him alone made it far too personal. The air crackled with the tension between them.

"Laurie it is, then," he said. His voice had grown huskier and his gaze dropped to her mouth, and he wondered what it would be like to kiss her. Instantly, he tried to pull his thoughts away from that track. This lady was in deep trouble, someone wanted her dead and her past could be filled with complications. And even under the best circumstances, he didn't want to get involved with anyone.

"You said you're single. Any woman in your life right now?" she asked.

"No, there's not. And there's not going to be anytime soon," Josh said, a little too forcefully, as if he were trying to remind himself of his situation.

She laughed softly, and he felt another jolt of his heart.

Why was she getting to him so easily? He guessed it was her beauty that was dazzling him. She probably turned men to mush everywhere she went, and he was no different from the others.

"You sound so definite. You don't like women?"

His brows arched. "Oh, yes," he drawled in a husky voice, "I do like women."

"So then why be so certain that you won't have a woman in your life?" she asked.

"I've got my hands full trying to run my ranch, and I have to deal with my stepmothers. I don't need another female in my life or another complication," he said, knowing he was skirting the real reasons. In this case, he absolutely didn't want to get involved because, in spite of her looks or maybe because of them, she was in trouble.

Yet his life was getting complicated right now, and every second with her drew him closer and involved him more with the lovely, mysterious stranger who couldn't remember her own name or why someone wanted to kill her.

"Even so, you're here with me," she said, echoing his thoughts. "Other than you and the sheriff, I don't feel like I can trust anyone. I can't even be sure about the nurses."

"You have a guard right outside your door and you can call him at any time. And for now, I'll stay with you."

"They told me I could go to the hospital cafeteria. I don't know when I last ate, but I'm getting really hungry. Will you go with me?"

"Sure," Josh replied, thinking he might as well be sinking in quicksand. He stood as she swung her legs out of bed. She was wearing only that short, blue cotton hospital gown. Her legs were long and shapely, and he drew another swift breath, having to make an effort to keep from staring.

"Can you hand me that robe?" she asked. Their fingers brushed, a feathery contact that he felt down to his toes.

With a graceful movement, she slipped into the short,

cotton hospital robe and belted it around her tiny waist. She lifted her long, silky hair over it and shook her head, causing her hair to swirl across her shoulders.

"Want a wheelchair to ride downstairs?" he asked.

She shook her head. "No. They told me I could get up if I wanted to. If I get light-headed, I'm to let them know."

"Since I'll be with you, the guard won't have to tag along."

"That could put you in danger."

Josh laughed. "I doubt if there's any danger in the cafeteria. The time it could be dangerous here is in the dead of night, when things quiet down. I'm not worried about it."

"You don't scare easily, do you?"

"Not easily enough," he remarked dryly, thinking that if he had any sense, he would get far away from her.

"The doctors told me that they'll wake me up through the night. If I can remember everything, I'll be released in the morning."

"I still think you'll have relatives or friends show up anytime now," he told her.

"I hope so," she said.

He hoped so, too, but he didn't voice it aloud.

As they left her room, Josh explained to the guard they were going to the cafeteria. They rode down in an elevator, and Josh was all too aware of the strangers around them. They were riding with two other men and a woman. On the third floor, another man got on. And then Josh realized one of the men was staring intently at Laurie.

Chapter 3

Josh tensed, every nerve coming alive. He moved closer to Laurie, slipping his arm around her waist. She looked up at him in surprise, but he kept his eyes on the stranger who was watching her. The man looked at Josh. His face flushed and he looked away.

Josh glanced around the elevator, saw *everyone* looking at Laurie and realized people simply noticed her because of her beauty.

He relaxed and took a deep breath, his arm dropping from her waist.

"What was all that about?" she asked when they stepped into the hall and the other people scattered.

"That guy was staring at you. My nerves are on edge. Then I realized they were all staring at you because you're pretty."

"Thank you," she said politely.

"I'm keeping watch." Walking along the hallway, he couldn't stop from regarding each stranger with suspicion.

Josh wasn't hungry. When they reached the almost-empty cafeteria, he got pop while Laurie ordered a ham-and-cheese sandwich. He chose a table in a corner, where he could watch the door and the people in the room. He wanted to be able to see everything that was happening.

Laurie smiled at him as she sat down. "So, Josh, tell me about your life."

"It's simple. I ranch, raise cattle, live on Cotton Creek. I've lived here all my life."

"Where did you go to school?"

"In Stallion Pass. It's the closest town."

"Stallion Pass? That's an interesting name. Do you know why it's called that?"

"There's an old legend about a ghostly white stallion— really an Apache warrior who was killed because he wanted to marry a U.S. Cavalry officer's daughter," Josh replied with a smile.

"So what's the legend?"

"The white stallion is still supposed to inhabit these parts and bring love to the person who tames him. What's funny is that there has been a real, wild white stallion in Piedras and Lago Counties for years. It's not the same horse, of course, but there's been one. Right now, I'm owner of the current one. A friend caught the stallion and gave him to me."

Her eyes twinkled. "So true love is coming into your life."

He grinned. Amused, he shook his head. "Nope. I don't believe that foolish old legend and I'm not looking for love."

"Why not, Josh Kellogg? I thought everyone was looking for love or had already found it."

"Naw. I told you, I have a busy life, too busy for marriage."

"Oh, my. Too busy for love? It must be cold and lonely. Maybe you need rescuing as much as I do."

Josh knew they were flirting, and it was a pleasant diversion to banter with a sexy lady, yet he also knew every second with her was a threat to his well-being.

"No rescue needed here."

She smiled. "So tell me more about your family and all those stepmothers."

"My dad is no longer living, and right now one of my stepmothers lives with me, as I said. But she'll be moving out in two weeks because she's marrying again. I have two younger brothers who are in college. Actually, they're half brothers. But we're pretty close." He waved his hand. "That's it."

"I suspect there's a lot more to you than that," she said, leaning closer and smiling at him, making him feel as if his life were of monumental interest to her. Her steady gaze shut out everything else. He forgot danger, other people, his surroundings, lost once again in her eyes and knowing he'd better rally more resistance to the pretty lady. "So tell me about your brothers."

Josh shrugged. "Kevin's the charmer. Like our dad. And he's irresponsible like our dad. Ben is reliable."

"Like you, I'll bet. What do you do for entertainment? Who're your friends?"

"Right now I'm busy working, so having fun is way down the list. I do like dancing with a pretty woman," he said, unable to resist. "I also like having lunch with a pretty woman."

"Oh, my," she said, tilting her head to study him. "I can't believe there's no woman in your life if you like things like that. And if you're busy with work, which means I'm keeping you from your work right now."

"It's worth it," he said with a smile. "My broken fences

will still be there tomorrow, and I can fix them then. In the meantime, this is a lot more interesting.''

''For a little while maybe I'll be Laurie and forget what's out there in the world waiting for me. At least until memory brings it all back. Somehow right now, it feels good to just be a woman talking to a good-looking cowboy, with nothing to fear or worry about.''

''That's great, but don't lull yourself into letting down your guard.''

''Against the bad guys or against you? Do I have to be careful around you, Josh Kellogg?'' she said teasingly.

''No, you don't,'' he replied. ''We won't have enough of a future together for you to have to be careful.''

''A person falling in love doesn't necessarily worry about the future. So what happens if I fall in love with my rescuer?'' she asked, her eyes sparkling.

Josh knew she was teasing, flirting for the fun of it. Even after the ordeal she had been through, she was coming to life before his eyes, radiating vitality. ''I think it's a whole lot more likely that your rescuer is the one who's going to do the falling. You're the prettiest gal around here, and this is the most enjoyable lunch I've had in a heck of a long time.'' He reached across the table to smooth her hair away from her face.

She laughed. ''That doesn't say a lot for me, because I'll bet you don't eat lunch at all, or you eat with your cattle while you're working. Right?''

He nodded. ''Yep, but it's the most fun I've had anytime lately, day or night.''

''*This* lunch? You must be working too hard! So when do you go dancing with pretty women? Every Saturday night?''

He grinned. ''Last Saturday night I delivered a calf, put out a grass fire that was started by someone tossing a cigarette and got to bed about four in the morning. I don't remember the last time I went dancing, but it's back there in my past somewhere.''

"The Saturday before last?''

He thought for a moment. "I worked until twelve on a hay baler that was broken.''

"I still say that maybe we both needed rescuing.''

"And you're ready, willing and able to rescue me?'' he asked softly, touching her cheek again.

She laughed and waved her hands. "Touché. No. I'm not ready to rescue you and not able to, either. I have to get my memory back before I do anything. I don't even know my name,'' she said solemnly.

"You will,'' he said.

She took dainty bites of the sandwich, but several times she closed her eyes to chew, as if she were eating a magnificent gourmet meal instead of a simple ham-and-cheese sandwich. "This is so good. I was terribly hungry and this tastes marvelous.''

"That's good. If I'd known you were so hungry, I could have brought something in that might be tastier.''

"This is great.'' She dabbed at her mouth with her napkin and studied him. "You take life pretty seriously, don't you?''

"Someone has to,'' he replied.

"Do you want me to stop prying into your life?''

"Nope. There's nothing there I mind anyone knowing, only it's not all that fascinating. It's pretty damn simple.''

"You don't care what I ask?''

"Fire away,'' he said. Laurie finished eating and pushed her plate aside. She leaned forward with her hands folded together on the table, and he reached over to touch her fingers. "You or someone else did your nails not too long ago.''

"I don't remember,'' she said, frowning and studying her hands. She took a deep breath and looked up at him. "Just now you said someone needs to take life seriously. Who doesn't in your life?''

"That's a question no one who lives in these parts has to ask. My dad was a charming, fun-loving, easygoing man. I told you, he drew women to him effortlessly. But he also didn't take responsibility for things in his life, so I've been trying to run our ranch and now I'm just trying to save it. He gambled, loved women and parties and a good time. And he spent money without a thought for how much he had or where the next dollar was coming from.''

"Wow," she said, growing solemn, and he touched her cheek.

"Don't look so serious. It's what I'm used to and have lived with for thirty-three years. I'm making a go of things. My dad always meant well, but he just didn't stop to think about consequences. He was lovable and, in his own way, good to me, and that's more than a lot of people have. Even with all the problems, I miss him. He died two years ago.''

"I'm sorry…. So you're the responsible one. What about the brothers you told me you have?''

"They're younger and in college, and I'm running the ranch, which is a good, productive spread on prime land.''

"And there's no woman in your life because you're so busy working? Is that it?''

"Basically, yes.''

"You ever want there to be a woman in your life or are you one of those confirmed-bachelor-forever men?''

"I guess I'm one of those bachelors. I watched my father go through all those marriages. I've lived too closely with hurt and anger. There have been enough marriages in my life to sour me on it forever. Besides, I might not be one bit better at making a marriage last than my father was. After all, a broken home is all I've ever known.''

"Yet you're not scared to flirt with me a little.''

"Naw. Twenty-four hours from now you'll probably be

gone from my life forever, so today I can flirt and come on a little strong and it doesn't matter.''

"You're toying with my affections."

"No more than you're toying with mine," he retorted.

She laughed. "Maybe it's a way of avoiding thinking about my problems."

"It sure as hell is a way to avoid thinking about mine. No, sitting here looking into your big brown eyes, wondering what it would be like to kiss you—that's a heck of a lot more fun than what I have waiting at home."

"Oh, my!" she said, fanning herself.

He was enjoying flirting with her, but he knew he should stop. "Ready to go back to your room?" he asked, feeling restless and on display in the cafeteria, where people came and went steadily.

"Yes, I am."

He moved close beside her and took her arm, aware of a faint scent of perfume mixed with antiseptic.

He was just as edgy going back upstairs to her room, but he had realized she was going to draw attention wherever she went. He hoped the Bexar sheriff was upstairs waiting, but to Josh's disappointment, when he asked the guard, the sheriff still hadn't shown up.

In her room, Laurie sat on the bed while he dropped back down into the chair. "I like having you here, but now I think I'm keeping you from all sorts of jobs you should be doing. When you want to go, it's okay," she said. "You don't have to stay."

"Now you're willing to send me on my way. You had a death grip on my arm earlier when I tried to leave you."

"You were my lifeline. You were the only person I thought I could trust."

"You didn't know you could trust me."

"Oh, yes, I did, after the first few scary minutes," she said, her big eyes as mesmerizing as ever. "When you lifted me out of the car into your arms, I was completely at your mercy. When you tried to help me, I knew I could trust you.''

''When I went after your attacker, you ran away from me, and you fought me like a wildcat when I found you.''

She blushed. ''Sorry. I heard gunshots and panicked. I just wanted to get away. I didn't even know where I was going.''

She looked around the room and moved her hand across the sheet that covered her legs. ''I can't wait to get out of this place, except I'll have to leave in my cut-up jeans.''

''I've been hanging around because I'm supposed to talk to the sheriff, but after I see him, I'll go get you some jeans if you'd like.'' His gaze drifted over her. ''You must be about a size four.''

''I don't even know, but you can check my jeans for the size. They're in that locker.''

He crossed the room to open a green metal locker, looked at tags in her jeans, aware of how personal looking at her clothing was. And much too aware of the filmy, pink lace panties tossed on top of her white socks in the bottom of the locker.

''I was right. You wear a four.''

''You guessed my size exactly, and yet you say there are no women in your life. I can't remember my life, but I don't think a lot of men can guess a woman's size just by looking at her.''

''I told you—it's all those stepmothers. I've bought clothes for them. I've taken care of them. I've been close to all of them. That's six mothers. You get to know women when you're close to half a dozen of them.''

''What about your real mother?''

''She died when I was two. I just have faint, fuzzy memories. I used to think if she had lived, my dad would have been different, but as I got older, I dropped that notion.

Probably they would have divorced, just like he did with all the others. At least Dad always brought home likable women. I've got super stepmothers,'' he said. Then he got to his feet. ''I'll be back in a minute. I want to see if the sheriff has appeared yet.''

She caught his wrist. ''You will come back, Josh Kellogg?''

He leaned down to look her in the eye, and felt sparks ignite between them. ''I wouldn't miss coming back to you for the world,'' he drawled, and she awarded him with a radiant smile.

With an effort, Josh turned and left quickly. When he stepped into the hall, Sheriff Cordoba was walking toward him. He offered his hand.

''Josh! Glad I caught you.''

''Where the hell is the Bexar sheriff? I've waited here all afternoon. I've called his office twice and they told me he was on his way to the hospital, but he hasn't shown up yet.''

''They had a homicide, and he had to go on the scene. When he can, he'll be here. Sorry you've had to wait.''

''That isn't why you came to see me.''

''No. I wanted to tell you that Les and I went over what we could of the wreck. I have one of her suitcases downstairs in my car. I was going to ask her what she wants me to do with it. A hospital has a lot of people coming and going, and is no place to keep big amounts of cash lying around.''

''She's got more cash?''

''Yep.'' As he stared at Josh, Will frowned. ''The license plate on her car must have been ripped up in the blast. We've found one piece and know it's a Texas plate, but we don't have a number. We couldn't find a purse, so there's no identification. Purse probably burned in the fire. Couldn't find another suitcase, either, but there must have been one.

This one blew clear of the car and it held another big chunk of cash, on top of what we found scattered around the wreck. So far, that cash doesn't have serial numbers on any list. It's legitimate. If you don't mind, come get the bag. Since you're here anyway, you can take it to her.''

"Okay, Will. Let me tell Jeff where I'll be in case that sheriff does get here.'' Josh spoke to the guard and then joined his friend.

The two men rode the elevator in silence and walked through the lobby. When they stepped outside, Will said, "With all that money, I imagine she was on the run, trying to get away from someone who wants her dead. With that kind of cash, she has to be mixed up in something terrible.''

"There are a million different things it could be. She could be running from an abusive husband, for one,'' Josh said.

"If she is, I'd think he'd already be checking missing persons. Or she could have stolen the money from somebody. I don't have any answers now and it seems that she doesn't, either. Damned convenient time to lose her memory.''

"I don't know, Will. I'd hate to lose mine if someone was after me and wanted to kill me.''

"Yeah, I guess,'' Will said as he unlocked his trunk and handed Josh a large, expensive suitcase.

"Thanks, Will. I'll take her things to her.''

"Are you putting the cash away for her or am I?''

"You keep it. As soon as I talk to the Bexar sheriff, I won't see Ms. Jane Doe again.''

"Let's get in the car. I don't want to open this out here.''

Josh climbed into the patrol car and watched while Will put the suitcase between them, partially in Josh's lap. When he opened it, Josh saw that it held jeans, sweaters, more lacy underwear, stockings and socks, toiletries, makeup and cash. The amount of cash she was carrying sobered him. She was on the run from something. What had she seen or done?

"That *is* a lot of money," he said grimly as Will took out the cash and stuffed it into a bag.

"Damn straight it is. Counting what you picked up, she has about one-hundred-eighty thousand in cold hard cash. Tell her I have her money and she can have it whenever she wants. I'll leave five hundred in the suitcase. That cash will more than cover her medical expenses, I'd guess."

Josh closed the case and carried it into the hospital. Once again he checked with the guard, and the sheriff hadn't arrived yet. When Josh opened the door to her room, Laurie stirred. Her hair was tousled, her eyes sleep-filled. As she sat up, she smoothed the sheet over her lap and smiled at him. She looked incredibly desirable.

"Here's your suitcase. You've got more cash, too. Sheriff Cordoba kept most of it for you. You can have it whenever you want, but he didn't think you should have that much cash in the hospital."

"I don't know anything about the money."

Josh shed his hat and jacket and dropped into a chair, trying to ignore his throbbing arm, which was hurting plenty now. He bumped his elbow on the chair and grimaced.

"Does your arm hurt? I heard you turn down their offer of a pain pill."

"It hurts, but I hate taking pills."

"At least they stop the hurt. I'm sorry you were shot. A bullet tore up your hat, didn't it?"

"Yep, but it missed my head, so that's what's important."

She rubbed her arms as if chilled, and he guessed he'd better change the topic of conversation.

"You've got jeans in your suitcase, but I'll buy you a new pair, since I cut up your old ones."

"You don't need to get new ones. You don't mind buying women's clothes?"

"Nope. I've been doing that all my life. I'd mind in Stallion Pass, because then it just starts rumors and questions—unless they know I'm buying something for a stepmother."

"Mr. Tough Cowboy who guards his heart and chases bad guys. Someday you'll fall in love, Josh Kellogg," she teased.

He leaned forward, closer to the bed, and ran his finger along her forearm. "Well, Laurie, if we were going to know each other for years, I'd make a bet with you on that one. And I'm not a betting man."

"I don't know whether I like to bet or not, but I'd bet that you fall in love. I mean, really in love."

"You'd lose. I'm thirty-three and it hasn't happened yet. I don't get involved in long-term relationships, and women don't tend to fall in love with guys who don't. Not really in love."

"I think you're wrong."

Amused, he continued to run his fingers back and forth on her arm, too aware that her skin was soft and smooth. "You don't even know me."

"I know you well enough now to know that you like women, you're sexy and good-looking, you like to flirt and women like you. All my nurses know your name now, and I think when you're here, they come in more often."

He laughed. "Yeah, right! Your nurses are just being efficient and doing their job."

"Sure, Josh." She smiled at him. "Now tell me about growing up and school in Stallion Pass, and who your friends are."

"It's just a small-town school and I had the usual friends, guys who grew up on neighboring ranches. All our ranches are on Cotton Creek."

"So who are your best friends?"

"Gabe Brant and Wyatt Sawyer. Only Wyatt isn't here any longer."

"Where is he?"

Josh shrugged. "Years ago, when we were in high school, Wyatt got involved in a scandal and left town."

"I'll bet all three of you did all sorts of wild things when you were growing up."

"Why on earth would you think that? I told you, I lead an ordinary life."

"You just said one of them had to leave town because of scandal. Tell me about him."

"Wyatt?" Josh leaned back in the chair. "Wyatt supposedly got a local girl pregnant, and Wyatt was a senior and not ready to get married. Wyatt's dad was downright mean—abusive is a better word—and between his dad and the scandal and townspeople snubbing him, Wyatt just vanished."

"He didn't even tell his best friends he was leaving?"

"We knew he was going, but not where. I don't think he knew. He just left and cut all ties. And as far as I know, no one in this town has ever seen or heard from him since," Josh murmured, momentarily lost in memories of another time. Then he shook his head. "Wyatt was wild. One time, on a dare, he rode his Harley through the courthouse. Gabe and I knew about the prank and we watched from outside, in Gabe's car. Wyatt had cops chasing him all over the county, but they couldn't catch him."

"Couldn't they just pick him up later?"

"His daddy always bailed his boys out when they got in trouble. Old man Sawyer didn't mind bribing or whatever he had to do to keep his boys in the clear," Josh said, gazing beyond Laurie and thinking about his childhood friends.

As he continued to talk with her, the hours passed by and the hospital grew quiet. Josh called his stepmother once again and didn't get her, and he left another message. Then he received a call. As soon as he hung up, he looked at Laurie.

"That was the sheriff. He was very apologetic. They had a homicide, so he's been busy, but he'll be here first thing in the morning."

"You should go home now," she said. "I have a guard."

"As late as it is, I might as well stay. I'd just have to turn around and come back as soon as I get up in the morning," Josh said, wondering if he was being honest with himself about his reason for staying. "I can sleep in the waiting room."

"You can't sleep out there," she protested.

"Yep, I can. I can sleep most anywhere."

"If you can..." She paused, staring at him.

"What?"

"If you can sleep anywhere, would you mind staying in here? I'd feel safer," she said hesitantly.

"Sure. This is fine," he answered easily, but he knew he was getting himself mired even deeper. Common sense told him to sleep in the waiting room. He didn't seem to be listening.

A nurse came in and Josh left, walking around the quiet corridors, finally returning to Laurie's room. By now he thought of her as Laurie. And even though he knew nothing about her, he felt as if he had known her a long time. He sat near her bed and they talked for another couple of hours, until finally she grew drowsy and fell asleep.

Standing, Josh moved close to the bed and pushed long, silky strands of hair away from her face. Her skin was soft, satiny smooth, and he wanted to keep touching her. With an effort he returned to his chair to pull off his boots and lean back, propping his feet on the foot of her bed. He looked at the closed door and hoped the guard stayed alert through the night. Anyone trying to get to Laurie would not only have to pass the guard in the hall, but Josh, as well.

When morning came, Josh again waited in the hall while Laurie was examined. The nurses had come and gone through the night, checking on her. Then, since he was still at the hospital, a nurse had insisted on looking at his wound and changing the dressing. Declining pain pills again, he was aware of Laurie watching him while the nurse hovered over him. He was aware, too, that he needed a shower and a shave. If the sheriff didn't show within the hour, Josh decided, he wasn't waiting any longer.

While Laurie ate breakfast, he sat and talked to her. Then she joined him in the cafeteria while he ate.

Finally the sheriff appeared, apologized for not coming Saturday and took Josh's report. As soon as he left, Josh headed for Laurie's room to tell her goodbye.

When he entered the room, Dr. Vandenberg was there talking to her.

"Sorry to interrupt," Josh said, and turned to leave.

"Not at all." The doctor stopped him. "Come in. I'm almost through." With a white coat over her yellow dress, she looked crisp and fresh and made him more aware than ever that he needed a shave.

While she turned back to her patient, Josh walked to the window to look outside. He was free to go. He just needed to tell Laurie goodbye, then get on with his life and forget the past twenty-four hours.

"You're doing fine except for your memory, which may return anytime now," Dr. Vandenberg told Laurie. "Physically, you're in good shape except for cuts and bruises. If you have a place to go, I can release you, but you need to be where someone will be with you, just in case you have any difficulties."

Josh glanced over his shoulder at Laurie, and saw her

slight frown. She bit her lip and stared at the doctor. "A hotel here won't be all right? There are people around."

"No, that isn't what I meant. Having people around— strangers—won't help you. You may be in danger, but won't know how to recognize the people who want to hurt you."

Josh was surprised and disappointed that no family had come forward searching for Laurie.

"I'll be careful in a hotel. I'll stay in my room. I can keep in touch with the police. Believe me, I'm terrified about the danger I must be in. Please, a hospital isn't the best place to stay."

"I'm sorry—"

"She can stay at my ranch," Josh said. The words were out of his mouth before he could think, surprising him as much as they must have surprised both the doctor and Laurie. Both women turned to stare at him.

Chapter 4

"**Y**ou don't have to do that," Laurie said, looking startled.

"I have plenty of room. I'll be there, and my stepmother is living with me right now," Josh replied.

"She might mind," Laurie argued, but the force had gone out of her voice, and he guessed that she wanted to accept his offer.

"No. Becky would love to have you."

"Well, if you don't mind, then I accept. And thank you," Laurie said, turning to the doctor.

The two of them began talking again, but Josh didn't pay any attention to what they were saying. He was still surprised at himself. Yet why shouldn't he have her at the ranch?

He knew why exactly. All his life his father had invited friends to their place. He had always let his boys bring friends, and one of Josh's best friends, Wyatt Sawyer, had lived at the ranch for long periods off and on while they were growing up. Josh's stepmothers brought people to stay, and even now, Becky had friends out occasionally. Laurie would just be one more in a long history of houseguests.

But Laurie wouldn't be an ordinary houseguest, and Josh knew it. Because they both thought their acquaintance was fleeting—or at least he assumed her reason had been the same as his—they had flirted all through the evening and into the night. More than once he'd had to fight the temptation to reach for her, to pull her into his arms and kiss her and end his curiosity.

It would be like having dynamite under his roof, having her sleeping just down the hall from him. A complication he didn't need.

And someone wanted to kill her. He was bringing home a woman in danger, and he might be bringing that danger down on himself, his men and Becky, something he didn't want to do. Yet he had already done it, and Laurie was discussing leaving the hospital to go with him.

He knew why he had blurted out that she could stay with him. He would have done it for any stranger he had helped, but in this case, he never should have, and he knew it to the depth of his soul. This woman was pure danger to his well-being.

Josh stepped into the hall and retrieved his cell phone to call the ranch, leaving a message for Becky that he was bringing a woman home who had lost her memory and whose life might be in danger. Then he paged Drake Browning to tell him the same news.

Walking farther down the hall, Josh stopped by a window overlooking the parking lot and called Will Cordoba.

"Will, it's Josh. Has anything turned up in missing persons? Have you found anyone looking for our Jane Doe?"

"Nope. There's nothing. No missing persons' description fits her. There is no family reporting a lost daughter that even remotely fits her description, or husband reporting a lost wife. I'm a little surprised, but I still think that pretty gal is in big trouble, and she sure has enough cash to cover her tracks.''

Frustration rocked Josh and he stared at the blue sky, considering the woman in the hospital room behind him. Someone had to be missing her. Why hadn't they reported it? What had she done? What was she mixed up in?

''Will, there has to be something. People don't just vanish without a trace. Or appear out of nowhere.''

''The instant I find something, I'll let you know. Are you home?''

''No. I'm still in San Antonio at the hospital.''

''Oh, jeez. It took the sheriff that long to talk to you? I assume he has talked to you?''

''Finally. I'm going home soon.''

''You watch your back,'' the sheriff told him.

''Will, they won't release her from the hospital unless she goes somewhere with someone who knows her.''

''The hell you say. You're taking her out to the ranch?''

''Yep.''

''If you need me, call. Call at the slightest thing. Josh, you're dealing with a would-be murderer, so don't take chances.''

''I won't go around without my pistol again,'' Josh remarked dryly.

''Hell, she ought to stay in the hospital under guard. You're putting yourself in more jeopardy, taking her there.''

''I'll be careful and I'll let everyone on the ranch know.''

''Call me anytime, day or night.''

''Thanks, Will.'' Josh turned off the phone, jammed it into his jeans pocket and waited for the doctor to emerge. When she did, she crossed the hall to him.

''It's kind of you and your stepmother to take her in. She doesn't need to stay here, but she does have checkups she'll have to come back for. I'll notify the sheriff so he can release the guard. I guess you'll be on your own at your ranch.''

"I'll be there and I have several men who work for me. I don't know how anyone would find her there. She'll be out of sight for a while.''

"I won't be giving out the information except to the sheriff and to your county sheriff if he calls. Her memory should return soon. She had a blow on the head, but it wasn't as bad as ones a lot of people receive who don't lose their memory.''

"You think she's faking it?''

"Oh, no. No one thinks that. Everyone just thinks her memory will return very soon. Frankly, we're surprised it hasn't already.''

"Yeah. I've seen a lot of guys lose it temporarily, but within an hour they're clear and remembering everything.''

"She said the two of you decided on the name Laurie for now. That's a good thing, because it's difficult not to have a name.'' Dr. Vandenberg smiled at him. "I told her to call if she has any questions.''

"Fine.'' As the doctor walked away, Josh knocked on the closed door and entered when Laurie called him in.

She was dressed in her jeans and a blue T-shirt. The bandage was gone from her head, with only a small pad taped over the worst of the cut. Her hair was tied behind her head.

"I'm glad some of my clothes survived the explosion,'' she said, smiling and turning in a circle with her arms out.

Josh drew a swift breath. Her figure was as gorgeous as her face. The T-shirt strained over full breasts and then tapered to a tiny waist, and tight jeans clung to long, long legs.

Several people had to be searching for this woman. He knew she couldn't possibly have lived in a vacuum. Not with her face and figure. Someone wanted her dead. But he

was equally sure that other people wanted her alive and
well. The clothes in the suitcases had designer labels. She
carried a huge amount of cash. Call girl? Actress? He eliminated the latter because he would have seen her in something. Dancer? He studied her long legs, and recalled how
she'd swirled gracefully, showing off her new clothes.
Dancer was a possibility. Model? Singer? With her looks,
it could be a stalker she was running from. There were a
lot of reasons for someone to run.

He already knew some things about her. She was stubborn, accustomed to getting her way, filled with vitality. She
enjoyed flirting, had a sense of humor. She was in deep
trouble. He knew he was taking five feet eleven inches of
trouble home with him. And he was attracted to her. As was
probably every man who ever laid eyes on her, Josh
guessed.

He had seen way too much pain and hurt with his father
and stepmothers. He certainly didn't know how to have a
normal marriage, and didn't want to get involved in any
committed relationship. All his adult life he had guarded
against that. Now he'd better double that guard, because
Laurie—or whoever she really was—was slipping past barriers too easily and too quickly for comfort. He found it
damned hard to resist her.

He walked up to her, moving in close and watching her
eyes widen and her smile vanish. "You're gorgeous and
you have to know what an effect you have on men," he
said.

"No, I don't know," she answered, and her eyes sparkled. "Except you just gave yourself away. Thank you for
the compliment."

"Has it occurred to you that our flirting is really putting
both of us on dangerous ground?" he asked softly.

"Scared of me, cowboy?" she teased, causing a storm of
emotions to surge through him. He wanted to shake her and

he wanted to kiss her. She was flirting, teasing, tempting, yet she should realize the risks she was running.

"Damn straight. I should be scared senseless."

"But you're not," she said softly, moving closer, her breath sweet and warm. She was taller than any other woman he knew. He could almost look her directly in the eyes.

He framed her face with his hands. "I'm beginning to understand how you could have gotten yourself in trouble. You don't mind stirring things up, do you?"

"I think your life might need some stirring up. You're too serious. Don't you ever just let go?"

"No, and I'm not going to now. You're going to my ranch with me, but that's the farthest you and I are going together. You're a complication I don't need in my life."

"Then don't take me home with you."

"Don't tempt me. Every lick of sense I have tells me to walk out that door and leave you here."

She laughed. "I'll be good, cowboy. Let's go before you do change your mind. I don't want to be left in this place. And life around you is much more interesting than here with the staff. You must be used to taking risks or you wouldn't be taking me home with you. And I feel a lot safer with you."

The tension was broken by her laughter, yet Josh was left with jangled nerves and a desire that smoldered. It had taken every ounce of willpower to keep from kissing her.

She moved away to get her bag, but he took it from her. As soon as she gathered up her other things, he held the door. She sailed through, thanking him cheerfully. He looked at her tight little butt and wanted to give it a good hard swat. The lady was stubborn, feisty, flirty, and knew, even without a memory of her past, exactly what kind of effect she had on men.

By the time she was in the pickup, he had gathered his

wits, although he kept watching the rearview mirror and every car around them. He didn't think anyone would find her this quickly, but it was easy to trace people, and San Antonio wasn't that far from his ranch.

As they reached the freeway and sped out of the city, she turned to him. "You're watching to see if someone is following us, aren't you?" she asked.

"Yes. I don't think anyone could pick up your trail this quickly, but nowadays it's easy to trace people, and we're not a long way from my ranch."

She rubbed her arms again and he knew she was worried. He squeezed her shoulder lightly. "Don't worry. You'll be safe on my ranch."

"It's just scary to know someone wants me dead, and I won't know the person when I see him."

"I'll be around, and no one will get to you on my ranch."

"You can't guarantee that." She took a deep breath and turned to look out the window, and he hoped she was reassured.

"It's beautiful out here," she said a little later.

"Next month is when it'll be beautiful. That's the beginning of spring. We'll have wildflowers blooming everywhere, including bluebonnets. Everything will green up. It's the prettiest place on earth."

She turned to look at him. "So you like where you live?"

"This is the only life I know, and it's what I love."

"Did you tell your stepmother about me?"

"I haven't been able to get in contact with her, but I left messages. Don't worry, Becky will love having you there. She brings guests home with her often and she thrives on people. She's a portrait artist and a pretty good one, but she doesn't give it a lot of her time. Even though she has showings in a gallery in San Antonio and a gallery in Austin, she likes people and parties and a social life more than art."

"I wouldn't think she would like to be out in the country if she likes people and parties."

"She often drives into the city, and she's just on the ranch temporarily. She and her fiancé are getting married the first weekend in March, and they're building a new house in town, so they've been living with me. Latimer is a diamond broker and often he's out of the country. Becky doesn't like staying alone, so she comes to the ranch when Latimer is gone. She'll move out of my house after the wedding."

"And you and I will be alone at your house?" Laurie asked.

"By then, you'll remember your past," he said, and smiled at her.

"Just when things might be getting interesting," she retorted, and smiled back.

With an effort he returned his attention to the road, exiting the freeway toward his ranch.

Laurie watched him drive, something easy to do. The tall cowboy was easy on the eyes with thick, wavy brown hair clipped short. His prominent cheekbones, firm jaw and slightly crooked nose gave him a rugged appearance, but it was his startling green eyes and that megawatt, melt-your-bones smile that made her pulse jump. She would bet anything there were broken hearts all over this area of Texas because of this solitary, determined cowboy.

Every time they were together, electricity zinged between them. She knew she teased and flirted with him and sent out challenges that she shouldn't. She didn't know one thing about her past except that someone wanted her dead and, from all indications, she was on the run. She might have a husband and she could be in deep trouble with the law.

She shouldn't be flirting, and she should have stayed at the hospital, but that place had scared her. Even with a guard, she felt vulnerable and alone. She was totally dependant on strangers, and how could she really know the good guys from the bad—until it was too late? However, leaving the hospital had been even more unnerving. Out in the open, she was aware of everyone, every movement.

Laurie found her rescuer, Josh Kellogg, irresistible. Which was all the more reason to put distance between them. She considered that moment in her hospital room when they had stood so close they were nearly touching. She'd thought he was going to kiss her and she had wanted him to. Laurie drew a deep breath, her pulse speeding up just thinking about it. There was something so controlled about Josh, yet she had a feeling that, if he ever let go, it would be awesome. He was fearless, sure of himself, a strong, sexy male who made her heart flutter.

She hoped her memory returned soon. She might be bringing danger down on Josh, and she didn't want to do that. Who was she? What was she involved in? Why was her mind so blank? There ought to be bits and pieces of memory, but nothing surfaced. According to the doctor, a person's mind could shut down after something terribly unpleasant, but memory would return. She had seen several doctors. Her doctor had been puzzled by her lack of memory due to the accident, especially since the injury hadn't seemed that serious.

She slanted another look at Josh Kellogg and then shifted in the seat to openly study him. A tall, tough Texas cowboy who had rescued her…. She could remember him racing after her attacker. The first few moments when he had carried her from her smashed car, Josh had looked so fierce he had frightened her. Which seemed ridiculous now. He had a smile that would melt stone.

From what he'd told her, in spite of the stepmothers who must drift in and out of his life on a regular basis, he had a lonely life. And yet he seemed to be quite friendly. Within hours, the nurses on her floor were calling him by his first name. So did the guards that took shifts in front of her door. Josh had a quiet way of reaching people—and a sexy way with women, but that probably just came naturally to him. With his rugged good looks and that gorgeous smile that put creases in his cheeks and a sparkle in those bedroom eyes, it was surprising he was single, and that he didn't seem to date much. It seemed he kept barriers up around himself to keep people from getting too close.

She disturbed him. Laurie knew that instinctively, and it was fun to know she unnerved the fearless cowboy. In the hospital she had wanted him to kiss her. She had been tempted to slip her arm around his neck and kiss him, and see what reaction she got, but she knew she better let well enough alone. It might be the same as disturbing a sleeping tiger.

She frowned and looked away from Josh. With what was in her past, she had better keep a wall around herself, too. She couldn't afford to fall in love, nor did she want anyone to think he was in love with her. She had no idea what her past held, but there had to be something bad in it if it included murder threats.

Thoughts about the attempted murder sobered her, and she rode in silence, looking out the window at the sprawling countryside, dotted with groves of blooming fruit trees. In spite of the sunny day and the tough cowboy beside her, she was still scared.

Someone wanted to kill her, and the killer couldn't be far away. She shivered and rubbed her arms, looking at the dark shadows in a thick stand of oaks. Anyone could hide in the woods. Was she being watched or hunted right now?

She turned to look at the empty road behind them, too aware that she wouldn't know the person after her if she saw him.

"Worried?" Josh asked.

"I can't keep from being concerned. I feel safe with you, but I still worry. Thanks for all you've done."

"Sure," he answered.

Minutes later, they came to a pair of prominent stone pillars supporting a wide wooden plank with *KL Ranch* burned into it. Josh turned there and drove along a rough, hard-packed dirt road. As they topped a rise, Laurie looked out at the rolling countryside, still brown from winter, yet holding a promise of spring beauty. Tall, live oaks were majestic sentinels on gentle slopes, and in the distance, Herefords grazed.

"Were you born here?"

"Yes. Right on this ranch. My great-great-grandfather started the business with longhorn cattle. He settled here because of Cotton Creek, which we'll cross in a minute."

"Have you ever lived away from here?"

"One year when I went to Texas A & M. Then it was back home to stay. Here's the creek."

They drove across a wide stone spillway that had a narrow, silvery ribbon of water running over it.

Laurie looked at the thin trickle of water. "Does this ever get deeper?"

"Yep. There's a bridge a quarter of a mile to the west, but this is the shortest route home, and most of the year, this way is fine. When the creek is up and running, though, you can't cross here."

Shortly, they passed a fenced pasture where a white horse raised its head and pawed the ground. He turned and raced away across the pasture.

"What a beautiful horse!"

"That's the white stallion," Josh said. "My friend couldn't tame him and I'm not having any success at it, either. Although I don't have much time to work at it. I'm beginning to think that horse isn't worth the trouble," Josh added dryly.

"You don't have to tame him to find love," she said with a smile. "According to legend, you just have to own him—right?"

"That old legend is bunk."

"Scared of love, Josh?"

"It just isn't going to happen any time soon and it sure won't happen because of that horse."

She laughed and turned to look at the ranch again.

They followed the road south until they rounded a curve, and ahead she saw a sprawling, two-story white frame house with wings extending to the east and west. A porch wrapped around the house. The yard was fenced and a large barn sat back from the three-car garage. There were smaller houses, a bunkhouse, a toolshed and a corral.

"This looks like your own small town," she said, looking at all the outbuildings. A shaggy black-and-white dog bounded out of the barn toward the car. "Your dog?" she asked.

"Yep. Toughie. He's one of the ranch dogs. He doesn't bite."

"Not even the bad guys?"

"Nope. Toughie doesn't bite anyone or anything except an occasional bone."

Josh parked at the back gate, stepped out, patted Toughie and retrieved her bags. "You might as well meet the men who work for me so you'll recognize the good guys from the bad."

"You sound reluctant to introduce me to them."

"I *am* reluctant. Most of them are young and single, and they're going to drool when they see you. Look, they're good men. I trust them and they're reliable."

"Why are you giving me a warning? What's wrong with them? Do you hire ex-rapists or something?" she teased.

"No, there's no one on the place who ever served time for rape," he said firmly, and a muscle worked in his jaw.

"Oh, my. They *have* served time."

"These are kids, nineteen to twenty-two. They've gotten in trouble, come from broken homes, been on the streets. They needed someone to give them a chance."

"Well, my goodness, Mr. Tin Man, you do have a real heart beating somewhere behind that steely barrier you keep up."

"I'm not heartless."

"You're only telling me this because you have to. Scared to admit you've got a kindhearted streak, tough cowboy?"

"You've got a smart mouth, missy. Over and over again I can see how you could get yourself in a peck of trouble."

"You're an irresistible target. I think there may be an unguarded spot, and I can't resist going for it."

"Do so at your own risk," he warned, and she smiled at him. "Listen, these guys look a little rough, but they are trustworthy. I just didn't want you to be caught off guard."

"I won't be. I'm with my protector."

She knew she was flirting and teasing, but she had been truthful when she said it was irresistible to try to get past his guard. What was it about him that made her want to do that? She couldn't answer her own question.

As Josh led her to a corral, he made a few calls on his cellular phone. In a few minutes men appeared from various directions.

Josh had been right. With the exception of one who looked older than the others, they were a young, tough-looking bunch. One was tall and black-haired, with a crooked nose and a scar along his cheek. Another was thick through the shoulders and chest, with powerful muscles, a square jaw and a belligerent scowl beneath auburn hair. The blonde was rangy and tall and had scars on his face. All of them were strongly built and all looked her over without glancing at Josh. Two more dark-haired, dark-skinned men joined them.

"I want y'all to meet my new guest, Laurie Smith. Laurie, this is Drake Browning, my foreman," Josh said, gesturing to the older man.

"I'm glad to meet you," she replied. The man was only a few inches shorter than Josh, and probably ten years older. He looked tough, but not as hardened as the others, and his blue eyes were friendly.

Next Josh told her each of the men's names, and she smiled and nodded as they said hello to her. All of them smiled back, looking less forbidding than when she had first glimpsed them.

"Laurie is going to be here awhile." Josh glanced at her. "If you'll wait near the pickup, I'd like to talk to them a few minutes."

"Sure." She turned and walked back to the vehicle. Soon the men dispersed and Josh was striding toward her, his long legs covering the ground swiftly.

"I told them your circumstances. They'll be on the watch for anyone or anything out of the ordinary."

"I'm glad you explained. They're a very rough-looking bunch, but not one of them looks like he would scare easily."

"They're good men. I don't keep them here if they aren't. Don't worry about them. They'll help guard this place and you. C'mon. I'll show you where you can stay." Josh scanned the horizon, looking intently at the stand of oaks beyond the barn, thinking about a rifle with a scope. Standing where she was now, someone could pick her off easily. He needed to get her inside the house.

She patted Toughie briefly and then followed Josh. They crossed the back porch and entered a small area cluttered with boots, a hat rack, stacks of magazines, baskets of laundry.

"This way," Josh said, leading her into a large, high-ceilinged kitchen with glass-fronted cabinets, a large double-door refrigerator, copper pots and pans hanging from hooks, a long wooden table in an alcove. A slender woman with black hair stood at the counter with a bowl of lettuce in front of her.

"Laurie, meet Endora," Josh said, and Laura smiled at the woman, who smiled in return.

"Endora, this is Laurie Smith, who will be staying with us for a while. I'll put her in the green bedroom."

"So you have help," Laurie said as she walked down the hall beside him.

"Two days a week. Compliments of my stepmothers. They don't think much of my housekeeping," he explained, grinning. He lead the way through a wide hall, pointing out rooms as they passed. "Here's the family room," he said, and she paused to look three steps down into a room that ran along one end of the house. It was finished in knotty pine, and had a plank floor, brown leather furniture, and an immense brick fireplace with a large picture window overlooking the ranchland.

They passed another spacious room that held another brick fireplace, a sideboard and a large mahogany breakfront, but was otherwise devoid of furniture.

"The dining room. My dad lost the table in a poker game," Josh said dryly.

They passed a sunroom, a game room with a bar and poker table, a room filled with pencil sketches and oils portraits. "Here's where Becky paints."

Another room held a sewing machine, chest of drawers and bolts of material, used mostly by another stepmother, he related. There were more empty rooms.

"This used to be a downstairs bedroom, but one time the electricity was cut off and Dad and his drinking buddies burned the furniture to get heat and light," Josh explained, stopping in a doorway.

"You're not kidding me, are you?"

"Nope. My dad knew how to party. Ask around in Stallion Pass, and people can tell you."

They climbed a wide staircase to the next floor where he showed her several bedrooms before stopping in one that had pale green walls, a deep green spread on the four-poster bed, and elegant mahogany furniture.

"This can be your room while you're here," he said, setting down her suitcase. "There's an adjoining bath. Becky's room is down the hall. Come here and I'll show you my bedroom." They passed another door and went to the end of the hall, to a large bedroom that also had an adjoining bath. "Here's my room."

The large room was cluttered with tools, ropes, books and magazines. Clothing was strewn about the place, and the desk was piled high with papers. "I didn't know I was having company," he explained.

Laurie stepped into the room, eyeing the big four-poster mahogany bed, the glass-fronted bookcases, mahogany rocking chair and large chest of drawers. She crossed the floor to look at the books, seeing fiction and nonfiction titles. "Do you read a lot?"

"Yep, I do." He stood in the doorway, one hand resting overhead against the jamb as he watched her move around his room. She was aware of the man and that this was his space, but she continued looking over his things, curious as a cat about him and his life. Laurie suspected whatever *her* past held, there was no one in it like Josh Kellogg.

Pausing in front of the bookshelf, she picked up an ivory cameo with golden filigree around it, hanging on a thin, gold chain. Looking over her shoulder at him, she asked, "A special necklace?"

"Yes. It was my real mother's." His voice had gone quiet.

"Ah, I see. This must be you with her," Laurie said,

picking up a small oval frame that held a picture of a young woman with a baby.

"Yes, it is."

She set the photo down and moved to another of three youths, one of them a thinner, younger Josh, with longer hair. All three were handsome, one slightly taller than Josh, one slightly shorter. They were all in boots and jeans. "Friends?"

He crossed the room to take the picture from her. "My best friends—the ones I told you about. In some ways, I'm closer to my friends than I am to my half brothers, because my brothers are a lot younger and moved out when my dad divorced their mothers. These two guys," he said, pointing to the picture, "have really been important in my life. This is Gabe Brant and this is Wyatt Sawyer. Wyatt's dad died suddenly this past year and Wyatt's brother, Hank, and his wife, Olivia, inherited the ranch and live there."

"Wyatt was the wild one who was involved in a scandal, right?"

"Yes. Shortly after this picture was taken Wyatt ran away, and no one's seen or heard from him since."

Laurie shivered, wondering if someone would say that about her someday. Josh saw her shiver and set down the picture, turning to look at her. "Something bother you then? Did you remember anything?"

"I just wondered if someone was saying that about me."

"Sooner or later, you'll figure out who you are. Wyatt didn't lose his memory, he left deliberately. I still see my other friend, Gabe, often." Josh touched her shoulder lightly. "Now you know all about me," he said. He stood close, and she gazed into green eyes that were intense and exciting. She could feel the tension jump between them.

"I don't know *every*thing," she retorted. "There's still a lot I don't know about you. A whole lot." She slanted him a quizzical look. "There are some things I'd really like to know."

He inhaled, and his broad chest expanded. "You like playing with fire, don't you?"

"There's something about you that brings out a reckless streak in me. I can feel your resistance, and as I told you, it's tempting to try to get past it."

He leaned closer and lowered his voice. "And maybe, like Pandora's box, you'll get there and wish to hell you hadn't."

"Just try me, cowboy, and we'll see," she said. Standing so close to him started her pulse drumming. She wanted his kiss and knew she shouldn't. He should be as forbidden as robbing a bank.

"Josh! I'm home," a lilting voice called out, breaking the spell.

For an instant longer Josh held Laurie's gaze, then he reluctantly turned his head. Heels clicked on the bare floor in the hall.

"We're in my room," he called.

Trying to catch her breath, Laurie stepped away from him as a short woman with a mass of blond curls came through the door. She was very striking, her lush figure set off by a clinging, deep purple skirt and blouse. Gold bangles clinked on her arm, long golden earrings dangled from her ears and her wide blue eyes were filled with curiosity as she approached.

"Laurie, meet my stepmother, Becky Kellogg. Becky, this is Laurie Smith—a name we picked for now, since she doesn't remember hers."

"Welcome to the ranch," Becky said, smiling warmly and making Laurie feel welcome. "We'll have to take good care of you here, won't we, Josh?"

Chapter 5

Becky warmed to Laurie instantly, and started making plans that Josh had to veto. When she learned Laurie had only one suitcase of clothes, she wanted to take her to San Antonio to go shopping, but Josh thought that was far too dangerous. Undaunted, Becky drove into the city herself, and returned laden with boxes of new clothes for Laurie. When Josh discovered Becky was buying clothes for Laurie in Stallion Pass, he put a stop to it.

Josh felt as if his life had turned upside down. He was accustomed to visitors at the ranch, but they tended to blend in, as comfortable to have around as an old shoe. From the first moment she had arrived, Laurie was different. At all times he was acutely aware of her presence, and each evening, he wanted to get home to her as swiftly as possible. Instead, he forced himself to work late, sometimes not getting home until ten o'clock at night, bone tired, yet feeling a current of excitement because Laurie was there at his house, waiting for him.

Wednesday morning he checked with the sheriff and was disappointed to hear that they still had nothing new. No missing-person report fit her description. No family had turned up in search of her. Josh spent the day trying to concentrate on his work, and that evening he didn't get back to the house until after ten.

He saw Becky's red convertible parked by the back gate, so he knew she was home, and he was both disappointed and relieved that he wouldn't be alone with Laurie.

As he passed the family room, he saw the two women looking at photographs together, and he guessed Becky had photos of her new house to share with Laurie.

"Howdy," he said, pausing a moment. Laurie was wearing a loose-fitting blue sweatshirt and tight, faded jeans. Her blond hair hung in a thick braid. Her bruises and cuts were healing, he noted thankfully. His pulse jumped at the sight of her, and when her gaze met his, a tingling awareness raced along his nerves.

"Come join us. Bring your supper in here," Becky urged.

"After I shower," he said, moving on. He shaved and showered swiftly, dressing in a T-shirt and clean jeans, slipping his feet into soft leather moccasins and going back to the kitchen. He looked at the covered dishes they had left for him.

"Need help?" Laurie asked as she crossed the room. "How's your arm?"

"It's healing," he said, gazing at her and losing his appetite for food to another hunger entirely.

"I see you found the leftovers. I cooked today. That's one thing I seem to remember—how to cook chicken. The potatoes were done in the microwave. Let me heat something up for you."

"All I want heated is a potato. I'll eat cold chicken and bread and butter, and I don't want anything else."

"That's not much dinner," she said.

All the time they talked, he was immobilized, gazing into her eyes. He fought the urge to reach for her. He knew he should step away from her, get his supper and go back where Becky would be with them.

"It isn't chicken I want," he said solemnly.

Laurie's eyes widened, and she inhaled swiftly. "I'll put the potato in to heat," she offered quickly, turning away from him.

He got a plate and bread, and when he glanced around, she had left the room. He closed his eyes and swore under his breath. He wanted her. He had wanted to haul her into his arms and kiss her until she melted against him. While he hadn't hidden his feelings at all, at least he hadn't given in to them.

"Keep your damn distance," he admonished himself, getting his supper and carrying the plate to the family room.

Laurie sat in a chair near Becky and he sat on the sofa, setting his plate and glass of milk on the coffee table.

"Laurie's helping me plan the decor for two of the bedrooms in my new house," Becky explained. "I just wish I could take her shopping with me."

"Well, you can't," Josh said dryly.

"I'll tell you what we can do," Becky said brightly, and Josh braced himself for what might be coming. She jangled an armful of bracelets, waving her hand at Laurie, who sat quietly with a faint smile. "This poor child has been shut away on this ranch for days now."

"It's nice here, Becky," Laurie said quickly. "I feel safe, and I'm so grateful to both of you for letting me stay. I didn't expect to be here this long," she added, her gaze sliding to Josh.

"That's wonderful, honey," Becky continued, smoothing her red silk slacks. "You're coming to my wedding, Josh."

"You know I wouldn't miss it," he said, staring into

Laurie's eyes and thinking Becky's description of "this poor child" missed describing her by a country mile.

"Well, you can bring Laurie with you."

Jolted by her words, Josh snapped his attention back to his stepmother. "Becky—"

"Laurie will be with you, so she'll be safe. You can't go off and leave her sitting here alone."

"That's sweet, Becky," Laurie said. "But it might not be safe."

"It damn well wouldn't be safe," Josh exclaimed, realizing that he should have seen this coming.

Becky waved her hands, her rings sparkling and her bracelets giving another merry jangle. "Nonsense. And someone may be a friend of yours who can help you with your identity."

"And the man who tried to kill her might be there," Josh snapped. "I didn't get a good enough look at him to recognize him if he's there."

"None of my friends are murderers," Becky stated with arched brows. "Really, Josh!"

"Becky, it might be dangerous to go out and drive around San Antonio. I'm not taking her to your wedding."

"You can't be that mean! I know you, Josh Kellogg. You're an intelligent man. Do you really think she would be in any danger from my friends?" Before he could answer, Becky continued blithely, "Of course not. Laurie, I'll get you a dress for the wedding, and you two can leave early if you're uncomfortable. There won't be a risk. You'll be in the car with Josh until you get to the church and the club. Once there, you'll be with my crowd, and then back in the car with Josh. I know you'd like an evening out. Now Josh, you have to be your sweet self and say yes. I just can't believe you won't be nice and bring Laurie, because common sense says it can't be dangerous."

"Becky, taking Laurie to your wedding doesn't have anything to do with common sense."

"Are you going to make her sit out here alone while you party? Make her miss my wedding when she and I have become friends? I won't forgive you if you do. Now, please, Josh. You must bring her with you."

"Josh, you don't have to take me to the wedding," Laurie said, smiling at him.

"Of course he does!" Becky intejected. "If you don't, I'll get Ben or Kevin or one of the cowboys to bring her."

"Now, dammit, Becky," Josh said, knowing once she got something set in her mind, she would work at it day and night. "All right. She goes with me, because she's sure not going with Ben or Kevin or one of the other guys," he said, looking at Laurie. "Do you want to go?"

She tilted her head to study him while she thought about it.

"Of course she wants to go," Becky announced. "It's settled. Laurie, I'll get you something to wear, as I said. And Josh, I'm going to leave my things here and pick them up later, if you don't mind."

"You know I don't mind," he said, aware that Becky was changing the subject as swiftly as she could before he could argue further. He barely heard what she was saying as she chattered on about the wedding. While she talked, he finished eating his dinner, then sat back, glancing at Laurie.

Ten minutes later Becky stood and gathered up her pictures and books. "I'm going to bed. I'll see you two tomorrow." She brushed Laurie's cheek with a kiss. "Thanks for all your help."

"I didn't do anything," Laurie protested lightly, while Becky crossed the room to kiss Josh, too.

"Thanks for agreeing to bring her to my wedding. You're a sweet man, Josh." She patted his shoulder. Perfume enveloped him and bracelets clanked in his ear and then she was gone.

He grinned at Laurie. "She's about as subtle as a monster truck."

Laurie laughed. "You don't have to take me to her wedding."

"Oh, hell. If I don't she'll rustle up some cowpoke or talk Ben or Kevin into taking you."

"So what's wrong with Ben or Kevin?"

"Nothing, except they're still kids. They're not going to watch for danger. They'll come on to you like hurricanes, and they'll party and have a good time."

"And that's bad?"

"In these circumstances—" he said, and she laughed, interrupting him.

"I'm teasing. I know it's bad under the circumstances, but I couldn't resist."

"Be careful, Laurie," he said, arching his brow. "You keep teasing and I won't be able to maintain this cool, impersonal manner I'm working like hell to project."

She slanted him a challenging look that was also seductive. "I'll try to remember," she said softly.

He inhaled, knowing they were moving onto dangerous ground. He propped one foot on his knee, picking at the frayed hem of his jeans and trying to get control of his emotions. "You'll be safer with me, and she's probably right," he said, staring at his boot while he talked. "I doubt if you know any of her friends, and it's not a huge wedding, although it won't be small, either. Becky's idea of small is about two hundred people," he added, finally looking at Laurie.

"Frankly, it would be nice to get out, but I don't want to risk my life over a wedding."

He shrugged. "She's probably right in saying that you

won't be in danger. If you go, you'll meet three more of my stepmothers, Caroline, Nina and Trixie.''

"They'll be at Becky's wedding?"

"I told you, my dad married very nice women. They get along like best friends. Except for the actress. None of us see her.''

"You better start teaching me who's who in your family.''

He shrugged. "It's over a week until her wedding. I still think someone will come along searching for you before then.''

Her smile faded. "Why hasn't someone shown up? I must have a family. Where are they?''

"I don't know.''

"It's worrisome because what's already a bad situation is starting to look even worse. What was I mixed up in that no one wants to claim me?''

Josh reached out to squeeze her wrist, a casual gesture until the moment of contact, and then he became even more conscious of her. Releasing her instantly, he stood, picking up his dishes. "I'll put these in the kitchen and be right back,'' he said, leaving hastily and knowing it wasn't his dishes that had sent him running.

When he returned he had two apples, and he offered her one, which she declined. Sitting as far from her as possible, he pulled out his knife to peel an apple. They talked until two in the morning, at which point Laurie stretched and stood up. "It's very late, Josh. I should go to bed. You must not require much sleep. I know you leave the house before dawn.''

He stood and jammed his hands in his pockets, wanting to walk her to her room, yet knowing he should stay right where he was and let her go. "I guess I don't need a lot of sleep.''

She smiled at him with a faint look of reluctance. "Good night."

"Good night," he replied, and watched her walk out of the room. Gazing after those long legs of hers, he wanted to follow. Instead, he went to the kitchen, poured himself another glass of milk and returned to the family room, turning out all the lights and moving to the window.

For a few minutes Josh stood looking out, his eyes adjusting to the darkness. Then he moved through the house, looking out other windows, studying shadows, hoping everything was as peaceful as it seemed and no one was out there, waiting for a chance to get at Laurie.

He tried to put himself in the killer's shoes. If he had been after her and knew she'd survived the wreck, then the first place he'd look was the last place he'd seen her. Josh thought about what might run through the killer's mind—the possibility that she was in an area hospital; the possibility that she'd survived the wreck and was in flight. But another possibility, one that couldn't be ruled out, was the ranch where she had crashed.

How safe was she here? She was sometimes alone during the day. Whenever possible, he worked close to the house, where he could see who was coming and going. Becky buying clothes for Laurie in Stallion Pass hadn't helped. His stepmother had no concept of the danger involved.

He was taking Laurie to Becky's wedding. It was a ridiculous idea, yet his pulse jumped excitedly at the thought. He reminded himself that someone might discover her identity before a week from Saturday, and she would be gone by then, back to her real life.

"You better hope she's gone," he said, knowing every hour with her tied him in knots more than before. As cool as he was to her and as much distance as he kept, he knew that when she moved out, he was going to miss her.

Returning to the family room, he sat down on the sofa

to sip his milk. Logs still burned in the fireplace. He stretched out his legs and stared morosely at the fire, tormented by erotic images of Laurie in bed.

By Thursday Josh was starting to feel slightly desperate. Once again, he had checked with the sheriff, who still had no clues about Laurie's identity. Each hour he spent with her, Josh wanted her more, and keeping his distance was tearing him apart.

She seemed to be avoiding him, as well, as if she knew the danger in becoming friends. Before she was up and dressed each morning, he ate and left the house. But when he came home, however late the hour, she was there, waiting for him.

This week Becky had been around as a buffer, fortunately, sharing her wedding plans with Laurie, both of them bending over numerous lists. Friday night all three of them gathered in the family room with a roaring fire, while Becky talked about colors for a room in her new house. Josh couldn't concentrate on what she was saying, for his mind drifted constantly to Laurie. He was too aware of the T-shirt molded to her full breasts, her tiny waist, and always, those compelling eyes.

After half an hour Becky said good-night and left. As she walked out of the room, the phone rang, and when Josh answered, he talked for twenty minutes. When he replaced the receiver, he explained to Laurie, "That was Ben. He's a sophomore at Texas A & M, and he'll be here next Saturday. But I won't see him until the wedding, after which he'll come back out here. He'll spend Saturday night and Sunday here on the ranch before he returns to school."

"Will I crowd you by being here? I can go back to town and stay in a hotel. Now that I've been released from the hospital, the doctor really doesn't have a say about where I go."

"No, you stay right here. You'll like Ben."

"What about your other brother?"

"The last I heard, Kevin will be here Saturday, too. He's a junior at Tech, and he'll stay with his mom until Friday. But Saturday night he'll come out here."

"Now I really think I should find a hotel."

"Nope. You'll be fine. They'll just be here Saturday night after the wedding, and will be gone by midafternoon Sunday. All of them are staying at the ranch Saturday night—Caroline, Ben, Nina, Kevin, and Nina's husband, Ethan."

"Then I should definitely move out! Why didn't you tell me?"

He ran his finger along her collar. "You don't need to move out. We have plenty of bedrooms, and Endora will have everything ready. I want you here and that's that."

"All right, but I'll feel like an intruder."

"Not with my family, you won't. They're as friendly as puppies. Believe me, they'll love having you here. Didn't Becky make you feel welcome?"

"Heavens, yes! She's been wonderful."

"You'll see. They're all like that. My dad could really pick winners."

"Maybe it's better to have loved all those women than to never love at all," Laurie said softly.

Josh raised an eyebrow. "Maybe, but it causes lots of pain at times. I'm a war-scarred veteran of divorces and separations and battles."

"You survived and turned out to be a very nice guy."

"Thank you. Now what's Becky got planned for tomorrow?" he asked. The conversation went from Becky and the wedding to questions about his life, and when Laurie finally stood to go to bed, he was surprised to glance at a clock and see it was again after two in the morning.

"Do you get this little sleep when I'm not here?"

"Nope. I turn in about eleven or twelve." He didn't care to tell her that since he had met her, he was losing vast hours of sleep. And what sleep he had was troubled by dreams of her.

"See you in the morning, Josh."

"Wait. I'll go with you."

"To my bedroom?" she asked, giving him one of her saucy looks.

"I'm going to my bedroom," he corrected. "You seem to like trouble, Laurie. Whatever you're mixed up in, I bet you brought some of it on yourself."

"Flirting with you is a very different sort of trouble than doing something to cause someone to want to kill you," she answered solemnly as he switched out lights and walked to the stairs with her.

"I guess it is, but you're playing with fire here and you know it."

"That's because you're going to see to it that nothing happens."

"Maybe," he said, giving her a look that made her draw a deep breath. "See you in the morning," he said as they reached her door. He strolled to his room and closed the door behind him, wondering if she had any idea what a turmoil she had left him in.

The following Monday he stepped out into the cold, crisp dark of early morning and strode toward his truck, his mind on Laurie. He had given her a safe place to stay, and Becky had befriended her, but that was as far as it could go.

"Yeah, keep telling yourself that," he said aloud as his boots crunched on the gravel drive. He was attracted to her more than any other woman he could remember, but she was completely off-limits. With her living under the same roof with him, the only defense he had was distance. When Becky moved out, Laurie would have to entertain herself, because he wasn't about to come in early and spend long evenings with her. He wasn't too certain how he was going to survive Becky's wedding. When it came right down to it, the evening would be a date. The two of them would be a couple, for he couldn't abandon her at the reception.

Common sense told him that attending the wedding would be safe for her. No one knew where she was, and the chances of her running into someone out to hurt her were unlikely. Unlikely, but not impossible, and the closer they got to Saturday, the more concerned he became.

His arm was still hurting him and ranch work was hard physical labor that often caused his wound to twinge. The bullet wound was a steady reminder of the danger.

Why hadn't someone turned her in as missing? There had to be a reason. A woman like her couldn't live inconspicuously, so where were the friends and co-workers she had seen every day? Where was her family? Where were the people—or man—who loved her? Josh was certain there had to be more than one person who cared about her. Something was keeping them from searching for her, and that was as disturbing as everything else about her. The questions spun repeatedly, and no answers came.

"Someone come claim her!" Josh said aloud, impatiently. He wanted her off his hands. Every day added to the tension around them. Who was after her? How was he going to get through an entire evening with Laurie as his date?

The man shifted impatiently, looking out the window of his office at landscaped grounds lightly dusted with snow. She was alive, but where was she? The wreck was roped off with yellow police tape. A cowboy had found her. Where was she hiding now?

Had she gotten another car and moved on, driving farther

and farther from him as each hour passed? Would she leave the country?

He clenched his fists, feeling hot rage well up. She had survived. He knew it. He could feel it. He wanted her dead and he wanted absolute proof that she was gone.

He tugged on his collar, sweat making his shirt stick damply. It was a cool morning, but he was hot with rage and frustration. The car had been completely smashed, yet she had lived. If she had died in the wreck, he was certain there would have been mention of it. The only mention in the hick papers had been a small article about a car wreck. No details. No death.

He didn't think she would leave the country. She had too much at stake here to run away and leave it all. She had family here; it was probably tearing her up to be away from them. This was the only life she had ever known.

He slammed his palm against the smooth surface of the desk with a bang. She had to die, *had to!*

Rage enveloped him, making him burn. She would regret every rejection, regret every success, regret all she had done. He tugged at his tie, loosening it. He would find her. She couldn't hide from him forever, and she couldn't come back to her regular life.

Moving toward a corner of his office, he opened the doors to a wet bar. He uncorked the whiskey, tilting the bottle to drink several big gulps. When he lowered the bottle, he wiped his mouth with his hand. His nights were sleepless because of the little bitch. Tomorrow night was the symphony benefit, and he would have to look relaxed, in control.

She had led a charmed life, surviving each attempt to destroy her. The next time he would see to it that she didn't survive. There would be no more failures. His reputation was spotless, and no one would suspect him. Not ever, no matter what happened to her or where she was when it happened.

It was going to pay big dividends to have her dead. The police had already questioned him over the fire in her condo, and he had been cleared because he had been at a party with a large group of people. He had reliable witnesses from the cream of society, and his time for the entire evening had been accounted for.

He had to think, to plan carefully so there was not a breath of suspicion, so nothing went wrong, so she could not possibly escape again. He wanted her to know, wanted her aware that he was still after her and would not quit until she was dead.

Think, he told himself. She was not invincible. Far from it. She was alone now, on the run. All he had to do was corner her where she couldn't escape and then finish the task.

The phone rang and he dashed across the room, knocking over a lamp in his haste to grab the receiver from his desk.

"I may have found her," a deep, masculine voice announced.

Aware of a bubbling anticipation, Laurie dressed with care. It was her first outing since leaving the hospital, an evening with Josh. For two weeks he had been cool and distant. No more flirting between them. She seldom even saw him. In spite of his remoteness, when they were together the air became electric. She was intensely aware of him and she suspected he was of her. And she understood his coolness, which she had tried to match. Her past remained a dark void that kept a wall around her, made any chance at a relationship complicated.

She felt uneasy, worried. Her memory was as blank as ever. Occasional headaches bothered her, but no memories had come back.

What had she been running from? She wondered if she really wanted to discover the truth. Since no one seemed to be searching for her, her foreboding had increased. What terrible thing had she been mixed up in that no one seemed to want her back? And why did someone definitely want her dead?

Becky had moved out this morning. All her clothes were still here and she would come back later to get them, but now Laurie and Josh were alone in the house, and Laurie was acutely aware that he was only a room away down the hall.

She brushed her hair, then caught it up, looping and twisting it so the locks in front cascaded loosely over her forehead. She studied the effect in the mirror, satisfied that her hair hid the injury on her temple fairly well. The deep cut was healing, but the scar was visible.

She was wearing a deep blue, sleeveless dress Becky had bought for her. Even though Laurie had begged her not to, Becky had insisted on paying for everything.

Laurie stepped into high-heeled pumps, pulled on her watch, then applied a smattering of eye shadow and liner and lip gloss. She gazed at the image of herself, turning first one way and then another, pleased with her image and relieved to see the bruises and small cuts from the wreck had healed.

Finally she dabbed on perfume, picked up a small black purse and left the room. She noticed Josh's open bedroom door and headed for the family room.

When she passed his office, he was standing inside, searching through his desk. He looked incredibly handsome in a snowy shirt and black tux, and the sight of him stole her breath. As she entered the room, she smiled. "I'm ready to go."

He glanced up, and she saw he had a pistol in his hands. A chill enveloped her until her gaze flew back up to meet his. When she looked into his green eyes, all worries about a gun faded completely.

"You look gorgeous," he said in a husky voice, his gaze slowly trailing over her. "There'll be a reporter at the wedding from the local paper. There won't be any way to keep him from taking your picture."

"I hadn't thought about a reporter." Laurie's initial pleasure at his compliment changed to worry as she realized that she might be running a terrible risk. What if the man who was trying to kill her saw her?

Chapter 6

He studied her without answering, and her worry and fear increased. Since Becky had talked her into going, Laurie had put qualms aside and looked forward to going out with Josh. Now the gun in his hand brought the reality of danger crashing back.

"You want to go, don't you?"

While she weighed the choices, the question hung in the air. "I want to live. That's what's important."

"It's up to you. I just didn't think about the press paying attention to you."

"I still have my brunette wig. I can go put it on—do a few things to change how I look."

"It would be safer," he agreed.

Laurie nodded and returned to her room, tossing her purse on the bed and getting out the brown wig. In minutes she had changed to a deep green dress with a long skirt and long sleeves. She removed makeup and earrings, studying herself in the mirror. Now brown hair hung to her shoulders and turned under slightly. Her legs were almost totally concealed. Her arms were covered and she didn't think she would be as noticeable as she would have been in the other dress. She picked up the purse and went in search of Josh, this time finding him in the family room.

He stood by the mantel and his gaze swept over her hungrily. "You'll attract about one percent less attention now. You're a very beautiful woman and there's no hiding it," he said in a husky voice, crossing the room to her.

Her pulse jumped. Since she'd arrived at the ranch, he had rarely come close to her. "Thank you," she answered. "You're a handsome man yourself, Josh Kellogg."

He gave her a wry smile. "I still hope to keep the press away from you. If you can possibly avoid it, don't let them take your picture."

"I won't," she said. "Are you taking your gun?"

"It's out of sight," he answered casually. "Let's go." He took her arm and she was intensely aware of him at her side. She could smell his aftershave, feel the warmth of his arm though his clothing, the brush of his hip against hers as they walked to the door. He was taller than she was and she glanced up at him.

"It'll be nice to get out."

"Just as long as you're safe. With no memory, you don't know whom to be worried about."

She caught his wrist. "I've ruined your evening, haven't I? Now you'll be on guard and you can't enjoy yourself and all the friends and family you'll see."

He gave her a long look that caused her insides to flutter. "You haven't ruined my evening at all," he said in a low voice. He gave her a faint, crooked smile. "It's the first wedding I've ever looked forward to attending."

She smiled in return, but she was worried. Laurie had the sinking feeling she might be making a mistake that would jeopardize her safety and Josh's.

All the way to San Antonio, they kept conversation light, on general subjects. The moment they arrived at the church, all Josh's attention was focused on watching for any sign of danger.

Guests mingled in the foyer, and several of Becky's friends spoke to him. As he introduced Laurie to other guests, he searched for any sign of recognition in their expressions. She was easily the loveliest woman there, and she attracted the eyes of every male in attendance. Josh's nerves were on edge while he tried to keep a constant watch over the crowd. The ceremony was to be performed in a chapel, with only about fifty guests attending. A large reception would be held afterward.

Josh and Laurie sat at the back of the chapel, and he was hardly aware of the ceremony or of Laurie as he looked out for trouble.

Becky wore a short, pale green silk dress and entered from the side, with her brother escorting her. Latimer, who was waiting at the front, took her arm as they turned to the minister for the ceremony.

The moment Becky and Latimer were pronounced man and wife and walked back up the aisle, Josh grabbed Laurie's arm and left by a side door, slipping out of the church to their car to avoid the other guests. As they drove toward the club for the reception, he glanced at Laurie.

"Enjoying yourself?"

She gave him a solemn look. "You wish I were back at your ranch, don't you?"

He shrugged one shoulder. "We're doing all right so far."

"If it makes you feel better, you can let me off at a movie, or at a hotel, where I could wait in the lobby while you go to the reception."

He shook his head. "No, I'm not leaving you in a hotel lobby or a movie theater," he answered dryly. "Men would be trying to pick you up while you waited. And Becky would have a fit.''

''No, she wouldn't. She's too busy now being a bride. I know you don't want to take me with you, because of the danger you think I might be in. And I know you're not worried about your own safety.''

''No, I'm not. You're the one who's in danger, not me. There's a killer after you. And he's out there somewhere.''

''You don't have to remind me.''

He glanced at her. ''I'll admit I'm concerned about the danger, but so far, there doesn't seem to be any. No one came up to you and recognized you.''

''No, no one did,'' she said, sounding disappointed. ''I wish someone had.''

Josh took her hand. ''Let me be the one to worry. You're supposed to be having an evening out. Relax and enjoy it. I'm your bodyguard and I'll keep watch. You have a good time. Becky's parties are always worthwhile.''

Her hand was soft and warm in his, and Josh drew a deep breath, glancing at her before returning his attention to driving. But she had smiled as she squeezed his hand. He didn't want to let go of her, and she didn't pull away, so he continued to hold her hand.

''Did anything stir any memories?'' he prodded.

''There are odd things I recall. Like two of the songs that were sung at her wedding tonight. I knew the words.''

''Maybe you were a singer.''

She laughed. ''I don't think so. I sing in the shower and my voice isn't bad, but it doesn't sound professional.''

Josh was immediately barraged with images of Laurie singing in the shower—her lush breasts, her long legs, her silky skin, with water pouring over her. He realized he was running his thumb back and forth over her knuckles, which he continued to do until they turned into the sweeping drive in front of the club where the reception would be held.

A valet opened the door for Laurie, and Josh went around to take her arm. They strolled into the club and were directed to the area for the reception.

"We're early," he said. "I'll get you something to drink—what's your preference? Champagne, wine, punch?"

"White wine, please," she said. "See? I think I know what I like to drink. Some things come back to me, just not enough and not the vital things."

"It'll come with time."

Round, linen-covered tables circled the dance floor and two long tables held wedding cakes, one with a five-tiered white cake and the other with a three-tiered chocolate-raspberry cake.

As the room filled with people, Josh and Laurie mingled with the crowd. He watched every person, particularly the men, to catch any sign of recognition, but after an hour they hadn't met anyone who seemed to recognize her. Josh did recognize Ty Horton, a reporter from the *Stallion Pass Sun* who had been at Becky's parties before. "Just a minute, Laurie," he said and stepped a few feet from her to talk to the reporter who shot her a long look and then smiled at her. Josh returned and took her arm.

"What was that all about?"

"I know him. I asked him to please not take your picture. I hinted at an obsessive ex-boyfriend and a restraining order. I'll explain to him later or if there's a story that's going to break anyway, we can give it to him."

She laughed and shook her head.

"Josh!"

When he turned to see friends approach, he tightened his hold slightly on Laurie's arm. "Here comes my best friend, Gabe Brant. I want you to meet him and his wife."

Laurie turned to see a tall, handsome, smiling man. His arm circled the waist of a beautiful, black-haired woman.

He said something to his wife and she smiled up at him. A look passed between them that made Laurie's breath catch. The two appeared to be incredibly in love, and Laurie had a pang, wondering if she had ever known love like that— or ever would.

Then the couple were smiling at Josh and her as the men shook hands.

"Gabe, Ashley, I want you both to meet my friend, Laurie Smith. Laurie, this is Ashley and Gabe Brant," Josh said.

"I'm glad to meet you," Laurie replied. "I've heard a little about you."

"Are you new to these parts?" Gabe asked.

"It's a long story," Josh interrupted smoothly. "I'll tell you later. Becky told me she'd invited both of you, and I'm glad you could make it. How are Ella and Julian?"

"They're great," Gabe said. He turned to Laurie. "In case you're wondering, Julian's our son and Ella's our baby girl. Here, I'll show you her picture. And, Godfather, you can look at her latest picture, taken with her brother."

"Gabe, for heaven's sakes—" Ashley began.

"I want to see the picture," Josh interrupted, grinning. "If you don't let him show it now, he'll just corner me later."

"You've got that right," Gabe replied. He handed a picture to Laurie, and Josh leaned close to look with her at a picture of a smiling little girl with enormous blue eyes and wispy black hair. Next to her, holding her hand, was a little boy with big brown eyes and dark hair.

"She's beautiful," Laurie said. "And this is your son?"

"Yes," Ashley answered. "That's Julian with her."

"She looks as angelic as her mom," Josh said, and Ashley laughed as Gabe pocketed the photo.

"Come sit at our table," Josh urged, and the four turned to walk to a table.

"Before we go get drinks," Josh said, turning to Laurie, "I want to tell you that we can trust these two with the truth and trust them to keep it to themselves."

Laurie listened as Josh sketched out what had happened since her car crash the day they had met. As he talked, Gabe reached out and took his wife's hand, and again, Laurie was struck by the depth of love apparent between them. Also, she was aware of receiving curious glances from both of them.

"Wow, that's something," Gabe said when Josh brought them up to date.

"I'm sorry," Ashley said. "If there's anything we can do, let us know."

"Thanks," Laurie said. "Every night when I go to sleep, I think I'll wake up the next morning and remember everything, but I still don't. Dr. Vandenberg expected my memory to return right after the accident. She doesn't understand why it hasn't."

"Let's get drinks," Josh said. "The bar is only yards away and I can keep an eye on you. I won't leave you unprotected."

"I'll be fine," Laurie replied. "There hasn't been a hint of danger tonight."

"What would you like, Laurie?"

Laurie smiled at Josh. "I still have my wine, thanks."

Gabe asked Ashley, and as soon as the men were gone, Ashley turned to Laurie. "I know Becky's been staying at the ranch, and now, with her wedding, she won't be. And I imagine Josh is working most of the time, so if you get tired of staying there alone, call me and I'll bring you to our place for the day."

"Thanks, that's so nice. But it wouldn't be safe for you. Actually, I've really enjoyed the time alone. I can relax, and with Becky coming and going, life's been interesting. I feel safe there, but I know something has to change soon because I'm imposing.''

Ashley laughed. ''From the way Josh looks at you, I wouldn't say you're imposing at all.''

''When you don't know what's in your past, though, you can't form real friendships,'' Laurie said, liking Ashley well enough to be admit what she felt.

Ashley's smile faded instantly. ''I'm sorry. I hadn't thought about that, but of course, you're right. That's awful. I hope your memory returns soon.''

''I do, too. But even that frightens me. I know I must have been involved in something terrible for someone to try to kill me.''

Ashley frowned. ''I don't think I'm doing much to cheer you up.''

''It's a relief to be with people who know. Of course, Becky knows, but we talked about her wedding and her new house most of the time.''

''No, Becky doesn't dwell long on life's problems. But Gabe says that she's good for Josh. Josh and his stepmothers—I guess you know about them?''

''Yes, I do. He said I'd meet some of them tonight.''

''I'm sure you will. Caroline is wonderful from what Gabe has told me. I imagine you'll like her.''

As the band began to play, Becky and her new husband had the first dance, and then guests joined them. Laurie sat and watched the couples dancing.

''Were you and Gabe childhood sweethearts?'' she asked Ashley.

The other woman laughed, and her blue eyes twinkled. ''Hardly! Brants and Ryders have been feuding since they came to Texas over a hundred years ago.''

''So how did you two get together?''

''It's a long story. Ask Josh. Here they come.''

"It's obvious you two killed the feud," Laurie commented.

"I think so," Ashley said, watching her husband, love shining in her eyes as he approached.

Instead of sitting down, he took her hand. "Will you two excuse us while I dance with my wife?"

Josh waved them away as he set a glass of wine in front of Laurie and a glass of water for himself. "Here's another glass in case you finish yours."

"Thanks. Do you ever drink?" she asked him.

"Sure," he said as he sat down and sipped his water. "But, because of my dad, I prefer not to. For most social occasions, I don't see any reason to."

"That's good enough for me. Your friends are really in love, by the way. She told me about the family feud. How'd they get together?"

"He asked her to marry him so they could join their ranches and have the biggest spread in Texas—and in the whole Southwest. Ella was a sperm bank baby. I believe Ashley thought she wouldn't ever get married, and she wanted a child. When Gabe proposed, it was a wonder she didn't go after him with her shotgun before he ever got a word out. There weren't any good feelings at all between the Brants and the Ryders until Gabe and Ashley got together." Josh touched Laurie's hand lightly. "Let's see if you remember how to dance."

On the dance floor she fit into his arms, featherlight, smelling of flowers, soft and warm. All of Josh's thoughts and worries of danger vanished as longing swamped him. He had dreamed of holding her like this, fantasized about it, and now here she was, pressed against him, her legs brushing his, moving with him, her hand in his and her arm around his neck.

Yet here was danger of the highest kind. Danger to his

way of life, to his peace of mind, to his future. He shouldn't dance with her. He knew he should take her home.

Home. The ranch. Isolated with just the two of them alone in his house for most of the coming week.

Josh was as hot as if he were standing in flames. He could feel sweat popping out and knew it wasn't due to the room or the dancing. It was his desire for Laurie. Hot, sweet desire that tore at him and tormented him. Even while he was telling himself that this should be the only dance, he tightened his arm around her waist and pulled her closer, not wanting to let her go.

She moved against him, tightening her arm around his neck slightly as he held her. The other dancers faded from his consciousness and he was aware only of Laurie, wanting to dance her out into the dark night and make love to her endlessly under the stars.

She looked up at him. ''I forgot about your wound. Does it hurt?''

''My arm is the last thing on my mind,'' he answered in a husky voice, pulling her close again.

The music ended and the band started a fast rock number. In spite of his silent arguments with himself, Josh began the second dance with her, twirling her around and watching her, her brown eyes volatile, every twist of her hips seductive.

He was mesmerized, caught by those big eyes and the blatant challenge they held. She turned, looking at him slyly over her shoulder, with a faint smile hovering around her mouth. Temptation and challenge.

Unable to resist, he caught her around the waist and yanked her up against him, dancing fast, looking down into her eyes as she gave him another searing, seductive look.

Then she whirled away from him, moving to the music, her hips gyrating. He wanted her as he had never wanted any other woman in his life. And no woman he had ever known was more dangerous to his well-being, more off-limits to him.

Josh clenched his hands into fists, wanting to swear, wanting to reach for her again and pull her tight against him. He yearned to kiss her long and hard, until she was flushed and breathless. Was all this hot desire just because she was forbidden? He had never had this intense reaction to any woman, but was it partially because he knew he couldn't pursue her? He didn't think that had a thing to do with what he felt. Where was his usual objectivity, his ability to walk away, to keep himself shut off and uninvolved?

The band took a break and he took her hand, leading her back to the table to join Gabe and Ashley who were already seated. "I'll return in a minute," he said, hurrying away from her. He had to get away, to cool down, to get more control over his thoughts, his feelings and his body.

He strode out onto the terrace. The night air was chilly and no one else was outside. He knew he had been abrupt with Laurie, but he'd had to be. He hadn't trusted himself to act any other way. He walked across the empty terrace, his boots scraping the concrete floor. Images of her smiling at him, laughing, giving him a tempting look, danced through his mind. Light spilled through long windows as he moved from squares of light to dark shadows.

Josh rounded a corner to find a man lounging in a chair, facing the windows and watching the people inside. When Josh appeared, the stranger stood up and left without a word, disappearing into the dark, hurrying off the terrace and into the night.

Josh stared after him, a chill running down his spine. He told himself he was being foolish, but he felt cold and uneasy. Moving into the shadows, he scanned the grounds, hoping to spot the man. He was tempted to go look for him, but that would leave Laurie on her own.

Josh glanced through one of the windows. He spotted

Laurie still seated at their table. The man had been sitting where he could see her, except when dancers blocked his view. Worried, Josh turned around, taking long strides back into the reception hall to join her.

When he reached their table, he sat facing her, his knees lightly touching hers. "Sorry to leave you. Hey, I see Caroline. Come meet her. You haven't met Kevin or Ben, either. They're all together. Excuse us, please, more of my family is here," Josh said to Gabe and Ashley. He took Laurie's hand and led her to a tableful of people.

Laurie stood back while Josh greeted his relatives with hugs and kisses, and finally turned to her.

"Okay, y'all. I want you to meet my friend, Laurie Smith. Laurie, this is my stepmom, Caroline Kellogg. Caroline, meet Laurie."

Laurie shook hands with a slender woman who had smooth, flawless skin, straight blond hair cropped just below her ears, and luminous blue eyes. She looked far too young to be the mother of a college sophomore. Ben, her son, had thick brown hair, blue eyes, a square jaw, and a dimple when he smiled. He was stocky, shorter than Josh, and she never would have picked them out as brothers.

"You're staying at the ranch?" he asked, shaking hands with her. "Kevin and I will be, too. At least tonight."

"Yes, I am."

His eyes were filled with curiosity, and she wondered what he had been told about her.

"And you can talk to her later," Josh said, taking her arm. "This is Nina. Nina, meet Laurie Smith."

Laurie shook hands with another slender, beautiful woman, whose thick brown hair curled under slightly just above her shoulders. Then she was introduced to Kevin, who was as tall as Josh, and had thick blond hair, a slender face, but resembled his mother far more than Josh. Next she met Nina's tall husband, Ethan Rosenkrantz, and finally, another attractive stepmother, Trixie Fulton.

"Come join us," Caroline urged.

"Thanks," Josh replied. "We're at a table with Gabe and Ashley Brant, but we'll sit here for a while. They've danced all evening, anyway, so they haven't been back to the table much."

Laurie sat with Josh beside Caroline. Ben immediately turned to Laurie and grinned charmingly. "Care to dance?"

She smiled and nodded, catching a sharp glance that passed from Josh to Ben. Then Ben took her arm and led her to the dance floor for a fast dance that eliminated any chance for conversation. When the music ended and a slow number began, Ben kept a hold on her hand.

"Dance one more with me, Laurie. Let me get to know you a bit better."

Glancing toward the table, she saw Josh deep in conversation with Caroline, so she nodded.

"Ignore him. Josh isn't into dancing," Ben told her.

"Is that right?"

"Nope. Josh isn't into partying, either. And that's enough about my brother. Tell me about you. I haven't seen you before, so you must not live around here."

"That's right," she said, assuming it would be safe to tell Josh's family about her situation. "Since you're family, I'll tell you."

"You get more interesting by the minute. My estimation of my brother has just jumped up a notch. So tell me."

She talked while they danced, almost laughing at the shock that crossed Ben's face when she began her story.

"Holy horny toads! That's wild. So that's why you're on the ranch. I thought Josh's cold heart was finally thawing."

"Josh, cold? He's incredibly kind!" Laurie protested.

"Josh is as good as they come, but he's pretty cool where women are concerned. He doesn't want to get married, after living through all the marriages our dad had. He won't ever get real close to any one woman."

"You make him sound as if he doesn't like women."

"Oh, no. He likes women and they like him—look at him with our stepmothers. They all love him and so do a lot of women in Piedras and Lago Counties. Haven't you noticed them coming up to speak to him tonight?"

"I suppose I have, but so do men. He's a friendly person."

"Well, women notice Josh, but he doesn't pay much attention to them. He's never gotten into any serious relationships. So you don't know one thing about your past? And someone wants to kill you?"

"That's right. I try not to think about the last too much."

"Wow. I ought to stay at the ranch and help protect you and try to help you find out about your past. Are you sure it's safe for you to be here?"

"Becky thought it would be. To tell the truth, I couldn't resist getting out. I haven't been anywhere outside the ranch house since I left the hospital."

"I bet I know whose idea that was. Josh can be as cautious as a ninety-year-old judge. No wonder you came tonight. And you haven't seen anyone who's recognized you?"

"No, I haven't. I've been avoiding the newspaper reporter all evening, so if you see the reporter approaching, we need to move away."

"Sure."

When the music ended, Ben looked over her shoulder. "Here he comes."

"The reporter?"

"No, my brother. He's claiming you. That purposeful look isn't aimed at me."

"My turn, kid," Josh said, taking Laurie's hand.

"She told me why she's at the ranch."

"Well, you keep it quiet. Family and Gabe and Ashley can know, but that's all."

"Sure. If I can help, let me know."

Josh smiled. "Thanks, Ben."

Ben strode away, and Josh pulled her into his arms for a slow dance. Laurie moved with him, relishing every second even though she constantly was aware that she shouldn't. "He's charming."

"Ben's nice. And before long Kevin will want to dance, and you'll see then what my dad was like. All charm, but beneath that charm, he's totally irresponsible. Both of them will want to help you, and their intentions are good, although the biggest motivation with Kevin will be coming to the aid of a beautiful woman. Kevin takes to pretty women like bees to flowers, and you have a very unusual situation. He won't want to go back to college."

"Well, I don't want to be the cause of your brother dropping out of school!" she exclaimed, aghast at the thought. "I'd move out tonight—"

"Don't worry. I'll send him packing. But you watch, he'll want to stay to help try to find out who you are. He'll want to guard you. Of course, halfway through the evening he'd forget what he's supposed to be doing, Especially around someone like you. But his intentions are good. Kevin's also a good kid and he's keeps things lively when he's around. And speaking of the rascal—here he comes."

He turned with an ironic smile. "I know, you want to dance with her," he muttered good-naturedly to the young man who approached.

"Damn straight I do," Kevin agreed, smiling at Laurie and never glancing at Josh.

Josh stalked to the sidelines, watching as Laurie laughed at something Kevin was telling her. Then he shifted his attention to the crowd, looking everyone over, trying to see if anyone else was watching Laurie with undue attention.

The minute the dance ended he returned to claim her.

"Sure," Kevin said. "She told me about herself. That's wild."

He left and Laurie moved into Josh's arms for another dance.

"You're right. He said he may stay at the ranch next week and help you protect me."

"The hell he will," Josh said. "Protection isn't what's on Kevin's mind."

She laughed. "He *is* charming, just like you said."

"Irresistible?" Josh demanded.

"No, not irresistible. He's young, too."

"That doesn't stop Kevin, ever. And he's not all *that* young. He's the perennial student because he keeps changing majors. I don't know if he'll ever finish college."

"I saw you studying the crowd," Laurie said.

"Everything looks all right," he replied, avoiding telling her about the man on the terrace. He didn't know anything for certain, and he didn't want to worry her. "You're just getting garden-variety attention from all the males—probably what you always get."

"You exaggerate, but that's sweet of you."

Josh smiled at her. He wanted to dance all night. That was the only way he was going to get to touch her and hold her.

Another song began to play and Josh pulled Laurie closer, moving with her and enjoying the contact without keeping up his guard. Without thinking, he wrapped his arms more tightly around her while they barely moved, and then he realized what he was doing and shifted her away, to stare down at her.

Her brown eyes were darker, with flames in their depths, as she gazed up at him.

The music ended and Josh took her arm, inhaling deeply, trying to get control of his emotions and his body. They started to leave the dance floor when a couple blocked their way.

"Sorry we didn't see you more tonight," Gabe Brant said. His arm was draped around Ashley's shoulders, while she leaned against him.

"That's fine. My family wanted us to join them."

"How's the stallion?" Gabe asked.

Josh shook his head. "Wild as ever. I haven't had time to work with him."

"I warned you," Gabe replied. He glanced over at Ashley. "We'll be going now. Both of you must come see us. I'll give you a call and we can plan a visit. It was nice to meet you, Laurie," Gabe said.

"It was a pleasure to meet both of you," Laurie told them, and watched them walk away.

"I hope I'm that much in love someday," she murmured. "Their relationship brings to mind the word *bliss*. I can't believe they used to be enemies in a feud."

"They didn't even speak until he proposed. Their marriage shocked everyone in this part of Texas," Josh said.

The musicians called a break. Reluctantly, Josh led Laurie from the dance floor. "I'm having a good time, but I'd rather get out of here before the crowd thins." Josh rubbed her arms lightly as they stood beside their table. "It's getting late enough that this shindig ought to wind down."

"Of course. I've had my outing and I've had a wonderful time," Laurie said warmly, giving him a look that sent his temperature soaring again.

"We need to say goodbye to Becky and Latimer and Trixie. I'll tell Nina and Caroline we'll see them at the ranch tonight." Josh took Laurie's arm, moving through the crowd and keeping watch for the reporter.

None too soon to suit Josh, he stood with Laurie under the long portico, waiting for the valet to bring the car. Josh casually looked around, searching the grounds, the entryway behind them, the few guests leaving, watching constantly for anyone who seemed to pay undue attention to them.

As he swung out of the lot, two other cars left within seconds. Beneath the bright lights at the entrance, Josh saw a low-slung red sports car turn into the street behind him.

After several seconds a nondescript dark green compact car turned behind the red car.

"You're watching to see if we're being followed, aren't you?" Laurie asked, looking into the side mirror and seeing the cars behind them. "I hardly think you need worry about the couple in the red car."

"I agree."

"You're watching the green car."

"I just want to check and see if we're being followed. If we are, then someone has discovered where you are and they know who you are."

She shivered, studying Josh. The evening had been wonderful. Too wonderful, she thought wistfully. She knew she had enjoyed his company too much, loved dancing with him too much. She was getting to know him too well. He couldn't be any part of her future until she knew her past.

Josh made a turn. She wasn't familiar with the city and she didn't know whether they were headed toward the ranch or not, but within minutes she realized they had doubled back the way they had come.

"We've got a tail, Laurie," Josh said grimly.

Chapter 7

"Are you certain?" Laurie asked, studying the headlights a block behind them while a chill ran through her. Fear gripped her, along with worry for Josh's safety. "How could anyone find me? I've been hidden at your ranch. It's impossible."

"No, it's not. Becky's been in Stallion Pass buying clothes that aren't her size. And she tries, but I'm not certain Becky can keep quiet about anything."

"At night, how can you be sure that's the same car?"

"They've stuck with us since the club. I'm going to call the sheriff."

"Josh, I'm sorry. I never intended to put you in danger. I thought you'd be safe or I wouldn't—"

"Forget it, Laurie. I did what I wanted to do. And I'm not worried about the danger. There's a big difference in going after an unarmed woman and going after an armed man. And one in contact with the police."

"I don't want you hurt."

"I won't be."

"You don't know that! Just stop at a hotel and let me out," she told him, staring at the headlights. She hated that she had pulled Josh into her problems and into danger.

"I'm not letting you out at a hotel, so you can just forget that one now." He handed her a cellular phone. "You call the police while I drive. Tell them who you are and that I think we have a tail. I'm going to stall him and see if I can find out who he is."

"You can't!"

"Stop worrying. I'll be all right," Josh said, slowing the car and unlocking the glove compartment to retrieve his pistol.

"Josh, I hate this. I—"

"Call the police, Laurie."

She dialed 911, wanting to stop Josh, yet knowing she couldn't. She was terrified for his safety and horrified that she had involved him, yet when she looked at him and saw the determined set to his jaw, she realized he was not afraid.

A dispatcher answered and Laurie briefly explained who she was and what was happening, giving their location. The dispatcher continued to ask questions, telling her a car was on its way, and then Laurie heard Josh swear.

"The tail is gone," he said. "He's turned off."

Laurie told the dispatcher the news. She talked a moment more and then shut off the phone.

"So we're on our own again."

"Sort of. There's a police car a few cars behind us now."

"Think that's why the person stopped following us?"

"Could be, or it might not be."

"Or it might not have been someone following us, only coincidence."

"The way I've been driving around, I'm pretty sure it was someone following us, but if he had a lick of sense, he would have realized I was making a lot of unnecessary turns. That could be why he disappeared.''

"You don't have a nervous bone in your body," she said, wondering if he had ever known fear.

He shot her a quick glance. "Oh, I have nerves all over, and right now I'm too damned aware of them," he said in a low voice. She knew he wasn't talking about the car tailing them.

"The cop is pulling us over," Josh said, his voice becoming brisk again as lights began to flash behind them. Josh pulled to the curb and stepped out of the car to talk to the officer. In minutes he slid behind the wheel again.

"He just wanted to see if we were safe."

"There he goes," Laurie said, watching in the mirror as the police car turned a corner. "If someone knew to follow me tonight, then they know where I'm staying. They know you and your ranch. Josh, I have to leave."

"No, you don't," he said, in a voice that was unyielding. "I'm not afraid. Not at all. In fact, I'd like to catch the guy. You should be safe on the ranch, and I'll have an alarm installed this week."

"Alarms are expensive, and you haven't felt the need for one before."

He grinned. "I haven't even locked the doors before."

"See?"

"Stop worrying about me or my house. What we need to worry about is who knows and what they know, and what they'll try to do next."

She shivered. "I felt so completely safe at your ranch."

"You probably would have been if Becky hadn't been around going back and forth into town every day. Her intentions are good, but I'd guess that's how someone found you. Besides, the wreck was on my property. That's where I'd start if I were looking for you and you disappeared after the crash."

Knowing he was right, she gripped his arm. "I can't stop hating that I involved you."

He inhaled, his chest expanding as he covered her hand with his, driving with the other. They were still in town, on a quiet street, and he slowed. She was aware of the contact, of his hand on hers and of his effort to keep his attention on the road. She started to pull her hand away, but he held it, lacing his fingers through hers.

"We shouldn't, Josh," she said quietly, withdrawing her hand.

He knew she was right and he clenched his jaw, locking both hands on the steering wheel and trying to get his mind back on the question of who was watching them.

As they left San Antonio, Josh couldn't tell if anyone was tailing them. They were in steady traffic for a few miles until he cut over to take a county road. Traffic thinned and for miles no one was behind them and there were few cars coming from the opposite direction.

He concentrated on watching the road and trying to get his mind off Laurie. He had been too aware of her in his embrace tonight when they danced. With every hour he wanted her more, yet she was as forbidden as she'd been the first moment he had met her.

He was relieved his family would be spending the night at the ranch with them. He wasn't going to worry about tomorrow, when they all left, until he had to. And he knew he'd better focus on protecting Laurie. If someone knew she was staying with him, she could be in grave danger.

He tried to keep his thoughts on how to protect her. He needed an alarm system, and he should talk to his men again. He had told his housekeeper about Laurie the first day, but he had to speak to her again because just by being at the ranch with Laurie she could be in danger, too. He considered hiring a bodyguard to stay at the house, knowing he could ask if any of his men wanted the job.

Josh shook his head in the darkness of the car interior. All of them would jump at that assignment. Should he stay home and guard her himself?

Laurie shifted and took a deep breath while she watched Josh drive. When he shot her a swift glance, she tilted her head. "What is it? Is someone following us again?"

"No. I'm trying to decide if I need to get you a bodyguard. Or if I should take that job myself."

"I don't think I need a bodyguard when I'm at your house. Particularly if you're putting in an alarm and you're on the property somewhere and have your phone."

"When I'm working, I could easily be a ten- to thirty-minute drive from the house. You need someone right here with you."

"I was just thinking about Endora. I'm putting you and everyone around you in danger. If you insist I stay, I think she should be warned. While I'm with you, I can cook and clean. There's not that much to do with just two of us," she said, too aware of how her words sounded. "Of course, I don't want to cause her to lose her salary or to leave you permanently."

"She'll get paid, anyway, but I'll tell her to take a vacation."

"I'm disrupting your life in every way," Laurie said, knowing she needed to pack and leave. But Josh was the only haven of safety she knew. "I'm moving out. Don't stop me. I've got money and I can keep moving around until my memory comes back."

"Don't do it, Laurie," he told her. "And don't you leave while I'm gone at work, either. Promise me, so I won't have to worry. I want you here, otherwise, without your memories, you'd be damned vulnerable. If I didn't want you here, I'd let you go. Promise me you won't just try to disappear."

"Josh—"

"I want you to stay," he said tightly.

"All right, but I hope we don't both regret it," she replied, knowing she wasn't doing what she should, but was giving in to what her heart wanted.

"That settles it. I'm your new bodyguard."

She laughed and shook her head. "I'm worried and upset, but I have to tell you, there's a part of me that wants you to be my bodyguard."

"I think your reaction is the same as mine, except my upset and my worry are for different reasons."

"What are your reasons?"

"I'm worried I can't protect you when I should, worried that I didn't find out who was following us tonight, upset that I might not be able to control what I feel for you...."

Her heart thudded, and she reached out to touch his hand. Instantly his fingers wrapped around hers, warm and strong. He rested their hands on his thigh and she felt the electric tingle spread over her whole body, too aware of the contact, wanting so much more.

"When will your family arrive at the ranch?"

"Nina and Ethan will bring Caroline, and they'll be out in about another hour or so, I'd guess. No one knows when Ben and Kevin will come in, but it'll likely be the wee hours of the morning."

"Your family is wonderful. You're very lucky to have your stepmoms and your brothers."

"We all get along."

When Josh turned the car into his ranch, he drove a quarter of a mile, pulled beneath a stand of trees and cut his lights and motor.

"What are you doing?" Laurie demanded, instantly aware of the intense quiet that enveloped them.

"I want to watch the road, to make sure no one is following us onto the ranch who shouldn't be here."

Laurie inhaled, dangerously aware of being shut in

the close confines of the car with Josh. Aware, too, of the danger.

"Whatever my background, I think I'm a city girl."

"What makes you think that?"

They spoke in soft voices, and she knew his attention was only half on her as he continued to watch the road.

"I notice the quiet out here. I think if I had been living in the country like you do, the absolute quiet wouldn't catch my attention so much. I notice it during the day at your ranch. There's no sound at all except a cry of a bird or the whistle of wind through the trees."

"You're probably right. I grew up out here and I never give it a thought. But in a city I notice the noise. Confounded racket most of the time."

Thinking about Josh as a child and the continual upheaval in his life, she asked, "Didn't it tear you up every time your dad got divorced? Particularly when Nina moved out and took Kevin, and when Caroline left with Ben?"

Josh was silent a long moment, and she wondered whether she had pried too deeply into a private part of his life, but then he answered, "Yes, it did. That's another reason I don't want to get deeply involved with anyone."

"Life without love is empty, Josh," Laurie said quietly, knowing he had been hurt as a boy by his father's divorces. "At least you remained friends with all of them, and Kevin and Ben are still part of your life. That's more than some people have."

"I know it is. Dad always brought home women who were pretty and nice to me. Besides, I grew up seeing my friend Wyatt and his dad, and watching them always made me count my blessings. That man was mean as sin. Wyatt didn't have a stepmother. He didn't even have a father who loved him. In some ways Wyatt was too much like his old man. They butted heads constantly. No, I always knew I had a lot to be thankful for, but the divorces still hurt, especially when I lost Caroline. After that I sort of withdrew from loving any of them.''

Laurie couldn't resist running her fingers lightly along his jaw. He instantly stilled, and she became aware of the extremely narrow distance between their bodies.

Knowing she shouldn't touch him, she placed her hands in her lap, lacing her fingers together and turning to look back at the road. ''How long do you intend to stay here?''

''I think we can go on to the house. I just wanted to watch for a while.''

When he started the motor, Laurie shifted in the seat, turning to watch him as he drove, wondering about the solitary life he seemed to lead, shut away, keeping barriers around his heart. Yet with his family he was warm and open.

At the house Josh pulled her inside, closing the door and moving to the phone without switching on any lights. He picked it up, punched numbers and carried it to the window.

''I want to keep watching for a little while. Hey,'' he said abruptly, speaking into the phone. ''We're home now. We might have been followed part of the way. Will you turn the dogs out and let them roam? Thanks. Talk to you in the morning.''

He broke the connection and replaced the phone, moving back to the window. ''Can you find your way into the family room without lights?''

''Sure, but I'll wait in here with you,'' she said, moving to another window to look at the moonlit yard.

Nothing moved except the gentle shift of leaves as the breeze played through the trees. Yet the darkness seemed menacing, and she was chilled. She was surprised by Josh's patience. She watched him as he stood without moving, staring out the window. Finally she walked over to stand beside him.

''You're very patient. Like a cat.''

He shrugged. "I've hunted before. You learn to be patient. Looks as if I'm wasting my time right now." He turned to her and moonlight splashed over both of them. She gazed up at him and her heart drummed in the silence that stretched between them, yet he wouldn't look away, and she couldn't. His eyes were in shadow, so she couldn't read his expression, but he stood close, his chest moving as he inhaled deeply.

Wanting so much, yet knowing she couldn't have anything, she turned away from him. Trying to put distance between them, she crossed the room.

"Want hot chocolate?" he asked. His voice was gruff, and Laurie knew he wanted to kiss her. Had circumstances been different, he would have.

"Yes, thank you. I'll help."

"No, you go sit in the family room, and I'll bring it. Go on, Laurie," he urged in a raspy voice that sounded almost angry. He was telling her to go, yet his tone was telling her something entirely different.

She left, hurrying to the family room, switching on a small lamp, moving around the room restlessly. She closed shutters, wanting privacy, then wondered if anyone ever closed them as she touched a fine layer of dust. She knew Josh paid little attention to shutters, and she was certain he never gave a thought to someone spying on him. And until she came, no one had ever had reason to, she was certain.

"Here's the hot chocolate," he said, setting steaming mugs on the low table in front of the sofa. He crossed the room to start a fire, and in minutes a blaze danced in the fireplace, taking the chill off the room. Josh switched off the light and she watched him move around the darkened space.

"Josh, you know it would be wiser for us to keep a light on," she remarked, too aware of the jump in her pulse.

He put on music and crossed the room to stand by her.

As soon as he shed his coat and tie and then yanked off his boots, he reached for her hand. "Come dance with me. It'll keep us moving, and I can still touch you, but that's all I'll do."

She reached up to place her hand in his, kicked off her shoes and moved into his arms. "I don't think this is wise, but I can't say no," she whispered.

"It's better than sitting on the sofa and trying to avoid touching each other. Remember, you don't get a broken heart over dancing."

She wondered if his words would echo in her mind forever. She was too aware of his warm breath on her when he talked, of his strong arms wrapped around her, of his lean, muscled body so hard against hers. They danced close, and he wrapped his arms around her and she wound her arms around his neck. They were living dangerously now, fanning the flames of desire just by moving slowly together in time to the music.

"I keep telling myself to wait, that your memory will return and then you'll know your past and we'll know where we stand. But I'll tell you now, absolutely," he said, leaning away and looking down at her, "I'm not into lasting relationships."

Something hurt deep inside, yet she knew that was foolish. "I don't know what kind of relationship I'm into, or anything else," she answered, too aware that Josh might protect her physically, but was probably going to hurt her emotionally. Even though she knew it was unintentional, he was already causing her anguish. And she was as much at fault as he. The first couple of days she had flirted with him, unaware that they would be thrown together for much longer and that the attraction burning between them would grow.

"So you're telling me caveat emptor," she said. "Well,

cowboy, the same back to you. This slow dancing was your idea, not mine.''

Desire blazed in his eyes and she knew she was taunting a tiger, yet his warning had made her want to fling one back at him. Dancing with him and feeling the tension exploding between them, she gazed into his eyes.

''Scared to kiss a woman with a dangerous, unknown past?''

''You little witch,'' he whispered in a husky rasp. He stopped dancing and wound his fingers in her hair, and her heart thudded so loudly it was a drumbeat in her ears.

''Whatever your past, you like taking risks,'' he said, grinding out the words in that husky voice. ''Well, I'm scared as hell,'' he said, and tightened his arms around her, leaning over her, his mouth coming down hard on hers and opening her lips to his.

The moment his tongue stroked hers, she knew she had gone way too far. She had goaded him into this kiss and she was going to pay an exorbitant price, because her knees had turned to jelly, her heart lurched and every inch of her responded to the touch of his lips.

She might as well have been standing in a bonfire, she was so hot. His tongue was waking nerves all over her body. She trembled, clinging to him, kissing him back, totally lost in sensations that ignited all the banked flames.

She had not only stepped over a line, she had stepped into a white-hot furnace of desire. Deep inside her an ache began, an age-old, female need. She was too aware of him, his mouth, his broad shoulders, his hard body. The need that had been building for days shook her now. She wanted this tall, tough cowboy—wanted him to love her. His kisses were driving her desire into a raging longing.

His kisses were more exciting than she had dreamed they could be. As he had predicted, she had opened Pandora's box and unleashed a world of trouble. There would be no going back from this moment. And if she had been drawn to him before, it was nothing compared to what was happening to her heart now.

Forbidden, forbidden, she tried to remind herself, her thoughts syrupy and dim from the heady rush of sensation. He was forbidden, his kisses couldn't escalate, couldn't lead anywhere until she had a past. And even if she learned that she was free to love, this wasn't the man. He had warned her repeatedly that he wouldn't give his heart to any woman.

She could feel that heart thudding beneath her hands, beating as swiftly as her own. She let go of her worries, giving in to him, knowing this might be the only time they would ever share such a kiss. She might have to tell him goodbye tomorrow.

Abruptly he stopped, his chest heaving and his breathing ragged.

She opened her eyes, gazing up at him, seeing a frown on his face.

"We're not alone," he murmured. He looked down at her, and for just a flash, recognition passed between them that was an affirmation of the desire they had unleashed during the past few minutes.

His words registered with her and she blinked, her thought processes beginning to work again. She stepped away as he turned to switch off the music.

For the first time she could hear dogs barking, and icy fear gripped her.

Chapter 8

When he switched on lights, she became fully conscious of what he was doing. "Someone's out there."

Josh relaxed. "Listen. The dogs are greeting someone. I'm used to hearing them bark. I know the difference between friends and strangers. My family is here."

She became aware of herself, wondering if she looked disheveled from his kisses and embrace. Her gaze raced over him, but he looked as collected as ever, except for slight wrinkles in his starched white shirt. And then she became aware of something else: he had heard the dogs while she had been lost in a hot, seductive kiss. Her roaring pulse had drowned out all sounds. While his kiss had blanked out the world for her, he had been able to stop instantly, and now he was completely composed.

She moved away, going to a mirror to look at herself. As she smoothed the brown wig, she thought she looked exactly like a woman who had just been royally kissed. Then she heard voices at the back door.

Josh jerked his head in that direction. ''C'mon. We'll greet them.''

Nina, Caroline and Ethan poured into the kitchen, and in minutes they all sat around the kitchen table with steaming mugs of hot chocolate. His family was warm, friendly and fun-loving, and Laurie envied him what he had, knowing in spite of all the upheaval and loss in his life, he still had some good, solid relationships with people who cared about him.

Did she have that kind of family? If she did, why weren't they searching for her? As talk swirled around her, these questions spun through her thoughts.

Shortly after one in the morning, she excused herself, leaving him alone with his relatives, certain they would enjoy having him to themselves without a stranger in their midst. She went to her bedroom and changed, pulling on a robe. She had left her purse in the family room and now she was thirsty, but she wasn't dressed and she had told them all good-night, so she didn't want to go back. Switching off the light, she sat beside the dark window while she replayed her time with Josh tonight down to the tiniest detail—dancing with him, kissing him.

Her past was still as obscure and dark as the night outside. Moonlight bathed open spaces in silvery light, but beneath trees and bushes were dark shadows that could hide anything. She shivered, easily imagining someone out there watching the house.

Had they really been followed tonight? Had someone found her? What could she have done in the past for someone to want her dead? What had she been involved in or witnessed?

The same old questions tormented her, so she returned to thinking about Josh until she heard voices and realized the family was finally going to bed.

When it got quiet, she crossed the room to the door and

tiptoed to the family room. The hall light was on and she didn't know whether someone would be returning downstairs or not. She hurried to get her purse and had turned to leave the family room when she heard voices. She realized Josh and one of his stepmothers must have been in the kitchen and were going upstairs now. Laurie started to step into the hall, but then heard Josh say her name.

Frowning, she halted, uncertain whether to continue or not.

"Look, Laurie needed help, Nina. It doesn't hurt anything for her to stay here on the ranch. I'm gone all day."

"You're in danger, Josh. If someone tried to kill her, you know he'll come back to see that the job was finished, and when he learns it wasn't, he'll be after her again. He may be after her right now. You could be in terrible danger."

"Could be, but I don't think I am. Like I told Laurie, there's a difference between going after an unarmed woman and going after an armed man who is staying in touch with the police."

"The nearest officers are in Stallion Pass. Too far away to help you. Get rid of her, Josh!"

"I don't see any need to," he answered quietly.

"I'm trying to take care of you! You don't know anything about her. Nothing! She could be a criminal involved in a murder."

"Could be, but I doubt it."

"You don't know what she is. She could be some high-priced call girl."

"Now I really doubt that one," he answered.

"Are you in love with this woman?"

"No, I'm not," he answered. "Nor will I be."

"You could have fooled me tonight. You practically hovered over her all evening."

"That's because I want to make sure she's safe."

"There you go! You *know* she's in danger. She'll be a

danger to everyone around her. She must be very selfish or she would have moved out of here first thing and not let you stop her.''

"I did stop her. Nina, she doesn't remember anything. She's totally vulnerable if she leaves here," Josh replied.

"So? She can cope with that. Send her to one of those shelters for women. She could stay there until her memory returns. You keep this woman out here alone on the ranch with you and you just might fall in love with her.''

"I'm *not* going to fall in love with her," he said. "You know I'm not a marrying man. It's late and I'm going to bed now.''

Their voices began to fade.

Laurie switched on a small lamp seconds before Nina walked into the room.

The two women stared at each other a moment. "I came down to get my purse," Laurie explained. "I didn't know anyone was still downstairs.''

"So you heard us. I'm just concerned about Josh," Nina said stiffly. Her blue eyes were cold and she stood with her arms crossed over her middle.

"I'm concerned about him, too," Laurie said. "He's been incredibly considerate to me, and I don't want to put him in danger or impose on him. I told him I should leave, and I know I should even though he's said he doesn't want me to go. I don't have a car, and if I call a taxi, he'll know.''

"He won't know if you call one while he's away from the house working, but you don't need to do that. If you would like, we can drop you off at a women's shelter when we leave. It really would be best for everyone here on the ranch.''

Laurie nodded. "If you don't mind letting me ride with you, I'll go. I know it'll be best for him.''

"You could be putting Josh in harm's way. It's because of you he was shot.''

"I regret that. I don't have many things, so I can be ready whenever you leave. But I should go to a hotel and not put women in a shelter in danger."

"No hotel. Shelters are set up to protect the women in them. You'll be safe." Nina sighed and gave Laurie a brittle smile. "Thank you for thinking of him. It relieves me more than I can say. Now we need to plan a little, because I know Josh. He can be very stubborn. He wants you to stay and he doesn't think he's in any danger. I think we should do this without him knowing about it."

"After all he's done, I'd feel terrible about sneaking away. He can't stop me if I want to go."

Nina gave her a look that made Laurie feel like a child who couldn't understand what she was being told. "My dear, this man is stubborn. I know Josh, and he's made his mind up about this. If you really are thinking of him, you'll do this my way."

Nina paced around the room, obviously deep in thought. Laurie watched her, torn between wanting to be truthful to Josh and wanting to protect him.

The older woman spun around. "How long would it take you to get your things together?"

"Not long. As I said, there's not that much. I haven't unpacked completely since I got here."

"Go get your things. Those shelters are accustomed to women showing up at all hours of the night. I've done volunteer work at one in Austin, so I know a little about them. I'll call and find one in San Antonio that will take you in. I'll drive you there right now."

"Tonight?" Laurie said, startled that it would be so soon. She wouldn't get to tell Josh goodbye, wouldn't get to thank him. But any goodbye would be painful, and this way might be best. This way he couldn't stop her.

"This is the perfect time. No one will know. You and I will be the only ones to know where you are. And anyone who might be watching the ranch won't spot us at this hour, surely. You should be perfectly safe.''

Laurie knew Nina was right, but it hurt to think of slipping out in such a manner and leaving Josh in the dark. She was breaking a promise she had just made to him hours earlier, yet it was for his own good.

''I'll get my things,'' she said. Hurrying to her room, she looked at Josh's closed door and thought about him in bed, asleep, remembering his kiss, wanting to be with him. She longed to tell him goodbye, but she knew Nina was right. This was the best way. Cut all ties, get out of his life, stop bringing danger to him and his men and to everyone around him.

She changed into jeans and a T-shirt, tossing her leather jacket onto the bed. She peeled off the brown wig, brushing her hair and letting it fall loosely around her face. If someone was watching the house, she wanted him to see her leaving, wanted everyone to know she was out of Josh's life. Once she was gone, Josh wouldn't be in any danger.

Feeling numb, she packed swiftly, carrying her suitcase to the back door. With every passing minute she hated leaving more, but every time she questioned what she was doing, she knew this move was for the best.

Getting a scrap of paper and a pen, she sat down and quickly wrote him a note. She folded it and carried it with her to the kitchen, where Nina was waiting.

''In case anyone wakes up and discovers us missing, I left a note,'' the woman said. ''If he couldn't find us, Josh would have the police searching for us in a minute. I have a cell phone, so if anyone does wake, we'll probably be getting a call. I'm parked by the back gate.''

Laurie paused to look around the kitchen, remembering the moments in it with Josh. She turned to Nina. ''Will you give this note to Josh?''

''Certainly.'' She tucked the paper into her pocket. ''I

know it's hard to leave, but you're doing what's best for him. I'll always be grateful to you for putting his safety first," she said quietly.

Nodding, Laurie picked up her suitcase and they left, Nina locking the door behind her.

They moved quietly through the chilly night. Laurie's gaze swept the barn and corral, the dark stands of trees beyond the outbuildings. Was someone out there watching her?

She hoped if there was, he was seeing her leave now.

On a thick branch of a sturdy oak, Finn Handly shifted and braced himself against the trunk of the tree. He was cold, uncomfortable and tired of staying in the tree, but earlier, the dogs had picked up his scent and found him, barking and whining until he thought he would have to shoot them and make a run for it. Then some family members or friends had come to the ranch. The dogs had raced away toward the arriving cars, barking and greeting people they obviously knew.

A ranch hand had whistled them in, and that was the last Finn had seen of them. He had watched lights go out in the house, but there were still several on, so he continued his vigil.

From what Finn had learned in town, the cowboy was Josh Kellogg, a solitary man, but one that had lots of relatives.

The small town was a wealth of information, but Finn had been very careful. Small-town people noticed strangers and were as nosy about them as they were about each other. He had kept his questions casual, his contacts to a minimum, gleaning little bits of information, and finally coming out to the ranch to see for himself.

He had seen Kellogg and a woman go into the house tonight, but the shutters had been closed and he couldn't get a good glimpse of her. He had watched her depart from the club's reception with the cowboy. Finn felt certain it was her.

When her car had skidded off the road and exploded, he had thought for sure he was rid of her. Job completed. But then nothing had shown up in the newspapers about a woman dying in a car crash. He had checked local hospitals and couldn't find any leads, no mention of a Jane Doe who fit her description, nothing. Nothing for too long, and he knew she had to have survived. That cowboy he'd shot at had to have found her. How Finn wished that one of his shots had killed the man! He couldn't be sure whether the cowboy had gotten a good look at him or not. Could Josh Kellogg identify him? That question had plagued him constantly.

Finn had gone back to the site of the crash. Then he had started checking on who owned the land. And eventually, in Stallion Pass, he had discovered that Josh Kellogg had a stepmother living with him at his ranch, but he had another woman living out there, too. That seemed to be a piece of hot gossip in the small town. Evidently the man didn't take his lady friends home to stay, and this was highly unusual.

Finn had learned about the wedding and had planted himself where he could see each guest go into the club. He had already found out what the cowboy looked like from old newspapers and rodeo shots. He'd gotten only a brief glimpse of the woman on Kellogg's arm when the two entered the club, but he felt certain it was her: same brown wig, same leggy stride. Then he had waited in the dark on the terrace and watched her dance with the cowboy. He had been tempted to try for a shot then, but his escape wasn't planned out.

He thought of the rifle in his car, one with a scope. There would be no misses this time, no failure. Once she was in the crosshairs of his rifle, he wouldn't miss. She would be his.

And so would the blackmail deal. Even if he pulled the trigger, he could get more money, because his boss couldn't risk a hint of involvement. All he wanted was an extra hundred grand. One time. He wasn't going to push it or bleed the man dry. And an extra hundred wouldn't hurt the guy— not with his wealth and with the woman out of the way.

The back door opened, breaking his reverie, and for a moment two figures were silhouetted against the brightly lit kitchen.

Instantly Finn was on alert, his aching muscles forgotten, dreams of money gone. He raised his binoculars and focused them. A woman he didn't know came out of the house. Then his pulse jumped. He focused on a tall blonde carrying a suitcase. Her face was in shadows, but he knew it was her. No wig this time. He recognized the cascade of golden hair, those long legs.

She was leaving! And leaving him at a disadvantage, he suddenly realized. He was over a mile from his car, which was parked up near the road. He watched the two women, his mind racing. By the time he got to the car, they would be gone.

He scrambled down out of the tree. If he ran, maybe he would get lucky and could make it by the time they reached the road. He jumped down, groaning as a pain shot through his ankle. He dropped the binoculars and had to scramble to find them.

The moment his hand closed over them, he was up and running, dashing through the hated woods. His next job would have to be a city job. He loathed the night creatures, the incessant bugs, the eerie sounds and the thick underbrush. He had heard this country was full of snakes. He shut his mind to that. Frantically he looked for the white strips of cloth he had placed on brush. Otherwise he never would find his way out of these woods.

At one point he tripped and sprawled on his face in the dirt and leaves. Swearing, he yanked up the binoculars and ran again, risking the flashlight to see where he was going. She was going to get away. She had a suitcase, so probably she was leaving the ranch for good. If he lost her now, he would have to start all over again.

Who was the other woman and where was she taking her? Why wasn't the cowboy driving her wherever she was going? Were they headed back to Kansas City? He tried to run faster. If he lost her now, he didn't want to have to report back about it. He didn't want to repeat the nightmare of searching for her.

Branches tore at his face, and his side hurt. He was gasping for breath even though he worked out nearly every day of his life.

Reaching his car at last, he flung himself behind the wheel and jammed the key into the ignition. When the engine roared to life, he shifted into gear and eased ahead, picking up speed as he bounced over the rough, open ground, not caring if they found tracks.

He drove over the fence he had knocked down and then he was on the road, accelerating, gritting his teeth. He couldn't lose her again.

Laurie sat quietly, her thoughts focused on Josh as they left the ranch. She answered Nina's chatter perfunctorily, barely aware of what she was saying.

"You're doing the right thing, and I thank you so much," Nina repeated. "Now I can go home and know Josh is safe. Since he's helped you from the first moments of your wreck, I'm sure you've come to depend on him, but you'll find friends at this shelter and women who will help you. The woman I talked to at the shelter is named Glenna

Thorne. She said they have a security guard on duty at all times.''

''I'm not worried. No one will know where I am,'' Laurie said, still thinking of Josh. Driving through the dead of night, she felt little fear for herself. She was doing what she should, removing any chance of danger for Josh, yet why did she feel so terrible about it? He would know why she hadn't said goodbye. And Nina was right. This was what was best.

In spite of all her mental arguments, Laurie was wrapped in gloom. She paid little attention to Nina until finally the woman fell silent.

Glancing at the mirror on the passenger side, Laurie became aware there were headlights in the distance behind them. Was it just an ordinary car, or was someone following them? As they approached the outskirts of town, the headlights were still far behind them.

''Nina, there's a car behind us. There's a chance someone could be following us.''

Nina shot her a worried glance and adjusted the rearview mirror. ''I don't think so, but I'll watch.''

In minutes they were in light traffic on the freeway into the city, and Nina shrugged. ''I don't think anyone was following us. Don't worry. Whether they were or not, you'll be safe. This shelter is accustomed to dealing with women who are trying to escape violent men.''

They were quiet until they stopped at an unpretentious frame building on an out-of-the way street near the center of town. A light burned over the door.

''I can take care of myself from here,'' Laurie said. ''You don't need to get out, and you should head back to the ranch. I'll say goodbye now.''

''I'll keep you in my prayers that you get your memory soon and things work out for you.'' Nina smiled at her coolly. "You're not going to call Josh to come get you, are you?"

"No, I'm not," Laurie answered, trying to be patient with the woman, who was merely being protective of her stepson. "Josh is out of my life."

Nina nodded. "Thank you for leaving. Goodbye, Laurie, and good luck."

Laurie got out, taking her suitcase, and as she approached the house, a uniformed man appeared out of the shadows.

"I'm Laurie Smith. My friend called ahead and talked to Glenna Thorne."

He nodded and held the door for her. Inside, Laurie met Glenna, a short brunette.

"Welcome, Laurie. You'll be safe with us," she said. "If you'll come with me and fill out a few papers, I'll show you to your room as soon as you're finished."

Laurie sat down with Glenna to fill out a few forms and answer questions. Finally she was given a narrow room sparsely furnished with a bed, dresser, desk and chair. She was shown where the kitchen and bathroom were, and was given a printed schedule.

She felt completely alone in the world, and it was cold and scary, yet she continually reminded herself that this was best for Josh, and eventually her memory would return. Her doctor had told her it would. She had said that memory could come back in bits or all in a flash.

Laurie changed and climbed into bed between clean, fresh-smelling sheets. She turned out the light and finally allowed memories to come, thinking of the moments she had stood in Josh's arms and he had kissed her senseless. Now it seemed eons away instead of only hours.

She had nothing to compare his kisses to, but she suspected when her memory returned, she would find that Josh's kisses had been the best of her life.

* * *

Outside, Finn stood in the shadows, trying to move with stealth. He had seen her under the bright, bare bulb of the porch light. It was her. There was no mistake. He didn't know what the place was, but there was a security guard.

He didn't care. When daylight came, he would find out about the place. No fast moves. He wanted to be careful, certain, but with his rifle, the job would soon be done.

He crept back to his car and climbed inside. Thankful to be in a city again, he headed for a motel. He could catch some sleep and then get back to work. She hadn't looked as if she was going anywhere else tonight.

He wouldn't call yet to report her whereabouts. He wanted to know as much as he could before he phoned in. Hopefully, she would be dead when he made that call.

Josh came awake, turning to stare at the glow-in-the-dark numerals on his clock. It was almost five. Memories rushed in of Laurie in his arms, dancing with him, kissing him. He stared into the night, seeing her, remembering her saucy challenge and then those kisses that had turned him inside out.

Just remembering her kisses aroused him. He wanted her as he had never wanted a woman before. Was it the forbidden part that made her so enticing? He knew it wasn't. Those kisses would have had the same effect if she had been completely available, willing and ready for any kind of relationship.

With a groan he flung aside the covers and strode to his bathroom to take a cold shower, hoping that would help his body cool down. He wanted to drive out taunting memories, wanted to get dressed and go to the kitchen and wait for her. Usually in the morning he didn't see her because he left early to do his chores, but he had made arrangements for his men to take over today so he would be free to spend the morning with his family.

Free to spend the morning with Laurie. He admitted to himself that's what he wanted. And this afternoon they would be alone. Eagerness gripped him at the thought, and he hurried, wanting to get to the kitchen so he would be there when she came down.

He knew she usually didn't wake until several hours after he had gone, but she might this morning. Dressing in a navy shirt and jeans, he pulled on socks and boots, fastened his belt and drew a comb through his thick hair.

He tossed down the comb, and his pulse skittered again as he left the room and headed down the hall. Laurie's door was closed, and delicious, erotic, enticing images of her asleep taunted him.

She's forbidden! He reminded himself constantly to keep a distance, yet he would probably toss aside wisdom again tonight, as swiftly as he had last night.

He hummed a tune under his breath, filled with anticipation, eager to be with her.

He switched on the kitchen light and soon had coffee brewing, bacon frying and orange juice poured. With his relatives here, they would eat an old-fashioned, calorie-filled breakfast. The boys would devour it. Tomorrow he could go back to the healthy stuff, but today was a celebration of everyone being together, his own private celebration that Laurie was there.

She won't always be here, he reminded himself. He knew that full well, but she was here now and he was going to forget caution and enjoy her company today.

Caroline was the first up, appearing in her thick blue robe, looking pretty even without makeup and just waking up. "I thought I'd find you puttering around the kitchen. Sit down and enjoy your coffee and juice, and I'll take over."

"Thanks, I'll do that," he said, pouring himself a steaming cup of black coffee.

"Josh, how much danger are you in with Laurie here?"

"I don't think I'm in danger. All my men know what happened, and I've asked them to watch for anything strange. I'm being careful, and when we went to the wedding, I carried my pistol."

"That's not exactly reassuring."

"I'll be careful. I'm not afraid."

"Maybe that's what worries me. Someone tried to kill her. He could try again."

"When her memory returns, she'll leave, and by then she'll know what's she's up against, whether the law will help her, if she has friends or family who can assist her."

Caroline turned to study him. "Please be careful. You're important to me."

"I will be," he said, smiling at her.

She looked up at him. "I talked to Mary Cordoba last night. She told me you got shot by the man who's after Laurie."

"It was nothing."

"I am just so worried about you."

He sipped his cold orange juice, aware that she was still studying him. "What, Caroline? Something else is bothering you, right?"

"What happens if you fall in love with her, Josh?"

Chapter 9

"I'm not falling in love with her and I won't," Josh replied, yet he didn't look at Caroline, and his denial was difficult to say.

She rubbed her forehead. "Men can be so obtuse. I saw you dancing with her last night. You've never in your life been deeply, truly in love, and I've always thought that when you did finally fall in love it would be the once-in-a-lifetime, this-has-to-be-forever kind."

"Well, I'm not in any danger of that happening. If she left today, I could say goodbye and that would be that."

"You really think so?"

"Absolutely. I'm not a marrying man. You know I've never gotten serious with any woman and I'm not going to now."

"I suppose. Why hasn't her family come in search of her? She's a gorgeous young woman someone, somewhere, has to have missed by now.

He set down his juice. "I'll admit, that's another bad

thing. She's on the run. She was carrying an enormous amount of cash," he said quietly.

Caroline closed her eyes and clutched her middle. When she opened her eyes, she looked pained, but murmured, "Just promise you'll be careful, okay? And remember, I'll be around if you need me."

Josh smiled. "Thanks."

"Good morning!" Ben entered the room. He wore plaid shorts and his hair stood up in tufts as he rubbed his face with his hand.

"Ben, go put on some clothes. We have a guest in the house," Caroline said.

He gazed at her with round eyes, then looked at Josh questioningly.

"Laurie, remember?" Josh stated dryly.

"I'm decent. I'm in shorts. This is what I wear to the beach."

"They look like the first deep breath you take, they're going to fall off," Caroline remarked. "But if you go out that way in public, I guess you can come into the kitchen that way."

"Put on some jeans," Josh said.

Ben shrugged and left, and Caroline looked at Josh. "Now how do you get that out of him, when I can't and his father couldn't have possibly?"

Josh smiled. "I'm the daddy who raised him, so I'm the voice of authority."

"That's too true," she said. "Well, thank goodness you're around and thank goodness he's a good kid, or I'd be in real trouble."

"I am around and he is a good kid, so all's well."

Minutes later Ben returned in jeans, and Caroline handed him a glass of juice and a glass of milk. He downed the juice in one long gulp and then moved to the table to sit down with Josh. "When does Laurie get up?"

"I don't think for another hour," Josh said, glancing at the clock, "but most mornings I'm gone, so I don't know for certain."

"She is one good-looking woman," Ben said. "Too bad she can't remember anything. You don't know whether she's married or not, do you?"

"No, I don't."

"Ben, the eggs will be done in a minute. Will you fix toast?" Caroline asked.

Ben crossed to the cabinet to get out a loaf of bread. "I hope Laurie gets up soon. Once Kevin comes in, he'll spend every second flirting with her. Unless you keep him from it," Ben said, shooting Josh a wicked look filled with curiosity.

"I don't care if he flirts with her."

"Hey, Kevin and I have a bet to see who can ride the white stallion the longest," Ben said. "Is that okay with you?"

Josh grinned. "Be my guest. I'll give you each two full seconds. And when you hit the dirt, you better be up and running."

Ben laughed. "We'll see. You haven't tamed him yet?"

"I haven't had time to do anything except see that he has feed and water."

In minutes the three were eating breakfast, yet Josh kept glancing at the kitchen door, watching for Laurie. He was only half paying attention to the conversation, enjoying Ben and Caroline, yet eager for Laurie to join them.

He knew Kevin would flirt with her, and the thought mildly annoyed him. He glanced at the empty kitchen doorway again and wished Laurie would get up.

They were finished with breakfast, Ben placing dishes in the dishwasher while Josh and Caroline sipped another cup of coffee, when Ethan joined them. Ten minutes later, Nina came in. She wore makeup and was dressed in pale yellow linen slacks and a linen blouse. The scent of her perfume floated in the air as Ben served the newcomers breakfast.

A half hour later, Josh was thinking about going to wake Laurie when he heard a clatter in the hall. He knew it was Kevin, who did nothing quietly.

The youth bounded into the room, barefoot, wearing a T-shirt and cutoffs. "Morning, all," he said. "I'm starving. What's for breakfast? It smells great."

He helped himself and pulled up a chair, looking around the table. "Where's Laurie?"

"How she can sleep through you being up, I don't know," Ben remarked, and Kevin made a face at him.

"Want me to get her up?" Kevin asked, his eyes twinkling as he looked at Josh.

"I think I'll do that," Josh said, standing. "I don't know how she's slept this long, either."

"It's still early," Caroline said. "Maybe she's one of those late sleepers."

"She left us early enough last night," Josh said. He started out of the room.

"Josh," Nina said. "Don't go."

He turned around. Nina's request was odd and unlike her, and his curiosity stirred. "Why not?" he said, sauntering back to the table. Everyone was looking at Nina, who fidgeted with a thin gold chain that hung around her neck.

"Why not wake her?" Josh repeated.

"She's not here," Nina stated, lifting her chin. She withdrew a scrap of paper from her pocket. "She wrote you a note."

Josh inhaled, trying to hold back his temper. "Why isn't she here? When did she leave?" he demanded.

Nina pointed to the paper. "Maybe you should read her note."

There was total silence in the kitchen while Josh scanned the simple note, written in a dainty, feminine hand: "It's best for you if I leave. I'm somewhere safe. Don't look for me because I can't come back. Thanks for all you've done. Laurie.''

He dropped the note on the table. "How'd she leave?" he asked in a cold, quiet voice, and Nina paled.

"Mom, what did you do?" Kevin asked. "Did you and Ethan take her somewhere?"

"I haven't been off the ranch since we got here last night," Ethan protested. "Nina, what's going on?"

"Where is she, Nina?" Josh repeated.

"I took her where she'll be safe and looked after."

"Dammit, she was safe here," Josh said. "Nina, where is she?"

"I'm not going to tell you."

"Nina, tell me where you took Laurie. Tell me now," Josh demanded in a chilly tone.

"I will not, because it's for your own good. And hers. She's safer where she is."

"The hell she is," Josh said, turning and heading for the phone.

"What are you doing?" Nina called after him. "You can't get her back. She's gone. I put her on a plane."

Josh spun around to look at her. "To where? Nina, don't lie to me."

Tears filled her eyes, and she put her handkerchief to her face. "Don't accuse me of being terrible when I'm just trying to be a mother to you."

"Darling, don't cry," Ethan said, patting her shoulder. She put her head against his chest.

"If y'all will excuse me," Kevin said, dumping his dishes into the dishwasher with his breakfast only half-eaten. He left the kitchen.

Remembering Nina's suggestion that he take Laurie to a shelter for women, Josh looked up shelter phone numbers, praying that she hadn't put Laurie on a plane, as she'd claimed. He had a tight feeling in the pit of his stomach. If anyone had followed them, he wasn't sure whether Laurie would know or not, but he knew for certain that Nina wouldn't.

"Don't try to get her back, Josh. She knows she's putting you in jeopardy by being here. She won't come with you. She's gone."

"Gone where, Nina?" he snapped.

She drew a deep breath. "I'm going home. I've tried to help, and it's not appreciated.

Josh jotted down numbers, glancing at the clock. It was Sunday, too early for most places to be open, yet he thought a shelter might be available twenty-four hours every day.

"I'm going to get dressed," Ben said, leaving the room. "This will cut short the family gathering. And there goes trying to ride the white stallion."

The room was quiet as Josh jotted down more numbers.

"She's right, you know," Caroline said, and he looked over his shoulder at her. "You should let her go."

"She doesn't have any memory. She doesn't know who's trying to kill her or why," Josh answered. "She's damned vulnerable, and I think we were followed last night."

"That's all the more reason," Caroline said solemnly. "I have to agree with Nina on this one. I don't want to see you risk your life for a woman who can't remember her past. She could be married. She could be in terrible trouble with the law or something worse."

Josh shook his head. "Sorry, Caroline. I know you love me and you're looking out for me, but I want her back here. If they were followed from the ranch last night, she could be in terrible danger right now."

"So you'll go get her and put yourself back in dreadful danger," she said. "Josh, don't do it."

He turned around to look at the woman who'd been the

closest thing to a real mother he'd ever known. "I have to," he said quietly.

She sighed. "Well, in all your cautious, responsible life, I guess you're entitled to do something that you shouldn't, but I'll worry about you. I don't want you hurt—not physically, not emotionally."

"I'll be careful. About both. In the meantime, I don't want her hurt."

"Put the phone down. I'll help you. I'll go talk to Nina. I can probably find out where she took Laurie. Just remember, Nina did that because she loves you."

"Yeah, but I'm old enough to make those decisions about my life."

"I know you are. Give me a few minutes."

"Kind of hurry her along."

"If Laurie's in a shelter, then they're accustomed to protecting the women who stay there. Just remember that."

"I'll try."

He folded the list of numbers and jammed them into his pocket. Then he finished putting away dishes and cleaning the kitchen, anything to keep busy and keep from watching the clock, or thinking about Laurie being so vulnerable. He suspected she wouldn't stay in a shelter long. She had cash and had talked about moving to a hotel, and he was afraid he would lose her. She had enough cash to buy some kind of car and flee the area.

He moved impatiently, glancing at the hands on the clock and wanting to shake Nina for her interference.

He went to his room to get his billfold and keys, putting his pistol in the pickup and driving it to the back gate. He strode back inside and stood impatiently by the window, alternately looking outside and turning to watch the clock again.

It was thirty minutes later before Caroline returned to

hand him a slip of paper. "Here's where she is. Where Nina took her last night. Nina's terribly worried about you, too."

"You two stop worrying. I'll be all right. No one is after me."

"If you keep protecting her, someone might be."

"I'm armed and in touch with the police."

She nodded. "Do you want to phone her first?"

"No, because she'll tell me she should stay out of my life."

"Well, then go get her."

"Thanks, Mom," he said, crossing the room to kiss her lightly on the cheek.

She hugged him. "You be careful. I love you."

"I love you, too," he said. He didn't call her mom in front of his other stepmothers, but he always did when the others weren't around. He jogged to the pickup and climbed inside, praying Laurie hadn't left the shelter yet. He had a gut feeling that she would leave this morning.

Laurie stretched and stared at the ceiling, looking around the unfamiliar room. Disoriented, she sat up and then remembered everything from the night before. She swung her legs out of bed and moved to the window, gazing out at a patio that held rusty lawn furniture, toys, a sandbox. A clothesline was stretched between two metal posts. A tall stockade fence enclosed the yard.

She should be safe here, yet if anyone tried to kill her, some of the other women—or children—could get hurt. She couldn't bear that. It was bad enough to put Josh and his men at risk, but they were tough, armed and ready, and on their own turf. None of these women or children would be.

She knew she needed to leave. The thought of a hotel was frightening, because she would have little protection, but she couldn't put the people here at more risk.

Also, Laurie knew that she needed to let the police know

where she was in case anyone showed up looking for her. She needed to let her doctor know. In spite of the security of the shelter, she felt she might be happier in a hotel. She could have more freedom, more independence.

She dressed in a T-shirt and jeans. She had been told there would be breakfast at eight, and she could hear others up. She heard the voices of small children.

She finally left her room. In the dining room she counted nine women and half as many children, seated around the two long tables. Colorful pictures decorated the walls, and the tempting aromas of hot coffee and bread filled the air.

Laurie sat between a pretty young woman named Adele with a little girl, Sonya, and a tall, slender brunette named Vi who held a baby in her arms while she ate. Laurie ate a little toast, but she wasn't hungry and soon shoved her plate aside. She heard a commotion in another part of the house and noticed some of the women grow still, worry coming into their expressions.

"Laurie!" a deep voice shouted. "Laurie!"

Startled, Laurie recognized Josh's voice. She excused herself quickly from the table, rushing out of the room and toward the office. In the front hallway, the security guard had Josh by the arm, and Josh was arguing with him.

"Josh!" she cried, too aware of the skip of her heart. In his black hat and jeans and denim jacket, he looked wonderful.

"Come home with me," he said. "I came to get you."

"You don't have to leave here," a woman said quickly. "I heard you arrived last night. I'm June Blankenfeld."

"C'mon, buddy. Out now!" the guard snapped, yanking on Josh's arm.

"You take your hands off of me while I talk to her," Josh said in a low voice that was filled with steel. The guard dropped Josh's arm and looked at Laurie.

"Laurie," Josh said. "Please come with me. It's what I want."

"Thank you," she said to June. "I'll go outside to talk to him so we don't disturb anyone."

"Are you sure?" June asked.

"He's been taking care of me and he's been very good to me. I came here to protect him, because someone I don't remember has tried to kill me."

"Oh!" June Blankenfeld looked startled. "Well, whatever you need to do..."

"I'll be back in a minute."

The guard stepped aside as Laurie hurried toward Josh. Josh took her arm and they left the house.

"Come sit in my pickup and talk to me," he said, shedding his jacket to throw it around her. "I don't like being out here in the open, where someone could take a shot at you."

"That's the precise reason I don't want to go back home with you. Nina was right."

"Nina is worried about me, but I can take care of myself. I'm worried about you and I want you to come back to the ranch with me. You're not as safe here and you know it. Someone can get to you. If I had come in the night, I could have gotten around that guard."

When Josh opened the door, Laurie climbed into his pickup. Skirting around to the driver's side, he slid behind the wheel and flipped the locks. "Scoot down in the seat a little."

She wanted to touch his hands, to feel his solid chest and strong embrace. Instead, she locked her fingers together in her lap, knowing she needed to say no to him. "I may not be safe anywhere, but I'll jeopardize your life at the ranch."

"You'll jeopardize the lives of these women and children here."

"I know that. I planned to go to a hotel today."

"Dammit, am I going to have to argue with you all day? I'll stay here and follow you to a hotel and stay in a room next to yours if I have to, but then my ranch will go to hell, and I can't afford that."

She closed her eyes and threw up her hands. "I believe you would do exactly that."

"Damn straight I will."

She stared out the window, her emotions churning. "You're making it difficult for me."

"I'm doing what I think is best."

She still continued to look out the window, fighting everything in her that screamed to go with him. She didn't want him in danger, yet she suspected he would do exactly what he said and stay with her at any hotel she went to. She looked at him. His green eyes flashed fire and his jaw was set with that same hard look he'd had the first moments she had met him.

"All right. I'll go home with you, but I'm scared for you and your men. Your family will hate me."

"Believe me, my family knows how to adjust to all sorts of things. And Nina and Ethan and Kevin have gone home, so they won't be around to protest. My men and I can take care of ourselves, and frankly, I would like to get my hands on the person who ran you off the road."

She rubbed her arms. "Maybe you should teach me to use a gun."

"Nope. That takes time and training, and I don't want an amateur packing a pistol. You might be more dangerous to us then than anyone else."

She shook her head. "You win. I'll get my things." Her pulse raced. She had to admit she was glad to go back to the ranch.

"Don't get out of the pickup. You're a sitting duck out here for someone with a rifle. Stay down. I'll lock you in and I'll get your things."

"Are you kidding? They would never believe that I'm all right and going of my own free will. Remember what kind of men they're accustomed to dealing with here. Nope, mister. I'll go get my things and explain to them I've decided I want to go back to your ranch. You sit right here so they believe me. Besides, the security guard is right there on the porch, watching us."

"So he is." Josh leaned across her, lowered her window and motioned to the guard to come to the car. Before he straightened up, he paused to look at her.

He was only inches from her, his shoulder touching hers, and she inhaled, her heart missing a beat. His harsh expression changed abruptly, and the look he gave her made her toes curl. Then he straightened and opened his door.

"What're you doing?"

"I'll get him to escort you." Josh stepped out of the pickup and talked quietly to the security guard, who turned to open her door. He glanced all around and then got behind her as she headed to the door, while Josh walked beside her. She hurried, suddenly feeling vulnerable, too aware there was a man behind her who could get shot for trying to protect her.

She scurried inside and turned. "Thanks."

"Let me know when you're ready to go back."

She nodded and rushed to the office to find June Blankenfeld and explain to her that she wanted to leave with Josh.

Thirty minutes later, Josh wound his pickup through town. When he left the city limits, Laurie glanced at him. "You must feel certain we don't have a tail."

"You're right. I'm sure we don't. So we can relax." He looked at her and smiled. "I want you back. I've been waiting to see you since I woke up this morning."

She drew a quick breath. "Josh, be careful."

"I will be."

"I mean about us. You know we shouldn't have kissed, and it shouldn't happen again."

"Yeah, but I can still enjoy your company and be glad to have you around." He took her hand, and she arched her brows at him.

"You weren't listening at all, were you?" she asked.

"Sure. You're the one who wasn't listening."

At the ranch Josh slowed and parked at the back gate, then rushed Laurie into the house.

Only Caroline and Ben were there, and Josh and Laurie spent the rest of the day with them. Laurie enjoyed them, and noted the closeness between them and Josh. Laughing often, Josh was more relaxed with his family around. As she watched them together, she felt a pang of longing, wondering if she even *had* a family.

Josh talked Caroline and Ben into staying for an early supper. They were all getting food on the table when Laurie glanced out the window and saw Josh's foreman, Drake Browning, striding toward the house.

"Here comes Drake, Josh," she said.

Yanking on his denim jacket, Josh left, closing the back door behind him. When he returned, he smiled, but the expression in his eyes was angry, and Laurie wondered what had happened. But as they sat at the table and began to eat, she forgot about the incident.

The sun was slanting in the western sky when they stood on the porch to see Caroline and Ben off.

Caroline took Laurie's hand. "I hope you get your memory back soon."

"Caroline, I want you to know I tried to leave here and stay away. Josh threatened to follow me to a hotel and take up residence there."

Caroline smiled, glancing at Josh as he talked to Ben. Both men stood at the foot of the porch steps.

"Josh can be stubborn sometimes," Caroline said.

"Nina's intentions were good—at least as far as Josh was concerned. She was just worried about him."

"I know, and she was right, but I couldn't see that it would help for both of us to be in a hotel. He needs to be here on his ranch."

"I hope when your memory returns, the things you've forgotten are only good things. You take care."

"I will. It was so nice to meet you."

Caroline gave her a half smile, but Laurie knew she was worried about Josh, and didn't blame her. As Caroline started down the steps, Laurie followed, until Josh glanced up.

"Laurie, stay on the porch," he said.

She stopped on the top step, hearing the solemn warning in his voice. She remembered Drake coming to talk to Josh and wondered why Josh was being so cautious.

"I'm taking Laurie inside," he told Caroline, and kissed her cheek.

Caroline turned to walk to the car, while Ben sprinted to the driver's side. "'Bye, Laurie, Josh," he called, before he opened the door and waved.

"Ben is waving at you, Josh."

"Let's get you inside," he said, standing on the lowest step and turning to wave at Ben. Then his gaze was drawn to the woods beyond them, as it had been time and again. A glint caught his attention and then he thought he saw a gun barrel. "Get down!" he yelled, too far away to reach Laurie himself.

The crack of the rifle sent birds flying, and shattered the quiet.

A piece of wood flew out of the wall behind Laurie, while to Josh's horror, she crumpled to the floor of the porch and then lay still.

Chapter 10

"Laurie!" Josh took the remaining three stairs in one long stride and knelt beside her.

Unable to breathe while his heart thudded so hard, Josh felt her throat. Relief swamped him when he found a steady pulse. He turned her over, saw blood spilling from a head wound, and yanked out his handkerchief to press it against the wound.

Ben reached the porch as Josh picked up Laurie. "Call 911," Josh snapped. "Then call Drake to let the men know a killer is somewhere on the ranch."

Ben dashed past Josh, while Caroline caught up with them and held the door open. Josh carried Laurie to the sofa in the family room.

"Get some gauze and antiseptic, Caroline," Josh ordered, placing Laurie on the sofa, yet wanting to hold her in his arms.

She stirred and moaned.

"Laurie?" he asked, lifting his handkerchief to look at

the damage. To his relief, the bullet had grazed her head, giving her only a superficial wound. But it was bleeding profusely.

She moaned again and opened her eyes to stare at him. "You told me to get down. What happened? I heard a shot."

"Someone was in the woods."

"I can't imagine Carter shooting at me like that," she said, holding her head.

"Carter?" Startled, Josh looked down at her. At the same time she gazed up at him with shock in her expression.

"Josh," she said, her eyes growing wide while she gripped his shoulder with one hand. "I remember a name!"

"That's great, Laurie," he said, waiting for her to blurt out more. But she gave him a dazed look.

"I don't know who Carter is. I just remember that name and know he's tried to harm me."

"That's better than not knowing anything."

Ben burst into the room at the same time Caroline brought bandages and first aid supplies. Trying to avoid hurting her, Josh began to clean Laurie's wound.

"The ambulance and Will Cordoba are on their way," Ben said. "I think I hung up on the dispatcher, but maybe that will get them here quicker. I talked to Drake, and he's taking some men to see if he can find anyone."

"Thanks," Josh said, getting antiseptic from Caroline. "This is going to hurt."

"It already does," Laurie said, closing her eyes.

Drawing a deep breath, Josh worked as gently as he could, too aware of each wince when he touched her.

"Josh, I can go help Drake," Ben said.

"And give your mother a nervous breakdown?" Josh remarked. "No way. You and Caroline get in your car and go. It'll be safe now, and you need to get back to college."

"Aw, come on," Ben grumbled.

"Please, Ben," Caroline said. "We're not needed here, what with the sheriff and an ambulance coming."

"Once they get here, you may have to stay for hours to answer questions," Josh said. "Take your mother and go."

"You're sure?" Caroline asked, and Josh nodded.

She bent to brush his cheek with a kiss. "You and Laurie be careful. Don't take chances."

"Go with them to the door and lock it," Laurie said, opening her eyes to look at Josh. "I'm okay, and we need to keep the door locked."

He left, and when he returned, she was standing in front of the mirror, dabbing at her wound.

"Will you sit down?" he demanded, and she turned to look at him, her eyes sparkling. He tilted his head. "What?"

"Josh, I have sisters. I can remember names and I know they're my sisters! Well, I remember first names," she said, her smile fading. "I don't remember the all-important last names."

"That's great! If your memory is returning, more will come." He took her hand. "Let me finish bandaging your head."

She ignored his words. Instead, she walked over to put her arms around him. "Hold me a minute before all the lawmen get here. Just hold me and let me know I'm safe and you're safe."

"I'm not going to argue with that one," he said gruffly, thinking about what a scare he had received, watching her go down as he heard the shot.

She looked up at him. "I'm getting blood on your shirt."

"I don't care."

"Josh, I'm not married. I just know I'm not. I can remember a sister named Emily and I can remember her house. I remember a restaurant and another sister, Talia."

"That's great. More will come. Just relax, and it'll come.

And you're single. At least I won't have to worry about angry husbands and a guilty conscience,'' he said lightly. But even if she was single, it didn't change a thing as far as his feelings on long-term relationships and marriage went. He wasn't a marrying man. Never had been, never would be. He didn't want a life like his dad's, with all that turmoil and upheaval and tearing up other people's lives. He raised his head. ''I hear sirens.''

''You have ears like a cat.''

''It's from living out here where it's quiet so much of the time. It's a wonder city folk aren't all deaf with that constant, infernal racket that surrounds them.'' He led her to the sofa. ''You stay here. I'll go meet them.''

''They're going to get tired of seeing me.''

''This is a different bunch. This is an ambulance from Stallion Pass, and you're not going to go to a hospital. I'll know these medics and I can talk them out of that. I don't think you're hurt that badly. They may clean your wound better than I did, but they'll be on their way soon. Now the cops—we'll have them with us all night. And I'm going with them to look for the guy.''

''Please don't,'' she pleaded.

''I'll be all right,'' he said tersely, and left, and she knew her protest was useless.

During the next hour paramedics cleaned and bandaged her wound, then packed their things and left. Police were in the house, and she knew they were on the grounds. At one point Will Cordoba came in to get information from her for his report on the shooting.

Long after dark, Josh returned, thanked the policemen who had been with her and locked up after they left. Then he came to sit down facing her. His angry scowl made her certain the shooter had gotten away.

''He's gone. The police will continue to search for him,

but they're sure he's gone and I'm sure he's gone. He saw you fall and he may think he's killed you.''

She shivered. ''So I'm in as much danger as ever, and I'm putting you in jeopardy.''

''Yes, but if your memory is returning, you'll be able to solve some of the puzzle, and then maybe the police can catch this guy.'' Josh stood to switch off some of the lights. While he built a fire, she watched him.

''I'm going to make the rounds and turn off more lights. Want anything? Some hot cocoa?'' he finally asked.

''That sounds great. I'll start the cocoa, and you check the house and lights.''

''Sit still and let me wait on you.''

''I'm all right. If I get woozy or my head hurts worse, I'll sit down and wait for you to do everything.''

''You don't take orders well, do you?''

''I take them better than you do,'' she answered, arching an eyebrow. Shaking his head, he left, and she could hear his boots scrape as he walked down the hall.

Later they returned to the family room. One small lamp was on, and a fire burned in the fireplace. As Josh entered the room, the phone rang and he picked it up. Laurie could hear his part of the conversation and realized something terrible had happened. As soon as he replaced the phone, he turned to look at her.

''That was Gabe. Remember, I told you we had another close friend?''

''Yes. Wyatt, you said.''

''Wyatt Sawyer. Hank and Olivia Sawyer, Wyatt's brother and sister-in-law, inherited the ranch last year when old man Sawyer died. Gabe just called to tell me that Hank and Olivia were killed last night. Hank had his own plane and was a pilot. Their plane went down in the mountains of Colorado in a snowstorm.''

''How awful!''

"Yeah. They have a baby girl. Gabe said the baby wasn't with them."

"Think your friend Wyatt will come home now?"

Josh shrugged. "From what I've heard, I don't think Wyatt has had any contact with his family since he left here. He probably won't even know. I imagine Olivia's family will take care of the little girl. It's damned awful."

"I'm sorry, Josh."

He shook his head. "I wasn't good friends with his brother. Hank was older than we were, and he and Wyatt didn't always get along, so I didn't know Hank that well. But it's too bad. If they put the ranch up for sale, I'm sure Gabe will buy it."

Laurie sat on a corner of the sofa with her legs folded under her, and Josh crossed the room to sit facing her in a wing chair. He held his cup of hot chocolate, while she set hers down on the coffee table near her.

"This afternoon, why did Drake come talk to you?" she asked.

Anger sparked in his green eyes. "Someone cut my fence and drove across part of the ranch. Whoever it was left in a hurry. I think the guy was here last night and had scoped out the place."

She felt a chill, thinking about someone spying on them.

"He probably was watching the house, saw you leave with Nina, and took off. I don't suppose you know whether or not you were followed?"

"When we got into the city, I couldn't tell, but early on, there were headlights far in the distance behind us. Still, that could happen on any public road."

"You probably were followed. Nina would never know, and when you're not in the driver's seat, it's hard to tell."

"I half wanted someone to see me leaving here so none of you would be in danger. But then, I didn't want to put all those innocent women and children in danger, either."

"You're going to have to stay inside," Josh stated grimly, looking at the closed shutters on the windows. "For a few minutes I thought we had a tail when we left the shelter this morning. If we did, the shooter saw you leave with me. He knew where to find you, so he probably just came back here, watched the house and waited for the right moment."

"You're scaring me again."

"Well, that's what I think happened. Drake and the men will take turns watching the house and grounds for the next few days and nights." Josh got up and moved across the room to sit beside her on the sofa. "How's your head?"

"They gave me something for a headache. I know the injury is there, but it's okay."

"Good. Now tell me what you remember."

Her eyes sparkled and she smiled. "I do remember more. I remember houses and I know one of them is my sister's house, and I remember her. I remember both sisters. I'm very fuzzy about Carter, but I can picture him and I know he wants to hurt me. I remember a bedroom and I think it's mine."

"And you don't remember a guy in it?" he teased.

She smiled. "No, I don't. I think I'm single."

"It doesn't change things a lot, Laurie. I'm not a marrying man."

"Maybe you should make a sign to hang around your neck. Then you wouldn't have to say it so often."

"Miss Smarty-mouth."

"I don't recall asking you to marry me or asking you for any such commitment," she replied in a saucy voice.

"No, you didn't. You warned me to watch out for my heart because I might lose it."

"So we're both forewarned," she said, teasing him, and Josh looked at her. Her blond hair framed her face in a silken fall. The red T-shirt she wore fit snugly, outlining her lush breasts and a tiny waist he knew he could span with his hands. Jeans covered her bottom half, but he knew how her legs looked and mentally stripped away the jeans. He caught her wrist. "Come here," he said.

Laurie's heart drummed as she gazed up at him. "Josh, you've been keeping your distance, as you should."

"Since when did you get scared of tempting fate?"

"As you said, you're a grown man, old enough to make your own decisions. You know you're playing with fire, so if you're willing to take the risks, I am," she said, scooting closer.

Swinging her around into his embrace, he cradled her with her head against his shoulder, being careful of her wound. He leaned closer. "You sure can drive a man wild," he said in a husky voice.

"Well, I wonder how many broken hearts *you've* left behind."

"I don't have to worry about yours. You've been taunting and tempting me since the first day I met you."

"Sexy, tough cowboy—how could I resist?"

He inhaled, tightened his arms and leaned the last distance to kiss her.

Laurie's heart thudded as she locked her arms around his neck and kissed him in return. His tongue stroked hers, while his arms tightened around her and he leaned over her.

Molding her body to his, she clung to him—softness against hardness, a fit that heightened desire. Each time they were together escalated a consuming hunger. Wanting him in spite of all the dangers and risks, she responded eagerly. He shifted, running his hand over her bottom and then around her waist, up to her breast. He caressed her there lightly and she moaned with pleasure, the sound lost in his kisses.

She felt him tug her T-shirt out of her jeans, and then his

rough, calloused hand was on her bare skin, pushing aside her lacy bra.

She tore her mouth from his. "I want your hands there, everywhere," she gasped. "But we can't do this every night."

"To hell with every night. We're going to tonight," he said, raising his head to look at her.

Her heart pounded at the expression in his eyes. He looked as if he could devour her, and she wanted him to. "You like this, don't you?" he whispered, stroking her breast.

She closed her eyes, feeling his hard shaft pressing against her hip.

"You want me to kiss you, don't you?" he whispered, his tongue touching her ear and his warm breath on her skin making her tingle.

"Yes, I do," she answered without thought, sliding her hand beneath his T-shirt to run her fingers lightly across his muscled chest. She pressed her palm against him, feeling his racing heartbeat. Pleasure rippled through her at the effect she was having on him. She had to kiss and touch him as much as she wanted him to kiss and touch her.

She ached with longing to tug away his T-shirt, to press herself against his bare chest, to love him with more than just kisses and light caresses, but she knew she shouldn't be doing any loving. She had to stop, yet she didn't want to. Every kiss was torment and paradise.

She caught his wrist and sat up, gasping for breath. "Your family isn't coming in tonight to stop us. And we do have to stop."

Hating what she was doing, she moved off his lap to the other end of the sofa, straightening her clothes. Noticing his silence, she looked back at him. His smoldering gaze stole her breath like a blow to her middle.

Knowing she had to move farther away from him, she closed her eyes and stood. "I'll go."

She hurried from the room, every step tearing at her because she wanted to be in his arms. She wanted his loving and wanted his kisses. She wanted to love him, and it was blatantly obvious that he wanted her.

Hurrying to her bedroom, she entered and closed the door. She should never have come back with him. How would the two of them stay out here alone, night after night, and be able to resist temptation?

While some of her memory had been jogged, not all of it had returned yet. She didn't know anything about her life except that she was single, a man named Carter wanted to kill her, and she had sisters. Not enough to lose her heart to a tough cowboy who had no intention of getting deeply involved.

She pressed her hands to her head. Why didn't the rest of her memory return? Was there something so terrible that her mind couldn't cope with it?

She showered and changed into a red silk nightie, pulling on a matching silk robe. Still lost in thoughts about Josh, she strained her ears for any sound of him going past to his bedroom.

His bedroom right down the hall... Where she could be in his arms, loving him, all night.

She shut her mind to those thoughts, because she couldn't cross that line. Their kisses were forbidden pleasures, and if she wanted to go home without a broken heart, she had to stop flirting with him, stop kissing him.

She switched off the lights and moved restlessly around the room, finally pulling a chair near a window and sitting down to stare outside, watching shadows, wondering about her past.

At night dark shadows were menacing, each one capable

of hiding a killer. Who was Carter and why did he want to kill her? What had she seen or done?

Downstairs, Josh paced about the family room. He couldn't sit still. He switched on the television, channel surfed for a ball game, then tossed down the remote control, heading for the kitchen.

He poured a glass of milk and got some cookies, heading back to the family room. He wanted Laurie as he had never wanted another woman. The realization of the depth of his desire shook him hard.

When Nina had told him that Laurie was gone, everything hurt. He had been worried about her safety, but more than that, he had to admit, he'd wanted her back just to be with her.

"Dammit," he swore, sitting forward, taking a long drink of milk and eating a cookie. He had to get someone else to guard her. He couldn't stay shut in this house with her day and night. He wouldn't last two days before he tried to seduce her.

Basketball players ran up and down the court, but he didn't really see them. Was she in her room asleep or was she as restless and tied in knots as he was? He imagined her in bed and groaned, images taunting him.

With his thoughts on Laurie, he stared at the television, watching an ad come on—of a gorgeous woman smiling from a boat, telling viewers what a wonderful life was possible if they only owned the vessel. Riveted, Josh stared at the television.

There she was! Her blond hair shimmered in the sunlight. The cookie in his hand fell unnoticed to the floor. His mouth hung open in shock.

There was Laurie, smiling, wearing bright red shorts and a red halter top that gave him a great view of her fabulous figure. Her lips were full and rosy, her brown eyes wide and thickly lashed, the touches of makeup highlighting her beauty. Her body took his breath away because it was easy to imagine her without the halter and shorts. She was stunning with that familiar, gorgeous smile.

A model! She was a model. There was no mistaking what he was seeing and her profession fit so well. She had the looks for it, and, the walk. She had the voice to be on television, the poise. And that sexy, come-hither expression was on her face, that familiar challenge dancing in her eyes.

"Damn," he repeated, coming to his senses and dashing across the room to hit the record button, trying to get at least part of the commercial. Different emotions raged in him, beginning with relief and joy to learn who she was and that she had a legitimate background. The relief and joy changed instantly to a gut-wrenching pain, because now he couldn't date her. She was a model with a glamorous, fascinating career in some big city. A city woman. Laurie had already guessed that much. There would be no future for her with him in it, and the realization hurt even though he had known all along that's exactly what would happen.

Somewhere deep inside, he knew he'd harbored a hope that he could see more of her when she learned of her past and her identity. But that wasn't going to happen. They were finished almost before they'd started. She was a beautiful, sophisticated model—completely beyond his reach.

Yet he hadn't wanted to get seriously involved with her, anyway—so why did it hurt so badly to realize that any future between them was impossible?

Sadness came with the hurt, and then concern for her safety. This was a high-profile woman, so what was she mixed up in? Now he could understand the cash, the flight, but from what? At least he had a place to start searching for her past. Why wasn't an agency looking for her? Why wasn't her family looking for her? There had to be a boyfriend. All this flashed through Josh's mind in seconds as he watched her on television.

Then she was gone, replaced by the next ad. Josh crossed the room to the phone, intending to call the sheriff. But as he thought about it, he halted, staring at the door. Before he told Laurie, before he told anyone, he wanted to make some decisions himself.

He glanced over his shoulder and saw that in his haste to record the commercial, he had spilled his milk.

He went to the kitchen to get paper towels, and in minutes had the milk spill cleaned up. For the next half hour, he surfed channels, trying to catch another ad with Laurie in it. All the time he looked at different commercials, he mulled over what to do next.

The one thing he kept reminding himself was that if she had been forbidden to him before, she was absolutely off-limits now.

Finally he switched off the television and strode down the hall in his sock feet. He stopped in front of her closed door. He didn't care what time of night it was or whether she was asleep or awake. She had to know what he had learned.

He knocked lightly, and then more loudly. "Laurie, get up. I want to talk."

"Josh, we shouldn't. Not tonight," she said, her words slightly muffled by the closed door.

"Come out here. I know who you are."

Chapter 11

Stunned by his words, Laurie yanked open the door to stare wide-eyed at him. "Who am I? How'd you find out? How'd you learn about my identity?"

Momentarily, he was riveted by the sight of her. She wore a red silk robe, loosely belted, with a deep V that revealed luscious curves, and he knew she wore very little beneath the robe.

"Josh?" she prodded, frowning.

"Let's go back to the family room where we can talk."

"Josh Kellogg, stop keeping me in suspense!" she snapped, stepping in front of him and blocking his path, holding his shoulders. "You know. Tell me now!"

He wanted her. He wanted to wrap his arms around her and kiss her and shut out what he had just learned. Sadly, he knew that was impossible. "You're a model. I saw you in a television commercial. I think I have a little of it taped."

"Then let's go watch it!" she said, grabbing his hand and dashing for the family room.

Grimly he hurried downstairs with her, then crossed the room to rewind the tape, get the remote and turn on the VCR. Laurie stood watching, and when the commercial came on, she said the words right along with the image of herself.

"I know the words!" she exclaimed when it was over. "I know the words. 'Want to put some fun in your life this summer?' I know it! And now we can call the sheriff and he can find out where I live and everything."

Her eyes sparkled, and Josh saw that she wanted to get back to her own life and out of his, and he knew he had to let her go. And this was best, anyway, for him.

"Wait, Laurie. I saw this almost an hour ago."

"Why didn't you call me or come get me then?"

"Sit down and let's talk. I've been thinking about what we should do."

"I want to call the sheriff."

"Sit down," he said, hitting the mute button and leaving the television running in case the commercial came on again.

"I can remember the words to the ad." Her eyes widened. "I remember the agency. Carter Dahl! Josh, I remember!" Her eyes sparkled and she looked jubilant, jumping up and waving her hands. "I remember!"

He grinned because her exuberance was infectious. It was also irresistible. He couldn't stop himself any more than he could stop breathing. He stepped closer, wrapped her in his arms and kissed her hard.

Startled, she stiffened for an instant, then closed her eyes and wrapped her arms around his neck, kissing him in return as he leaned over her, molding her to his body, tasting and taking and shutting his mind to their discovery.

She was bubbling, radiating energy, and he wanted to take that energy and transform it to passion. His tongue played over hers and he kissed her deeply, one arm banding her tiny waist tightly while his other hand caressed her throat and slid to her breast beneath her robe and nightie. Her flesh was soft, filling his hand as his thumb caressed the taut peak.

She moaned, moving her hips against him while she tightened her arms around his neck.

Josh relished kissing her, knowing she was responding wildly to his touch and kisses. Her fingers wound in his hair while she clung tightly to him.

He pushed away her robe, shoving the flimsy nightie off of her shoulder to caress her breast. He leaned down to take her nipple in his mouth, his tongue stroking her. Dimly, above his roaring pulse, he heard her moan. Her fingers wound in his hair and slipped beneath his shirt.

He wanted to peel her out of her robe and gown and take her now, to know all her fire and passion. Instead, he swung her up and released her, holding her lightly, with one hand on her hip, while with the other he stroked her nape. He pulled her gown and robe back in place, but not before catching a tantalizing glimpse of bare breast.

"I couldn't resist," he said.

"I didn't tell you to stop," she answered in a sultry voice.

"Don't push your luck," he snapped gruffly. "I'm on the edge."

She laughed and danced away from him, looking at the television and then at him. "I remember so much! Josh, my sisters are Emily and Talia. And, I'm Ivy. My name is Ivy!" she exclaimed, waving her arms, and he had to smile at her. "Ivy James."

"Ivy," he said, knowing that to him, she would always be Laurie.

"I'm so excited! This is wonderful! I remember!"

"I'm glad, Laurie." He picked her up in his arms and moved to the sofa to sit and hold her. "Now tell me what you know."

"I inherited the modeling agency. Carter and I both worked for his uncle." She frowned and shook her head. "Right now I can't think of the uncle's name, but I should know it if I know my own and Carter's."

"Don't worry. It'll come. And you own the agency. You must have been a very good businesswoman."

"I don't even know," she said. "Carter is a playboy. I think he's the one who tried to kill me when I was home. That's why I left."

"He'd have a motive, if he wanted the agency. I'm surprised he didn't take you to court, though, and fight it that way. Especially if he is a blood relative, and you aren't. Do you know where home is?"

She frowned again. "I can see things. The Plaza. I remember the Plaza at Christmas. Kansas City! It's Kansas City, I just know it is."

"So you think Carter is the one who ran you off the road?"

She frowned again and ran her fingers idly along the collar of Josh's T-shirt. He knew she was unaware of what she was doing, but he wasn't. The slightest touch stirred him, and he was quite conscious of holding her on his lap, of her soft curves and sweet smell, of the silken nightie and robe that provided almost no barrier. Continually, he fought the urge to kiss her. With her memory coming back, they needed to think about the killer, the future, and what the wisest course of action would be.

"Josh, I know Carter. He's a spoiled playboy, charming, a salesman type. He would never get up in a tree and take a shot at me. Never."

"People can be driven to do all sorts of things. And your memory may not be serving you so well just yet."

She shook her hair, long golden strands brushing against his cheek and neck. "No. I know Carter. I can remember. I think he's the one who set my condo on fire." She looked startled and twisted to face him. "I just remembered the fire. Things come back out of the blue."

"You might not be right."

"Oh, yes, I am. The night my condo burned, before I was going to bed, my sister Emily called and wanted me to help her with something. I don't remember what, but she said to come spend the night at her house. I did, and my condo burned that night. The fire started in my place. I didn't think about anyone doing it to harm me, but the fire chief said it began with an unknown substance, and later he said the fire was deliberately set."

"What about the money, Laurie? You have a lot of cash."

"I was fleeing for my life and I didn't want to leave a paper trail. I liquidated some assets from my inheritance and took some of my savings. I didn't want to run short of money and I didn't want to use a credit card. I had more than two hundred thousand dollars when I left Kansas City."

"That's a hell of a lot of money," Josh remarked grimly.

Laurie toyed with Josh's hair, winding her fingers in it, but her gaze looked beyond him, as if she were lost in memories. "Josh, Carter could do something like sneak around and set something on fire, but to get up in a tree out in the middle of nowhere and shoot at me? Never. This man moves in high social circles and supports the symphony and loves museums. He'd never dirty his hands that way."

"Whoever shot at you wasn't a country boy. He didn't know a thing about getting from his car to where he could watch the house. He had little strips of cloth tied to trees to find his way out."

She laughed. "I can imagine what all of you thought of that!" She sobered to look at Josh. "It wasn't Carter. He's too subtle to tie rags to trees. Maybe I was wrong."

"Or maybe he hired someone to find you and do the dirty work," Josh said quietly.

"That sounds more like Carter," she agreed, sobering. "I remember—Jeff Dahl was the man I worked for, and he was Carter's uncle. He owned the agency. It's Dahl Stars Modeling Agency in Kansas City, Missouri."

"Good. More puzzle pieces."

"When Jeff died over a year ago, he left the agency to me instead of Carter. I don't know which one of us was more surprised. I never expected that, and Jeff never told me, nor did he tell Carter, who flew into a rage when they read the will. I remember all of that now. And Carter did take it to court, but I won. That wasn't so long ago."

"So you modeled and inherited the agency. You must be very good."

"Maybe, but Carter was very irresponsible. He was charming, but unreliable."

"I can relate to that one."

"Josh, I should call Emily."

"Fine. Why Emily instead of your sister Talia?"

Laurie blinked. "I don't know. I just think it should be Emily."

"Do you remember the phone number?"

She concentrated, and Josh leaned forward to kiss her throat lightly. He heard her swift intake of breath and then she pushed against his chest.

"Let me think," she whispered.

"I didn't think you'd notice," he said.

She leaned closer, trailing her tongue over his ear and kissing his own throat. He inhaled and caught her face, framing it in his hands. "Okay, you proved your point. We better leave the kisses until we make some decisions and some calls."

"My sister Emily should be the first call. She may think something happened...." Laurie turned wide eyes on him. "Why didn't she turn in a missing-person report?"

"I've been wondering about that. Two sisters. Even Carter. He could have legitimately gone to the police if you'd disappeared from your work. Do you know if you both still worked together after you inherited the agency?''

She rubbed her head and frowned. ''Yes, we did. I need to call Emily. After that I should call the sheriff.''

''There's just one thing to consider before you do. You have a high-profile job. Remember, someone tried to kill you. If you call the sheriff, there are things he will have to do, and the newspapers will get the story.''

''What do you propose? I can't just hide here when I know this much!''

''I'll tell Will and see if we can keep things quiet, but I wouldn't count on it. You call your sister before I call Will. As a matter of fact, since it's now ten past two in the morning, I think we should call the sheriff when he gets to his office later on.''

''Josh, I remember the restaurants. My dad had a chain of restaurants and now Emily runs them. Mom and Dad are deceased. It's coming back.''

''Good.''

''I'll call Emily now.''

Josh stretched out his long arm and snagged the phone to hand to her. ''Want me to leave?''

''No, but don't start kissing me or I'll lose my train of thought.''

''Will you really?''

She wiggled her nose at him. ''You keep your distance. I'll take all kinds of revenge if you don't.''

''Sounds more tempting by the minute.''

''Josh Kellogg!'' Suddenly she wrapped her arm around his neck and leaned forward to kiss him. This time he was surprised, but only for a second, and then he wrapped his arms around her tightly, reveling in her soft curves pressed against him. From that first day, she had done as she pleased, often surprising him.

He kissed her hungrily. She had started this, and this time she was going to have to be the one to stop. He slipped his hands beneath her nightie, cupping her breasts. He leaned down to take her nipple in his mouth, to flick his tongue over her taut bud.

"Josh," she whispered, winding her fingers in his hair and then tugging up his T-shirt. He paused, yanking the shirt over his head and tossing it away, and then he bent to kiss her again, first one breast and then the other. They might be worlds apart in their lives, but this moment they were here together, and she was willing and eager and passionate.

She shifted, twisting and hitching her leg so she was astride him, facing him. His pulse roared and he felt as if he were going up in flames as she wriggled out of her robe, yanked her nightie over her head and tossed it away. She still wore narrow, red bikini briefs that matched her nightie.

He couldn't breathe, and he couldn't stop looking at her as he cupped her full, soft breasts. She was gorgeous, even more beautiful than he had imagined, and he thought he was going to burn to cinders any second. Except he wasn't. His body was hard, ready, and he wanted her. He leaned forward to take her nipple in his mouth again, circling the bud with his tongue while he caressed the other breast with his fingers.

Then he slid a hand down to the silk panties between her legs. She cried out as he caressed her intimately.

"Josh, Josh!" And then she pushed against his shoulders. She swung her long leg over him and stood, yanking up her robe to pull it on again. She turned to look down at him. "That got out of hand way too quickly. I need to find out about my past and fill in the gaps. I should call Emily," she said solemnly.

He was torn between doing what she wanted and pulling her down to seduce her. As if she could read his thoughts, she moved away from him. "I really need to call Emily," she said quietly.

"All right. Come sit down. I'll leave."

"No! I want you here," she said, approaching him as if

he were a crouching tiger. She sat with one knee bent, facing him as she reached past him for the phone.

Josh watched and waited, his body cooling only slightly. Tousled and aroused, she looked more desirable than ever.

"I don't know how to get the number," she said, looking at him.

He took the phone from her and ran his finger along her jaw. "Someday you'll start something that can't be stopped."

"Maybe, but I know you'll always stop if I want you to."

"There's a point of no return."

"If we get there, then I won't want to stop, either. But we're not going to get there, Josh, because I don't want to go home to Kansas City and leave my heart back here in Texas."

"And I don't want you to take my heart away with you."

"That's impossible. You've made that all too clear."

He picked up the phone and began to punch numbers. In a few minutes he handed the phone to her, too aware when his fingers brushed hers. He still simmered with desire, wanting her, thinking about seduction, knowing he should focus his thoughts elsewhere. *A model.* He should have guessed. In fact, the possibility had occurred to him. A woman as beautiful as Laurie had to be an actress or a model or a singer. Even though he knew he should keep his hands to himself, he couldn't resist reaching for a lock of her hair.

Laurie's pulse raced in anticipation as she listened to the phone ring.

A woman answered and Laurie gripped the phone tightly. "Emily?"

"Ivy? Thank goodness! Is that you?"

Chapter 12

Laurie closed her eyes with relief and ignored the tears that spilled from her eyes.

"Ivy, are you all right? Where have you been?"

"It's a long story, but I've had amnesia."

"Amnesia! Talia and I have been wild with worry. We finally filed a missing-person report yesterday."

"Why did you wait so long?"

"You asked me to, remember? You made me promise not to do anything if I didn't hear from you. Where are you? How'd you get amnesia? Do you know how long it's been since we've heard from you?"

Laurie laughed as the questions spilled out without giving her time to answer them. "Emily, listen. Let me tell you what happened and what I know. First I have to tell you— I was in a car wreck and haven't remembered anything until today. Yesterday, actually."

Hearing the excitement in her voice, Josh felt a pang. As he listened to her, he knew that with each second that passed he was losing her. But then he'd never really had her, not in any real sense. Yet how he was going to miss her! He didn't want to think about coming back to the empty ranch house when she was gone. That startled him, because never before had he thought of the ranch house as empty, or lonely.

"I have so much to tell you. I just got my memory back. I'm in Texas. Ivy, am I married or do I have a boyfriend?" After a pause, she said, "Really?"

Josh wondered what that comment was about, but she didn't discuss a man, so maybe there was none in her life. But it didn't matter. There was another vast, unbridgeable chasm between them, and she was not going to be a part of his life much longer. And even if she were plain Jane Doe, with no life to go back to, that still wouldn't change how he felt about lasting relationships or marriage. It wasn't for him.

He listened to her account of everything that had happened, including some talk about him that made him want to leave the room.

"He's tough and reliable and he's armed."

Josh shot her a look and shook his head, standing to leave the room, but she motioned for him to stay.

He sank down again and listened to her relate more of what had happened to her, and then as she talked, he heard uncertainty in her voice. He reached for the phone.

"Laurie, let me talk to your sister."

She glanced at him and said, "Emily, this is Josh Kellogg." Laurie held out the phone.

"Thank you for all you've done for my sister," said a woman with a whiskey voice. "It sounds as if she wouldn't have survived if it hadn't been for you."

"Look, she's still in danger. That hasn't changed. This is as good a place as any for her to hide until this is over.

Until they catch the guy, he's going to come after her again, and when he does, she's safer here with me.''

''It puts you in danger,'' she said.

''I don't care about that, and I'd like to catch the guy. I'm having alarms installed and I'll be her bodyguard. Would you like to come visit so you can see her?''

''I want to see her, but I want much more for her to be safe. If she's better off without seeing me, so be it.''

''He already knows where she is. He shot at her a few hours back, but she's okay.'' Josh saw Laurie waving her hands at him, trying to get him to stop telling her sister about the shooting.

''Oh, my heavens! A few hours ago? That rules out our prime suspect, because he was on the news tonight at a gala. He certainly wasn't in Texas. Maybe we've been looking in the wrong direction.''

''She told me about her condo burning.''

''That and the time someone tried to run her down.''

Josh glanced at Laurie. ''I don't think she remembers that yet. I'll let you talk to her about it.'' He handed the phone to Laurie. As she talked, he leaned down to nuzzle her neck. Her voice dropped a note and she wriggled away, twisting around to give him a look.

''Talk as long as you want,'' he whispered. ''I'm going to mosey around outside and see what I can see.''

Picking up his jacket, he left. The chilly night air was refreshing and he stretched his legs, moving swiftly toward the barn, drifting into shadows and walking over his land, watching for anything amiss. The boys kept the dogs with them at night, but they should turn them out instead, he decided. Hopefully, the dogs would bark at a stranger. His dogs were pets. They weren't ferocious guard dogs. It had never been important before.

A model whose family owned a successful chain of restaurants... How long would it take him to forget her? He suspected the rest of his life.

He told himself that she wasn't vital to his well-being. They hadn't known each other long. Or intimately. He would forget with time.

Like hell he would.

He put off going back inside, finally stopping in the oak grove far from the house. He stood in the shadows, watching and listening for anything unusual. His skin prickled. Why did he feel something was amiss? Was it a gut instinct? Was it because he was upset over Laurie, anyway? Was it the quiet, dark night? He rejected the last, because he had camped out on many quiet dark nights and never felt the unease he did now.

He moved closer to the trunk of a tree, easing between low branches and then standing absolutely still. He heard a noise and held his breath, wishing he had thought to bring his pistol, but it was locked away in his office.

Hairs rose on his arms, and he felt as if someone were watching him. His gaze moved slowly around the area. He scanned the branches above him, but saw nothing amiss. Still, he couldn't shake the feeling that something was wrong. He had no idea how long he stood quietly waiting, but he heard nothing unusual. The normal night rustlings continued, uninterrupted.

Finally he headed back, walking much more cautiously than when he had come out, staying in dark shadows. He was careful with each step, trying to make the least noise possible, still straining to hear any strange sounds.

He worked his way back to the barn and slipped inside one of the open doors. In the darkness he stood waiting, just as he had outside.

He had no idea how long he stood in the barn, but he couldn't hear or see anything amiss. It was empty; all the animals were outside.

He eased toward the bunkhouse and saw it was dark. The men had gone to bed, and he knew the dogs were inside with them or else he would have seen them by now. They didn't roam too far from home.

He headed toward the house, and as he neared the porch, he was momentarily startled to see a figure there. Then he saw golden hair, pale in the darkness, and his pulse jumped with eagerness.

He climbed the steps. "What are you doing out here in the cold?"

"It's not that cold, and I was watching for you. Where have you been?"

"Looking around." He kept his voice low and turned to look behind him, still feeling uneasy.

"What is it?" she whispered.

"I don't know. Something just doesn't feel right."

"Now you're scaring me."

"You're in a white sweater that's way too visible. So is your hair. Go inside, Laurie."

He heard a slight shuffle and then heard the back door. He turned to follow her, but stopped in the darkest part of the porch and stood still, his gaze searching the yard. He was still uneasy. It could be his imagination after the incident earlier, but he still felt as if someone was out there. He needed those damned alarms installed, plus yard lights.

Reluctantly, he turned and went inside. Laurie sat at the kitchen table, her eyes wide. He knew he had scared her, but she needed to be more careful.

"Don't go outside like that again."

She nodded. "Sorry. It was dark and I didn't think my cardigan or my hair would show that much. I was worried about you. Did you carry a gun?"

"No. It's here in the house."

"You think someone is watching the ranch?"

"I don't know. I've prowled all around the place and into

the barn, and couldn't find anything amiss. Want something to drink?''

''Pop would be good,'' she said absentmindedly. ''Should you call the sheriff?''

''Nope, not until morning. There's nothing to call him about. We're locked in and I'm with you. Relax.'' Josh poured glasses of pop over ice, and together they went to the family room to sit on the sofa. He turned to face her. ''Now, tell me what Emily said.''

''She isn't coming here because I think it might put her in danger.''

''You're right. If the motive is what you think—Carter's jealousy over your inheritance—then you're really the only one the killer wants, but she could be caught in the backlash.''

Taking a long drink of pop, Laurie set her glass on the coffee table. Forgetting her fear, she smiled at him, her eyes sparkling. She looked radiant, he decided. ''That was wonderful and weird at the same time, because I still have gaps in my memory. But now I know that I have a family, and I know why they didn't come searching for me! I've felt unloved and unwanted and alone, and if it hadn't been for you, I would have really been unhappy.''

He arched an eyebrow. ''I'm sure you haven't had a day of your life when you were unloved and unwanted, and probably not too many when you were alone.''

She laughed, and he ached to pick up her and hold her and kiss her. Instead, he sat quietly, waiting to hear all she had to tell him.

''When I left Kansas City, I asked Emily not to expect to hear from me. After the car incident, I fled.''

''What car incident?''

''After the fire at my condo, I hired a bodyguard, because I was scared. One morning as I was going to work, a car tried to run me down. The bodyguard pushed me out of the way and took the hit. It put him in the hospital, and that's when I figured I should leave town and sell the agency.''

''You're selling your agency?'' Josh asked in surprise, wondering what she planned to do.

''I don't remember that part of it, but Emily told me. I hope these gaps fill in soon.''

''They will. Look how far you've already come.''

''I know. Anyway, when I left Kansas City, I made Emily promise not to look for me, but to wait until I contacted her. Talia made the same promise.''

''There you are—a good reason why they didn't search for you. You didn't want the publicity or to stir anyone up. With your background, if they had reported you missing it could easily have become big news.''

''I never thought about asking my family to keep quiet if I disappeared.''

''Did she know where you were going or what you were going to do when you left Kansas City?''

''Yes. We have a family home out of Seattle. I remember it now.''

''See there?'' he said, smiling at her, and she stuck her tongue out at him.

''Don't say I told you so,'' she said.

''I didn't say it even though I did tell you,'' he teased. ''Go on.''

''I was going to try to hide there. I would have been all alone, and it's very quiet and peaceful.''

''How'd you get down to Texas if you left Kansas City for Seattle?''

''I remember that, too. I travelled around a good part of the United States to make certain no one was following me.''

''Ah, good for you.''

''Emily said I was checking in with her nearly every day until I reached Houston, and then she never heard from me until today. They kept waiting, knowing I had asked them not to search for me, and finally, yesterday, they went to the police. We should get a call from your local sheriff, because if they are keeping up with the missing-person reports, they'll recognize my description.''

"I'm going to call him early, anyway.'' Josh took a sip of his pop. "So what about your parents?''

"I'm the youngest of three sisters. Our mother died when we were young. Our father died three years ago. We inherited the family business together—a chain of restaurants being run by my sister Emily. Our middle sister, Talia, is a news anchor in Chicago. Emily said that over a year ago I inherited the modeling agency, where I've worked since high school.''

"Wow. Impressive family.''

"My sisters are nice.''

"Now you have answers to all your questions. No boyfriend? No husband?''

"Nope. Emily said I didn't have time in my life for men.''

At one time that answer would have thrilled him, but it didn't now. "Right after you asked about a man in your life, you said, 'Really?' What was that all about?''

"There's someone I date occasionally, and according to Emily, I only think of him as a good friend and he's boring. She thinks he's adorable.''

"So I can seduce you with a clear conscience?''

She gave a throaty laugh and slanted him a mischievous look. "Maybe I'll seduce you first.''

"There's a threat I like.'' He set down his drink and reached for her. She slipped away and stood.

"Not yet, cowboy. Let's go look on the Internet at the Kansas City newspapers and see what we can find out about Carter Dahl.''

They went to Josh's office, where Laurie sat in front of

the computer and did the search while he pulled up a chair beside her. He draped his arm over the back of her chair and in seconds, shifted his attention from the screen to her. A model who owned an agency. From a successful family of women who had inherited their father's business. Sophisticated, wealthy and completely off-limits.

Yet how he wanted her! He studied her flawless skin, her profile, her thickly lashed eyes. Her hair spilled over her shoulders and back, and he couldn't resist picking up strands and twisting them through his fingers. She glanced at him with curiosity in her eyes, but her attention was on the computer and she turned back to it swiftly.

Though he wanted to lean the few inches necessary and brush kisses across her nape, he knew he had to leave her alone. How many times was he going to have to remind himself?

"Here he is," she said, and Josh turned to look at a tall, blond man who was smiling into the camera, standing in a cluster of women. He had his arm around a beautiful, slender brunette. If he was vice president of a modeling agency, he probably dated beautiful women constantly.

"Here's another picture of him. He's very social and in the papers a lot. He wanted us to date, but I wouldn't go out with him. Carter is a womanizer and doesn't mind bending the truth to suit himself."

"If he has enough of an ego, that could add to his motive to get rid of you," Josh said. "You inherited the agency he expected to get, and you wouldn't go out with him. That would be enough to drive some men to violence."

"Yes, but now Emily questions if I was right in thinking it was Carter. She said she couldn't imagine him trying to run me off a road. She said he's in the news constantly, and the time the police questioned him about the night my apartment was set on fire, he had an alibi." Laurie turned to stare at Josh with wide eyes. "If it isn't Carter, I can't imagine who it is, or why."

"Why didn't Carter turn you in to missing persons?"

"Emily said Carter told everyone I took a leave of absence and needed some rest. He probably was happy to have me gone."

She shut down the computer and turned to him. "So you want me to stay even when you know all that about me?"

"Yes. You'll be safer here. Tomorrow there are things I need to repair here in the house. I'll be around to give you protection."

"Fine. So what do you see happening? Am I going to keep living with you for the next month? The next year? Josh, I have sisters. I should go home."

"Not yet. You left that home when you had your memory. Don't go back there when you don't remember fully." She was only inches away from him and he was struggling to keep from reaching for her.

"That's true, but I can't stay indefinitely."

"I don't think you'll have to. He has to be getting more desperate."

"That's scary in every way."

"You've got to let him get into the open so this doesn't drag on."

"Finding out about my past has changed you," she said, studying him. Her mouth was only inches away. Soft, luscious, tempting.

"Maybe it has," he said, standing abruptly and moving away. "We're going to part soon, so we'd better start keeping a little distance now." He headed back to the family room and she followed. Josh added another log to the glowing embers, building up the fire again to take the chill from the air.

"I only went a year to college because I was too busy

modeling," Laurie said. "Since Emily liked the restaurants, Dad didn't care if Talia and I did something else."

"Where did you get the car you were driving when you had the wreck? It must not have been a rental or someone would have missed it."

"No, I had cash and bought it off a lot in Houston."

Josh settled back against the chair, listening to her talk, still wanting her in his arms. Even at three in the morning, she was bubbly and excited and more desirable than ever.

They talked for another hour. He didn't want to leave her, and he knew he wasn't going to sleep, anyway.

Finally she stood. "I should go to bed and try to sleep for a few hours. You should, too."

"I know how to solve that being unable to sleep."

She arched a brow and she gave him a sly smile. "Do you really, now? What do you suggest?"

He stood, moving to her. On his way, he switched off a light, leaving only a dim glow from the hallway and the flickering light from the dying fire.

"I'm losing you. I never really had you, but our worlds are spinning apart now. Dammit." He stepped back abruptly. "Good night, Laurie. Ivy. I guess I should call you Ivy, but all I know is Laurie."

He turned and left the room swiftly, without looking back, and she felt as if she had just lost something important.

She had learned her identity tonight and been high on the discovery, and high from talking to her sister. Now she came crashing down, because Josh's words hurt. He was right. They were worlds apart, but she was going to miss him when she left. She knew she taunted and flirted with him, sometimes goading him into kissing her, and she knew she should stop. But there was something irresistible about him and she couldn't keep from trying to get past the barriers he put up. She couldn't recall any man in her life who had kept up barriers around her.

She knew Josh wasn't a man she should taunt. He was forceful, and if she ever completely broke through that reserve, she might regret it. She knew she was flirting with danger, tempting the man who could steal her heart as no one in her life had ever done. She suspected it would be incredibly easy to fall in love with Josh, and she knew she should be guarding her heart as much as he guarded his.

She went to the hall to switch out the only light left on, and returned to the window, raising one of the slats of a shutter and peering into the darkness. She shivered. Something out there had disturbed Josh, and she suspected that was a rare occurrence here on the ranch.

Then she became aware of the silent, dark house, how solitary she was in the family room with Josh gone. She felt chilled, frightened and alone. Frightening memories of Kansas City, and of being on the run, came back to her.

She turned to look at the darkened room. Josh could move through the dark like a cat, she knew. Laurie was tempted to call out to him, but that seemed ridiculous. She was safely locked in the house with him, she reminded herself. Covered with goose bumps, she moved across the room and switched on a light, looking around to reassure herself that everything was all right.

Her nerves were jittery. She went into the hall to switch on that light and returned to turn off the one in the family room, then rushed upstairs. Before she stepped into her room, she looked at Josh's bedroom door, which was slightly ajar. All her fear evaporated, replaced by longing, and the hope that they catch her assailant soon.

She went to bed, aware of Josh so close, yet growing further away from her by the minute. Her lifestyle would separate them soon enough. Stay away from him, she told herself, yet she ached for his kisses, his loving. How easy it would be to cross the hall to his room. She knew he wouldn't send her away.

It was another hour before she fell asleep, only to dream about Josh—a strange dream in which he kept slipping away from her.

Outside in the night, Finn shifted restlessly. Damned cowpoke. He'd thought the man was going to patrol the grounds all night long. Finn shifted the binoculars in his hand and looked at the house. The shutters were closed and she had gone inside. He had been tempted to take a shot when he had seen her come out on the porch, but then the cowboy had walked up, quiet as some damn cat creeping through the underbrush. The cowboy had been close enough to catch him if he had fired at her, so he'd lost that chance. The cowboy had been too damned close, period. Finn had held his breath, praying no insect or night critter would crawl over him, and that no animal would discover him. At least the man didn't have his dogs with him, but the last time he had been there, he'd fed the dogs some steaks and dog treats. Now they no longer barked at him. They weren't killer watchdogs, they were spoiled pets.

All Finn needed was a minute to take aim, make certain he had her in his sights and then squeeze off a shot, and she would be gone.

His problems would be ended and cold hard cash would await him. Only a few minutes with her in view. She had to come out of that house again at some point. He'd thought he had gotten her earlier, but then, as he watched the house, he had seen her move past the door.

The days had been growing warmer lately. She had to be getting tired of being shut in his house day after day. There was no way to keep her constantly hidden. She would come out of the house again, and when she did, he would be ready.

He climbed down and headed for his car. He would be back.

And if she didn't come outside—then the house would have to go, be it with a fire or some other method. She should have used up her luck by now.

He felt his pager vibrating and picked it up. Only one person could be paging him.

Chapter 13

The next morning Josh was working in the utility room when Laurie went down for breakfast. She followed the sounds of the hammer and found him repairing a shelf. He wore a T-shirt, faded, torn jeans and his scuffed black boots. The gunshot wound was healing, leaving a fresh scar on his muscular arm. He looked fit and sexy, full of animal magnetism that played havoc with her senses.

"Hi," she said, leaning against the doorjamb.

He glanced over his shoulder, his gaze sweeping over her and she was aware of her cutoffs and T-shirt. Every nerve in her body tingled and her pulse jumped again when he smiled.

"Morning," he said, and put down his hammer. "I've been waiting to eat breakfast with you."

"And you've been up for how long?" she demanded.

"I'm accustomed to getting up about the time we went to bed last night, so I overslept. I slept until eight, which is a first. I can't remember ever sleeping that late."

"You're a workaholic, Josh. I've slept past eight plenty of times when I was up late. And it was wonderful to sleep in this morning," she said.

His brow arched, and she studied him. "You're giving me a peculiar look." As he approached her, her pulse jumped again.

"I'm imagining you asleep." He propped his hand over her head, leaning against the doorjamb only inches away from her, so close she was certain he could hear her pounding heart. "Now, there are some circumstances where I would be perfectly willing to sleep in," he drawled.

"You flirt, Josh, but you just go so far and no further."

"I told you, I'm ready, willing and able to go as far as you want to."

"Your body might be, but your heart isn't."

"And yours is? I don't think so. You flirt and tease, but you don't want to give your heart any more than I do mine, so don't make it sound like I'm so different from you. This is one place where we're birds of a feather."

"*Au contraire.* I can hope for a long-term relationship. I don't lock away my heart like you do."

"I like to date."

"When this is over, we can see each other."

"Hardly," he drawled in a cynical voice, while his green eyes were devouring her. "I'm on the ranch. You'll be in your big city. Our lifestyles aren't compatible. You have a glamorous career. I don't think a cowboy and a struggling ranch fit into that picture. If we were off-limits to each other before you knew your identity, now we're really forbidden to each other. There's no future between us at all."

"Is that right? Then you'd better keep your distance."

"Not necessarily. A few kisses fall under big-time fun, and there won't be any hurt in that."

"You sound so sure of yourself. Just kiss and forget, huh?"

"That's not all bad."

"Not to you, since it's what you live by. Someday, cow-boy, someone is going to kiss you, and you won't be able to forget her or walk away."

"It hasn't happened yet, Laurie. And it obviously hasn't happened yet for you, so there you are—we're two of a kind."

She shook her head and smiled at him. "No. I'm not scared to live, like you are. You're oh, so tough when it comes to chasing bad guys and getting shot at and dealing with wild bulls and horses, but you're scared where your heart is concerned. You're scared of me."

"Yeah, right. I'll show you how scared," he said, and her heart thudded.

He slid an arm around her waist, yanked her against him and leaned forward to kiss her hard, opening her mouth, kissing her with a force and hunger that made her forget the discovery of her identity, made her forget the past and future, the plans she had just made, the excitement she felt. Everything vanished, consumed in a kiss that possessed and seduced, that shattered every thought in her head.

How could anyone want her this much? Her pulse gal-loped and she turned to mush, melting, changing, transform-ing into a woman in need. His kiss laid claim to her in a way none before had. It was the kiss of a fierce warrior returning from battle to his woman, the kiss of a hungry lover ready for seduction. It was the kiss of a lifetime, and she trembled, returning it avidly.

All her arguments were gone, but dimly, she knew she had been wrong. He wasn't scared to kiss her at all.

Suddenly he released her and stepped away. His breathing was ragged and he looked torn and hurt, so much so that she was shocked. Yet she was still lost in that kiss, which had stunned her.

"Our lives are worlds apart," he said roughly.

She touched her lips lightly with the tips of her fingers. "It's your call," she whispered, still thinking about his kiss and absorbed by her reaction to it.

He stroked her cheek. "You'll have a good life to go back to," he said, and then he was gone, and she heard the back door close.

She stepped into the kitchen and sat down abruptly, feeling weak-kneed. That kiss had taken her breath, and taken a little bit of herself that she didn't think she was going to get back.

Whatever happened, if they never saw each other again after the next few days, she knew she would remember him and his kisses the rest of her life.

She would remember *that* kiss the rest of her life. Would anyone else ever kiss her like that? Would she ever want anyone to?

Josh was right, she began to realize. Their lifestyles weren't in the least compatible, and their flirting was dangerous to both of them.

That knowledge hurt, and for the first time, she saw why he had been so grim. Even though they had told each other over and over that they should leave one another alone, she had always thought there would be a possibility of dating when she knew her real identity. But Josh had told the truth. They had entirely different lifestyles. She didn't want to fall in love with a tough cowboy who kept a wall around his heart. A cowboy who would never leave his ranch.

She touched her lips again with her fingertips. She would be telling him goodbye so soon now. She sobered and glanced at the empty doorway, understanding his hurt, but feeling part of it was of his own choosing. He was the one who didn't want a lasting relationship. He didn't want any woman around long. He had told her that from the first.

"If that's the way you want it," she whispered.

Trying to get her mind on other things, she went to the

kitchen to pour a glass of orange juice and fix some bacon and eggs. Yet she had lost her appetite, and it was impossible to think about breakfast or mundane things. Was she in love already, forever in love with a cowboy who wouldn't love in return?

Laurie shook her head, knowing she had to get her mind off Josh. She moved around the kitchen, doing the same things twice, barely aware of her actions.

She stopped abruptly and looked down at herself. No wonder food tasted so good! And no wonder her clothes had gotten tighter. In her past, she probably had been very careful about what she ate, to keep her weight at a certain level for modeling. Since the wreck, she had let go and eaten whatever and whenever she wanted, relishing every meal and snack. Now she could guess why the food had seemed so wonderful. She had probably deprived herself for years.

As she scrambled eggs, she heard the back door open and turned to see Josh.

"Sorry you kissed me?" she asked, unable to resist, and wondering what it was about him that brought out a devilish streak in her. Maybe it was that cool facade that was just too tempting to try to break through.

"Hell, no. Come here and I'll do it again if you'd like," he said lightly, and she knew he was back to the flirtation that meant so little to him. But when she looked into his eyes, her breath caught.

"Not until we have breakfast," she said, trying to keep things as light as he was. "And call the sheriff."

"I'm ahead of you there. I phoned him early, and he was going to call us. He spotted the missing-person report and intended to call your sister today. I told him you had your memory back."

"Oh, Josh, it's wonderful!" she said, throwing up her arms and sending a little fleck of scrambled egg flying through the air to land on the counter. "Whoops," she said, laughing. "You can't understand because you've got your life," she said, wiping up the egg and turning to stir the pan again. She looked over her shoulder at him. "In spite of the danger, I'm deliriously happy. My life has been a black hole, but now light and answers are spilling into it. I remember my first grade teacher, my first kiss, my first dance. I remember my first modeling job—well, not really. I remember my family talking about it because I was one of those little kids that got to be in a commercial. I tutor kids—or I did until I left town."

"You, a tutor?"

She arched her brows. "You think you're the only one who can help people? Or don't you think I know enough to tutor little kids?"

"No, I don't think that. I'm just surprised. It doesn't fit in with this model image of you."

"It doesn't fit your preconceived notions, you mean."

"Don't get so indignant. You couldn't believe I hired kids who had been in trouble."

"Okay, so we both have preconceived notions. Mine are just more justified."

"Like hell."

"I remember everything!" she exclaimed exuberantly, throwing up her arms. She looked at him. "I'm sorry if I'm acting goofy about it. I know for you life is just the same."

"My life isn't quite the same," he said.

"Oh, yes, it is. You still have that wall around you."

"Not this morning," he said. "I seem to remember kissing you a few minutes ago."

"That you did. Your eggs will be ready soon."

"You must have known I was coming back."

She looked over her shoulder at him and gave him a smug smile. "Maybe I'll always get you back."

"No, you won't, Laurie. When you leave for Kansas

City, you'll tell me goodbye forever. I'm a cowboy rooted to this ranch like one of those big trees outside. And you know what happens if you uproot one of those trees."

"You don't look like a tree to me."

"I'll leave that one alone. I'll wash up and take over cooking." He left and was back in minutes to take the spatula from her.

"I can do this," she said, laughing at him. "You think I can't cook?"

"If your family has restaurants, I'm sure you can cook, but I'll do it. Sit down and let me wait on you."

"Thanks. Anyway, I can help."

Too aware of him, she moved around the kitchen, putting things on the table, and soon she was seated across from him with their plates full. Yet her appetite fled and her pulse still skittered and she was too aware of his intense gaze focused on her.

"Do you have any pasta on the place?" she asked.

"Sure. I've got a well-stocked pantry."

"Then let me cook dinner tonight. I have a penne specialty."

"Any specialty you have, I'll be tickled pink to try," he drawled.

"Well, you know the old saying, 'The way to a man's heart is through his stomach.'"

"The way to my heart definitely involves a different part of my anatomy."

"That's pure lust."

"There's nothing pure about it."

"Okay, dinner tonight. What time shall I plan to have it ready?"

"Seven."

"Seven it is. So what's the schedule today?"

She listened while he talked about things he would do around the house. Men were coming later to install an alarm system and outside lights, and she knew it was just as well they wouldn't be alone, because neither one of them could resist flirting.

Josh helped her clean the kitchen, and she was intensely aware of every brush of their fingers, of him standing close. Then he left to go work on something in his bedroom, and she wondered if he had picked that spot to get away from her. She could hear him hammering while she called both her sisters again, talking for over an hour to each one. Then she went downstairs to plan dinner and see if he had everything in the pantry that she would need.

She didn't see Josh again until noon. She went ahead and fixed sandwiches, knowing she would go get him when she had everything ready. Before she could, he strolled into the kitchen.

"You look good enough to eat," he said easily.

"So do you," she answered. "Tall and tasty."

He inhaled swiftly. "You're playing with fire again," he said, crossing the room to her, and her pulse jumped.

"Maybe because I know I'm going to be leaving the blaze all too soon. Besides, you said someone will be here at noon to install an alarm. That's going to force us to be good."

"*Good* isn't the right word. Circumspect maybe, but this is what's good," he said, putting his arm around her to kiss her.

She wrapped her arms around his narrow waist and kissed him in return, wanting more kisses like this morning, wanting Josh. The threat of goodbyes vanished as the need she felt escalated. Kisses weren't enough, but they were better than the constant reminder that Josh and she would be parting before long.

Laurie was barely aware when he moved back against the wall and spread his legs, pulling her up tightly against him. But she was aware of his thick shaft pressing against her.

His hands slipped beneath her T-shirt to cup her breasts, and she moaned, trembling as she kissed him hungrily. She wanted him, wanted him with a growing desperation, yet she couldn't yield completely because she knew if she did, she would leave her heart behind with this tough cowboy who had come to mean so much to her.

His fingers were calloused and rough, yet he touched her so gently, light caresses that were exquisite torment.

He was the one who stopped abruptly, pulling her T-shirt down. She opened her eyes to look up at him, and the raw need revealed in his expression made her tug his head down again. He caught her arms, holding her away.

"Here comes the man about the alarm."

Surprised, she blinked, and heard the rumble of an engine coming up the drive.

"That blue-ribbon hearing of yours again," she said. "How could you have heard that? Someday, I'll kiss you until you don't hear what's going on, like you do to me."

"Do I now?" he drawled, studying her.

"You know you do," she snapped, straightening her shirt and moving away from him. "You'd better start trying to cool down yourself if you're going to go meet him."

"I'll cool down," Josh answered with amusement in his voice. He started past her, then paused and leaned down to brush kisses across her nape. "I'm glad to learn that you have a little trouble cooling down."

She whipped around, but he was already striding toward the door, whistling a tune and acting as if nothing had happened between them.

She, on the other hand, was tied in knots—hot, bothered, wanting him. Every kiss made her want him more, made her long for him when he was nearby. He had to know the effect he was having on her. She wasn't certain of the effect she was having on him, but he responded. Saints alive, how he responded! When she left, would he remember these times together? Would he miss them? She had little idea of exactly how he felt, except on rare occasions when he let go and became earnest and open.

All afternoon the workers drilled and hammered, installing the alarm system. When they finished, hours later, she watched Josh try it out, and then he wanted her to try it. Finally the men packed their tools and drove away.

As they disappeared down the road, she saw Josh's foreman approaching the house. "Here comes Drake," she noted.

"He's coming up to do some repairs to the porch. I'm going to leave for a while."

"Why do I get the feeling I've got baby-sitters?"

"*Bodyguards* is a better word," Josh said, grinning. "I want to leave and I'll feel better knowing someone I trust is with you. And I'll get a porch step fixed all at the same time."

"And I didn't have any say-so in the matter."

"Matter of fact, you didn't. You don't need a say-so," he said, laughing as he dashed out of the room before she could reply.

"Josh Kellogg!"

Josh laughed, hearing her call his name as he closed the back door. His amusement faded when he went to meet Drake. They talked a few minutes, and then Josh headed toward the trees, in the direction the shot had come from. The local police had searched the grounds yesterday, and they would have trampled the undergrowth and smashed twigs, but Josh wanted to look himself. He still felt someone had been out there in the dark, watching him last night.

He moved slowly through the woods, kneeling, looking at grass and weeds, picking up twigs, turning to study the house, finally deciding where the shooter had been standing when he took the shot at Laurie.

Laurie…Ivy. He couldn't think of her as Ivy. Out here,

in his world, she was Laurie. She always had been Laurie to him and she always would be. When she went back to her world, she could be Ivy James again.

Josh looked at the trees around him and then spotted one that would be easy to climb. He scrambled up, pausing to study the house and where he had walked last night.

The man could have been in a tree.

He felt certain someone had been in the woods last night, waiting, watching him as he prowled around. Josh needed to talk to Drake. They had to let the dogs out every night.

Josh guessed it was a hired killer after her. The only reason the shot had just grazed her yesterday was because Josh had yelled at her to get down, and with that split-second warning, she had moved. It was a miracle she had survived the car crash. If Josh hadn't been around, the guy would have come back to finish what he had started when he had run her off the road. Even with the incidents in Kansas City she had been lucky. Josh could see how she had escaped each time, but her luck was bound to run out any moment.

Carter Dahl could have hired a killer in order to keep himself in the clear. If it was a pro, he would make the hit and then vanish, and Carter would have an alibi and that would be that.

Something had to happen soon. Josh suspected the man had come back last night to watch and see if his shot had killed her, or if she was still alive. She had come out on the porch, and he was bound to have seen her, so he knew he would have to try again.

A chill ran down Josh's spine as he realized the killer would try again, and soon. If he were in the man's place, what would he do?

Sabotage the cars? Wait for another clear shot? The killer had tried to burn her apartment. He might set fire to the house.

Josh climbed down and began to study the ground, moving slowly toward the road, seeing if he could pick up tracks. In a few minutes he found a strip of white rag tied to a low branch. He shook his head. The city guy couldn't find his way through the woods. He headed back to get his pickup to go look for his men. He would ask a couple of them to stay in the woods and wait and watch tonight. Maybe someone would catch the guy, who was clearly unfamiliar with prowling around after dark in the country.

The men who worked for Josh hadn't been country boys, either, not one of them, but all had worked for him long enough now that they had grown accustomed to being outside, and they had learned about the land and about animals. He thought of Rudy and Hector—two who had taken to ranching as if they had been born in the country.

Josh drove across the ranch, his thoughts jumping back to this morning with Laurie. He had let go when he had kissed her. She goaded him into losing control. She knew what she was doing. She had a wild, mischievous streak in her that pushed him to his limits.

Her kisses were pure fire. She had almost incinerated him this morning. They were playing with dynamite each time they were together. So seduce the lady, he told himself, and his pulse jumped at the thought. Seduce her and then let her go back to her exciting city life.

Except he didn't want to find out when she had gone that he had fallen in love with her. Right now he knew he could walk away and forget her.

"Yeah, right," he said aloud to himself. How long would it take to forget her? Maybe never. He didn't want to seduce her and find that every other woman forever paled in comparison. And he didn't want to fall in love with the minx. He could imagine the broken hearts in her past.

And tonight she was cooking dinner for him. Was she planning a seduction scene? He wouldn't put it past her. He was getting hot just thinking about tonight and her. And maybe seduction would be the best thing—satisfy himself and get over her. She would goad and torment him if he didn't. She was constantly throwing challenges at him, so if the beautiful model wanted seduction, that's what the little minx would get.

Josh took a deep breath, and realized he was driving aimlessly. He changed course and soon found some of his men, warned them about the intruder and asked them to keep watch.

Driving home he stopped at the pasture with the white stallion. The horse trotted to the fence and eyed Josh, pawing the ground.

Josh got out of the car and stared back at the horse. "I don't have time for you and you don't like being penned up, do you?" Josh approached the gate and the horse spun around, racing away. Josh unlocked the gate, drove inside, closed the gate again and went to check on the water tank.

It was six o'clock when he pulled back into the garage, closed and locked the door. It was the first time he could ever remember locking his garage.

As he strode to the house, anticipation rippled through him. Seven o'clock, dinner with Laurie.

He ran up to his room to bathe, shave and dress.

An hour earlier Laurie had left the kitchen to get dressed for dinner. All the time she bathed and dressed, she hummed a tune. Excitement bubbled in her. Eagerness for their dinner date made her tingle all over. She applied blush and mascara lightly, studying herself, looking at the new wound on her scalp and the white scar on her temple. The recent wound had a bandage, and she brushed her hair carefully, looping and pinning it to hide the fact as much as possible. She left some tendrils loose to curl around her face.

"Try keeping that wall around yourself tonight, Josh Kellogg!'' she whispered into the mirror. Then she stepped back, looking at herself. She wore a plain, black silk dress that Becky had bought for her. It was sleeveless, with a deep V in front and a slit in the side of the skirt. She wore high-heeled black sandals. Laurie dabbed on perfume, then went back to the kitchen.

The table was set with candles. She had had to search to find any, and she'd found crystal candlesticks. She put on music, then went to check the pasta, which was keeping warm in the oven.

"Wow," Josh said, and she turned to find him looking at her, his gaze trailing slowly over her. "You're gorgeous, but then you know that. That's why you're a model."

"And you're sexy, but then you know that. That's why you flirt."

"Want a glass of wine?"

"Yes, please. Red this time."

He poured her wine and poured himself pop. He handed her drink to her and raised his. "Here's to the return of your memory."

She touched his glass with hers. "I'll drink to that." She sipped her wine and raised her glass. "And here's to the toughest cowboy of them all, the man whose heart is fiercely protected from love."

"And I'll drink to that one." He sipped his pop and studied her. "You're the most beautiful woman I've ever known, and that's saying a lot, because Texas women are gorgeous."

"So are Texas cowboys."

"You're going to turn my head."

"That doesn't begin to describe what I'm going to do to you tonight," she said in a sultry voice, and his green eyes darkened, pinpoints of fire in their depths.

Without taking his gaze from hers, he took her drink and set it on the counter alongside his. Her pulse drummed, and she was mesmerized by the look in his eyes.

"How about a dance before dinner?" he asked.

Chapter 14

Taking her hand, Josh pulled her close and started dancing slowly. He never shifted his gaze from hers, and she was lost. She wanted his loving, wanted to make love to him. Was she going to wind up back in Kansas City, having left her heart here in Texas?

Deep down, she knew Josh had been right. They were planets apart. She couldn't leave her life behind even if he were into commitment. If he proposed tonight, she would have to say no. The full realization sobered her, because she hadn't faced it before. First, he had been totally off-limits to her because she hadn't known about her past. Then, when her memory returned, she had been so jubilant she hadn't given a thought to the future and leaving Josh.

As they danced, moving together in unison, Laurie felt devoured by his gaze, which held the green of summer and the heat of sex.

She could remember the men in her past. They had been few and disappointing, and had never come close to stealing her heart as this one cowboy had.

"Why did this happen to us?" she asked quietly. "We couldn't fall in love even if we both wanted to. You're right. Our worlds are impossibly different. We can't date. All we can do is say goodbye."

He nodded. "That's right. You'll go back to your life— which should be exciting enough to make you forget Texas completely. I'll bet you've traveled all over."

She wanted to shake him, to stir him out of that cool, remote stance he could keep so easily.

"Yes, I've traveled. So how long will it take you to forget me? A week? A day? A month?"

His eyes darkened again, and her heart missed a beat as she gazed back steadily. "You know damn well I'll never forget you," he said gruffly. Joy flared in her. So maybe he cared more than his cool exterior showed.

The music changed, and she wriggled away from him. "I've cooked all afternoon for you, so let's eat."

He helped her remove from the oven a pasta casserole thick with golden, bubbly cheese and red tomatoes. She had hot, buttered garlic bread and tossed salads, and they sat facing each other to eat.

In the flickering candlelight, Josh gazed at Laurie. He wouldn't ever forget her. She was stunning tonight, tall, willowy, sexy. With her hair up, and dressed so sleekly, she looked sophisticated, cool, absolutely unreachable. Yet he wanted to peel her out of her dress and kiss every delectable inch of her.

She must have finally faced the fact that under no circumstances could they have any kind of future together. Not even a few dates. Gone was her saucy flirting, and she kept looking at him with a solemn expression he had seldom seen. Yet he knew that when they'd danced, her pulse had been racing.

They were dangerous to each other's well-being, yet couldn't stop the spontaneous combustion that ignited every time they were together. It didn't keep him from wanting her and it didn't keep her from responding to him.

And she could cook. The dinner was fabulous and when he told her so, her eyes sparkled.

"Thank you. I like to cook. I don't get to cook very often and I've never eaten like I have since the crash. I can't imagine how much weight I've gained, but I'm not sure they'll want me back as a model."

"You couldn't look any better than you do now," he told her.

"You don't know the modeling world."

"You weren't one of those sticks when I first found you."

"They're not sticks. They're slender, and clothes hang better on a slender figure," she protested.

"I don't see how clothes could hang any better than they do on you tonight."

"Thank you! But I know what I'm talking about. I started eating more when I first left Kansas City, so I'll bet I had already put on weight when you found me."

"If you'll come over here and sit on my lap and let me squeeze a little, I'll tell you whether you've changed since the wreck or not."

She laughed. "I'm not sitting on your lap tonight. I'm finally taking your warnings seriously."

"I'll wager you on that one. I'll bet you'll be on my lap tonight. Loser has to cook dinner tomorrow night. No leftovers. I'm saving these for another time."

"I'll take you up on that, but it doesn't count if you use force."

"Now that pains me. Have I ever used force?"

"Not physically, but you order me around sometimes."

"Yeah, like yelling to get down when someone is shooting at you."

"All right, I apologize for the remark about force. But

the bet is on, and I saw some thick steaks in the freezer that I would like tomorrow night.''

''Do you know how to cook them?''

''I won't have to know, but yes, I do.''

He leaned back in his chair, watching her finish her dinner and then he took her hand. ''We're not cleaning up tonight. Come here and dance with me again.''

She moved into his arms, and as they slowly danced, he watched her steadily. How long before he kissed her? she wondered. Earlier, she had wanted to make love tonight, but then she had thought ahead, and knew she was going to have to tell Josh goodbye soon. And never see him again. Was she already in love with this tough cowboy who could be so sexy and appealing?

''So you have the agency up for sale. What will you do when it sells?''

''Invest, maybe open another agency where I don't have to deal with Carter.''

''If he's behind the attempts on your life, you won't have to deal with him anyway, once he's caught.''

''I don't know whether it's Carter or not. Carter definitely isn't down here in Texas. He's either hired someone or I have the wrong suspect in mind.''

''So you ran the Dahl agency for over a year?''

''Yes, and I liked doing it. I can't model forever, so I have to find something else. I'm not fond of the family business. And I couldn't possibly do what my sister Talia does.''

''The news anchor?''

''Yes. That's not my field, either. I'll have to do something in pubic relations or modeling.''

''If it turns out that it's not Carter, would you still sell the agency?''

''Yes. We can't work together. He hates that I've inherited, and he hates that I wouldn't go out with him. No, I don't want to work with Carter ever again. So many people think he's delightful and charming, but there's a darker side to him.'' She tilted her head to study Josh. ''Will you be lonesome here when I'm gone?''

''Now what do you think?'' he asked with amusement.

''I don't think you'll miss me at all. You may be glad to have your house to yourself again.''

''No, I'll miss you very much. My life will go back to being quiet and dull.''

''Right.''

''So why are you suddenly taking my warnings about us seriously? You never have before.''

''I didn't think about it before. I wanted to break through that barrier you keep around you, but I didn't think what might happen to me if I did.''

''So now you're scared?''

She thought about his question. She had never met a man like Josh. Suppose she never did again? Suppose her future was filled with dull guys, as her past had been? Was she going to miss something here because she was afraid of falling in love?

''No, I'm not scared. And I still want to get past those barriers, and I really thought my cooking might do the trick.''

''Your cooking is good enough to tempt me to let go of the barriers, but—'' he shrugged ''—I'm set in my ways. Guarding my heart is an old habit now. On the other hand, that doesn't mean I can't enjoy a night of love.'' He danced her over to the wall, then placed his hands on both sides of her so she was hemmed in. ''And I've waited, Laurie. You have your memory. You're free to love, and you've flirted and tempted and toyed with me from the first day.'' He slid his arms around her waist and pulled her against him.

''Don't say I didn't warn you,'' she whispered, and dragged his head down to kiss him.

Josh tightened his arms around her, leaning over her while he spread his legs. His hand slid to her bottom to pull her up against him. Laurie felt his thick shaft and knew he was already aroused. He kissed her possessively, as he had earlier, driving all thoughts from her mind.

Sensation and need enveloped her. She desired this strong, tough cowboy, who offered both excitement and risk. Being careful of her wound, he gently removed pins from her hair until it fell freely around her face. His warm fingers brushed her back along her zipper, and then cool air spilled over her shoulders.

Josh pushed away the dress and leaned back, drawing in his breath and knowing there would be no going back this night. She wore a lacy black bra and a wisp of black lace for panties. Her breasts were full, and her legs so long they were a dream.

He flicked the clasp on her bra and pushed it away, cupping her breasts and circling her nipples with his thumbs. She tugged at the buttons on his shirt, twisting them free while she gasped and threw her head back and closed her eyes.

As he caressed her, she pulled his shirt open and trailed her fingers lazily over his chest. She shoved his shirt away and ran her fingers along his arm, above his healing wound.

"You took this for me," she said, brushing kisses on his arm below the scar. Then she tugged at his belt, struggling to get it unbuckled. He was aware of her unfastening his jeans, freeing him, and he paused to yank off his boots. Stepping out of his jeans, he flung away his shirt.

"You're gorgeous!" she gasped, hooking her fingers into his briefs to shove them down.

"I'm the one who's supposed to say that," he said in a husky voice. "Damn, you're beautiful!"

He swung her into his arms and carried her to the family room, where he sat on the sofa and pulled her onto his lap.

He kissed her breast, his tongue drawing lazy circles over her nipple.

"Josh!" Laurie gasped, running her fingers through his hair. She twisted to straddle him, kissing him hungrily and stroking his thick, hard shaft. Her heart pounded and she was on fire, burning with urgency. He was solid muscle and hard planes, his chest well sculpted. He was so male and so ready for her.

His hand slid between her legs and she was wild with need as his fingers stroked and circled and entered.

"Josh, please…"

"You like that? And that?"

"Oh, yes! I want you!"

He kissed her savagely, possessively. She kissed him back, trying to drive him to a need that equaled hers. She wanted to do things that would make it impossible for him to keep that heart of his locked up. She wanted to make him unable to blithely send her away.

"Try to forget this," she said, scooting away from him and pushing him down on the sofa, coming over to kiss and stroke him, her hair spilling over his belly and thighs.

He gasped and wound his fingers tightly in her hair while she continued, relishing the feel of his male body, wanting to touch and kiss him all night long.

He inhaled, making a guttural sound deep in his throat as he sat up. When he picked her up, she wound her arms around his neck, too aware of their naked bodies, hers still tingling from his kisses and caresses. He took the stairs easily, two at a time, and then crossed his room to stand her on her feet beside his bed. The only light spilled from the hall, highlighting his muscles.

Wanting to give him a night he couldn't ever forget, Laurie pulled his head down to kiss him, moving her hips against his. His arms wrapped tightly around her while he kissed her long and deeply in return.

Josh fought to keep his control, wanting this night to last, wanting to make love to her for hours. He shifted slightly, caressing her, his fingers trailing over her warm, soft breast, sliding down over her flat stomach, down between her legs where she was wet, ready.

But he wanted her to be a lot more ready. He wanted her wild with need. He stroked her and she thrust her hips against him, moaning softly while she clung to him.

He was on fire with wanting her. She was cream and pink and golden, and those dark eyes held mysteries in their depths.

"Josh, please!" she gasped again, moving against him. All the pent-up desire he had felt for her since that first day boiled up in him, and he vowed to love her through the night.

He shifted and picked her up again, to lay her gently on the bed, and then he moved to her feet, watching her as he caressed her.

Laurie inhaled, her hips moving compulsively. She was caught in Josh's gaze, unable to look away. He moved slowly higher, his tongue hot and wet, an exquisite torment. Kissing the skin along her calf and stroking behind her knees, he shifted between her legs, his kisses trailing higher. His tongue flicked along her inner thigh and she closed her eyes, gasping and winding her fingers in his hair.

And then he spread her legs, sliding them over his shoulders and bending to trail his tongue where his fingers had been, kissing her intimately.

"Now I'll kiss you like you've kissed me—all over. I've dreamed of this, Josh," she said, pushing him down and trailing kisses from his throat to his flat nipples, feeling the rock-solid muscles of his chest. Her fingers fluttered over him, caressing him and sweat beaded his brow. He started to get up, but she wouldn't let him, moving astride him again and looking down at him.

''Let me kiss you,'' she whispered, and then leaned down to trail her tongue over his nipple again, moving lower, down across his flat, muscled belly. She scooted lower still, caressing his thighs and then taking his shaft to kiss him, her tongue stroking him.

''Laurie!'' He nearly growled out her name as he sat up, his hands framing her face. He looked at her, a hungry gaze that made her heart thud, and then he kissed her, hauling her into his arms as he sat back on the bed and leaned over her.

How long he kissed her, she didn't know, but suddenly he stopped. ''We've barely started here,'' he said, his voice a deep rasp. He pushed her down, turning her over to kiss and caress her back, his hands playing over her bottom while he moved down to kiss her behind her knees.

Each time she tried to sit up, to reach for him, he pushed her down gently. ''Wait, Laurie, wait. Let me love you. Give me time to love you,'' he whispered.

His kisses and caresses burned her to cinders. She felt boneless, on fire, wanting him more than she would have ever dreamed possible.

There was no world beyond Josh. Each time she tried to twist away—to kiss him, stroke him, discover him—he gave her only a few minutes, then was kissing her again.

She was in sweet torment, wanting him, never wanting him to stop. Finally he moved between her legs. ''Are you protected?'' he asked.

When she shook her head, he moved away to return in a moment. As soon as he was between her legs, he opened the packet in his hands to remove a condom. Watching her, he slowly lowered himself. She cried out, arching against him. ''Josh, now, now,'' she whispered, wrapping her legs around him.

He slowly entered her. She pressed forward eagerly, wanting him.

"Josh, please!" she cried out, clinging to him. How long she had wanted him! Night after night she had dreamed of this moment, and the reality of it was far more exciting.

He turned to kiss her, slowly filling her and then moving back.

She was wild in his arms, passionate and sweet. Sweat poured off Josh as he started thrusting against her, nearly mindless with pleasure. Yet he wanted to make the moments last, to take her to the heights with him.

She was as exuberant and responsive as all her earlier eagerness had hinted. He was enveloped in her softness and warmth, and for these few minutes, she was his woman.

Josh held her tightly, kissing her, loving her, still moving slowly, although it was costing him more by the second. Still he tried to hold back, to make it last for her. Her hips arched and she moved rhythmically with him, an age-old dance that bound them completely.

And then his control was gone. He couldn't hold back any longer, thrusting and pumping and feeling her match him, hearing her cries of pleasure and need, until he shuddered with release. She cried out, arching one last time and then letting go.

Laurie burst over the summit, satisfaction rocking her as she felt Josh's shuddering release. She held him tightly, knowing that at this moment all differences between them were but ephemeral shadows that hovered in the background. For now, she and Josh were one and there were no barriers. He was hers and she was his. For now, she laid claim to him, to his heart. And she knew she loved him. Wisdom had nothing to do with the decision. How could she keep from loving this tough, exciting man who had just shown her rapture and ecstasy?

He was a mass of contradictions, fearlessly chasing the killer who was after her and then cautiously guarding his heart. So tough and responsible as a rancher, but caring enough to hire young men who had been in trouble and needed help.

So seemingly controlled and guarded, and then unleashing passion that consumed her.

She held him close, mentally saying *I love you,* but knowing that wasn't what he wanted to hear.

His back was covered with a fine sheen of sweat and his weight felt good on her. She wanted to hold him for hours. He shifted and raised his head to look at her, and then he kissed her, long and slow and sweet.

When he raised his head again, he rolled to his side, taking her with him and holding her close. He stroked her hair away from her face. "That was just a beginning," he whispered.

"A beginning?"

"The night is long and I want to love you every minute of it."

"That feeling is mutual," she said, running her fingers along his jaw and feeling the slight stubble. His hair was tousled and he looked sexy and marvelous to her.

He hugged her tightly, stroking her throat and then running his hand down her bare back. She leaned away to look at him again.

"You're beautiful," he said, kissing her temple. "I can't stop touching or kissing you."

"That's good. I like that," she answered honestly.

"I think you melted my bones."

"I hope so. At least for now, those barriers you keep around yourself are almost gone."

"I don't really keep barriers. It's just the way I am."

"No, it isn't, but I don't want to argue with you about it. Everything is too good right now."

"It is good," he said in a husky voice. "I don't want to let you out of my arms."

"That suits me, too. You'll at least keep in touch with

me by telephone when I go back to Kansas City, won't you?'' she asked.

"Sure.''

"I don't think you mean that, but I'll call you.''

He held her quietly for a few minutes, his hand stroking her while their heartbeats slowed and their breathing returned to normal.

"Come here. I'll see if I can stand up, and if I can, we'll totter into the shower.''

He slid off the bed, then reached down to scoop her into his arms. "There. It's a good thing you're light as a feather because tonight I'm not up to much.''

"Seems to me you were up to plenty a few minutes ago,'' she teased, and he chuckled while he nuzzled her neck.

"How did someone who is so beautiful get brains and personality, too?'' he asked. "It isn't fair to normal mortals.''

"As if you're a run-of-the-mill mortal.''

"I'm just a country boy, ma'am. Born and bred in Piedras County.''

"Oh, sure.''

He stepped into the shower and turned on the water, adjusting the nozzle so the spray wouldn't hit her scalp wound. Then he started slowly spreading soap lather over her smooth, wet body.

"Josh,'' she said, desire igniting again. She did the same for him and finally he picked her up, braced himself against the shower wall and let her slide down his body. His thick shaft entered her and she moved with him, holding him tightly until they both burst over the brink of ecstasy once more.

He finally let her slide back down to her feet, and she leaned against him while he held her close. Their racing hearts slowed, and then they washed and he dried her off after she had dried him.

"Back to bed before I collapse," he said, picking her up again and carrying her to bed, to pull her close in his arms.

To her joy, they made love all through the night, and the sky was growing light when he finally fell asleep in her arms.

Laurie marveled at his stamina and energy. She toyed lightly with locks of his hair, her heart filled with love. It would hurt when they parted, but she would never regret this night. "I love you, Josh," she whispered softly, knowing she was wildly in love with him, knowing that he had warned her repeatedly against that.

She didn't want to sleep at all. Excitement and joy bubbled in her. She wanted to look at Josh and touch him. She would never get enough of either one. He was a marvel to her, incredibly sexy.

She lay beside him, facing him. He had one arm flung over her waist, holding her in his sleep. She wasn't going to think about tomorrow or the future. It would come all too soon and wreak its havoc. Right now they were in each other's arms, and she could relish that and store up memories.

In spite of wanting to stay awake, she finally fell asleep for a while, to wake once more in an erotic haze. Laurie opened her eyes to find Josh watching her while he drew lazy circles around her nipple with his fingers.

She reached up to slip her arm around his neck and pull him to her for a kiss.

They loved for hours. She could see sunshine slipping through slits between the shutters, and knew the morning was passing, but she didn't care. All she cared about was Josh, being with him, exploring his body, storing up more memories.

"You're sex-starved, cowboy."

"Yeah, ain't it nice," he drawled, and she laughed, hugging him close. He tightened his arms around her.

Twice the phone rang, but they let the answering machine take the calls. The third call was from Drake, with a message for Josh about lost cows.

With a groan, Josh crossed the room to his desk to pick up the phone. Laurie rolled on her side to look at him, her gaze roaming slowly down the length of him, over his muscled back, his firm butt, his long legs. She paid little attention as he talked to his foreman, except when he glanced over his shoulder at her, his gaze traveling with as much deliberation over her as hers had with him.

When he replaced the receiver and turned to come back to bed, she saw that he was aroused again, ready for her.

She smiled, holding out her arms, and he came down eagerly to kiss her. Then they were lost again in another rapturous hour of loving.

Laurie had no idea what time it was, but she knew the day was far advanced when she stirred. His eyes came open and he looked at her, tightening his arm around her middle.

"Josh, I am starving."

"So am I," he said, nuzzling her.

"No. I mean for breakfast, lunch, whatever. My stomach is grumbling."

"I can end that," he said, shifting to kiss her stomach.

"No, you don't!" She pushed against him and slipped out of bed, going to his closet to rummage around and finally take one of his shirts. "May I?"

"Sure. It'll look a whole lot better on you than it ever has on me."

"That's debatable."

He got out of bed and she left the room quickly, afraid that if he crossed the room to kiss her, she would be lost to more lovemaking, and her stomach was rumbling fearfully.

It was half past one in the afternoon. She busied herself, heating the leftover pasta casserole, swiftly making another tossed salad. As she worked, Josh appeared in jeans and cleared the dishes from the table from their supper the night before. In minutes he had the dishwasher running and water poured, bread on the table, and was holding a chair for her.

Lifting her hair, he brushed a kiss on her nape when she was seated. Her skin tingled at his touch, and she marveled how he could do that to her with such a feathery kiss after their marathon lovemaking.

"You're such a good cook, I'm surprised you didn't want to stay in the restaurant business with your sister."

"No, that's not for me, but thanks for the compliment."

"I told Drake I was taking the next few days off, and not to disturb me unless it's an emergency."

"Few days?" she said, laughing. "We're staying in bed for the next few days?"

"You object?"

She reached over to take his hand. "Never!"

"I have to let Will Cordoba come out here sometime soon and get his report from me on this last incident, but I can put him off for a few days."

"So we're just going to hole up here and make love wildly, and hope no danger comes slipping up while we're distracted?"

"I've got alarms now, and lights, and the dogs are out at night. I think we're pretty safe. Are you backing out?"

"Not on your life!"

He pushed back his chair and caught her wrist. "Come here," he said in a husky voice.

She had eaten plenty and now she wanted to be in his arms again, so she went eagerly, sitting down in his lap to kiss him.

The next three days were a time of passion and discovery. They talked for hours, learning more about each other, and they loved wildly, with as much exuberance and need as the first time.

Laurie was amazed he would take so much time out of his busy schedule, because she knew how hard he worked. Yet she wanted every minute possible with him. Time was fleeing, and soon Josh would be gone from her life.

He told her how much he liked being with her. He told her how beautiful she was. He told her he had never known anyone like her. But there were no words of love, no promises of tomorrow, no asking her to stay.

And then their days were over. The morning came when Josh made love to her and then left her, going to shower and shave and dress.

Finn sat in a corner booth in a San Antonio bar and watched the door, dreading to face the man who had hired him. Finn was angry that the man had come to Texas, angry that the woman wasn't dead. He'd hit her with that rifle shot. He had come so close. He'd watched the ambulance arrive and had waited, hoping they would take her body out, but instead the paramedics were at the house only a short time and left just as they had come—without a passenger.

She was still alive.

He had tried to get close to the house, but it was harder now because the cowboy's men roamed the ranch.

For the past two nights he had been able to watch the house. It was risky. One of the cowboys had passed close to him during the night.

And no one was coming or going from the house. They had to come out sometime.

His employer had gone into a rage over the phone when he was told that she was still alive. And now he was coming to Texas himself.

Finn drew a deep breath. He didn't want help. He didn't want to deal with the man, who went crazy when he was angry.

Finn knew he couldn't ask for more money now. He wanted a lot of distance between them when he did that. He would do it by mail. It could be handled. The man would have to pay. He couldn't risk having it known that he was involved in murder.

He was a perfect target for blackmail. Wealthy, ambitious, prominent in society. He would pay and pay.

Only tonight, Finn had to deal with the man, and cope with that violent temper. Why was he coming? Did he think both of them could do better than just one—and that one a professional?

This should be a one-man job; it would be tidier. But this way, he would have more leverage to get the man to pay. Finn slipped his hand in his pocket, fingering the small recorder he would switch on while they made their plans.

And he had protected himself. He had made a video and paid someone to hold it until he picked it up. But if he didn't pick it up at the end of the month, the man was to send it to the police.

He was dealing with an amateur. A violent, nasty-tempered amateur. Finn wanted this job finished, and he hoped it was over in the next twenty-four hours.

Then the man entered the bar. Finn waited and watched. Tall, blond, wearing a tailor-made suit, he stood out in the bar crowd. Stupid amateur, Finn thought. People would notice him. Women would notice him. Finn glanced around and saw women already watching the man. And then he spotted Finn and headed in his direction.

Chapter 15

Carter Dahl tried to control his smoldering rage. He wanted to grab Finn and throttle him for botching the job. Finn was supposed to be so good. And this should have been easy. How did the bitch survive everything?

Well, she wasn't going to much longer. It would all be over tonight. After some careful planning, Carter would take care of the job himself. Use Finn as a decoy to lure the cowboy out of the house, away from her, and then Carter would finish her quickly. But not so quickly that she didn't know who and why.

Carter spotted Finn, barely able to see him at first glance where he sat in the corner of the last booth, a dim blur hidden in dark shadows.

Carter nodded at Finn as he slid into the booth.

"She's like a cat with nine lives," Finn said.

"She won't survive the next attempt. That's why I'm here."

"Am I through?"

"No. I still need you. I want you to lure the cowboy away from the house. Just give me time alone with her."

Carter studied Finn. The man was as plain and unremarkable as the floor of the bar. No wonder he didn't have a police record. Carter doubted if anyone had ever given a decent description of him. Brown hair that was neither short nor long. Hazel eyes that probably looked blue if the man wore a blue sweater, green if he wore green and brown if he wore brown. He was medium height, medium build. There were no scars or distinguishing marks. No one would notice him in a crowd. And no one could ever pick him out of a lineup. He was perfect for what he did; just too bad he wasn't a better shot.

He'd said the cowboy had warned her. Finn had heard the cowboy yell and guessed sunlight must have glinted on the gun barrel at just the wrong moment.

By tomorrow it wouldn't matter. Tonight Carter would finish this job himself. And then… It took his breath away to think of the possibilities.

"How the hell am I supposed to lure him out? They've been shut in that house for days now. Probably in bed."

"Not her," Carter said, feeling another hot rush of anger. "She's cold and arrogant. She won't want a cowboy."

"Well, they're shut up there together. Now how can I lure him out of the house? The hired hands prowl the grounds at night. Dogs are no problem—I've been feeding them steaks. Best-fed mutts in the U.S.A."

"It won't matter. We'll set his land on fire on the far side from the highway. That'll bring him out of his house, and he'll leave her behind."

"It'll bring the neighbors and the fire department."

"Not at first. But it'll draw his hired hands. Then we'll come in from the other side, and you'll cover me when I go into the house. I want to get her myself."

"I think it would be simpler if you left it up to me. You could stay in the clear."

"I want this. I want her to know. You can cover the house in case he comes back. That way I won't have to worry about being surprised."

"Whatever you want. It's your money. Suppose he just stays in his house and lets the hired help take care of things?"

"Didn't he go after you after the crash? He had to have left her, even without knowing how badly she was injured, while he chased after you."

"Yeah, I guess you're right. He'll come. He prowls around. Up until the last few days, he's been out there himself. You're probably right."

"I know I'm right."

"But if you're not, you'd better be ready. I shot him. I saw him take the hit and he still kept coming after me. He jumped on the car as I was leaving. I don't want to tangle with him again. And he's like a cat out there in the dark."

"I'll be ready for whatever happens. Just make sure you watch the house. I'll take care of her and then I'm gone. Now I want to drive out there and look over the land and the ranch, pick our spots."

"What are you going to do for an alibi? You're not in Kansas City now."

"I rode down with one of our models. I've got a plum of a shoot for her today. This is a huge jump in her career, and she knows it. As soon as I leave you, she and I will spend the day at the shoot. We're dating. Seriously dating. We'll spend tonight together, drive home in her car tomorrow. She's my alibi."

"She's willing to say you were with her every minute?"

"She knows the stakes. She knows her career is poised to take off with this shoot, and she knows if I marry her, she'll own what I own. Yes, she's willing."

Finn shrugged. "Fine. We need to stop at a grocery so I can get some boneless steaks. A few more nights of this and someone is going to notice that those dogs are fattening up."

"There won't be a few more nights. After tonight it's over. I'm not leaving until it is. I'll do this myself."

"So suppose I run into the cowboy or one of his men?"

"Take 'em out. No one can tie you to this. And I have an alibi."

"And you have the rest of my money? When we part tonight, that's it."

"Yes. I'll give you part of your money as soon as we get back together. And after you drop me a block from my hotel, you get the rest. You and I will go our separate ways, and we won't ever see each other again. I can count on that, can't I?"

"Sure, Carter. I'm a professional." Finn squinted. "I told you, the cowboy installed an alarm system and yard lights. The lights won't matter if everyone is up and moving anyway, but the phone cable is on the back of the house on the east side. You can cut it and disengage the alarm."

"I'll take care of the alarm."

"I hope you can move fast."

"I can."

"Carter, if either one of us gets caught, we don't know the other person exists. I won't tie you to this, but don't you tie me to it."

"Of course not. You deal too much with dumb thugs, Finn. I would never link you to this. Besides, I don't know your real name, do I?"

"You probably don't," Finn replied quietly, and raised his beer. "Here's to success."

Carter lifted the beer and touched Finn's bottle lightly. He hated beer, but he drank. Less than twenty-four hours and it would all be over literally. And Ivy James would be out of his life forever. When Ivy died, he was certain her sisters would go ahead and sell the agency. Ivy wouldn't sell it to him, but they wouldn't care whether he bought it or not.

The agency would be his. All his. Rightfully his. And the money would flow. The business would be without Ivy. And he would pay her back for her rejection of him.

Laurie ran her fingers across Josh's chest. "So are we going to live the rest of our lives in this bed?"

"No. Actually, I think another few hours today and then we have to get back to reality. There are some things here on the ranch that I've let slide, and I can't keep avoiding them. Drake will stick around while I go to work this afternoon."

"I still feel like I've got baby-sitters."

"That's what you call this?" he asked, running his hand across her bottom.

She laughed and made a face at him. "Maybe not this, but having Drake come up here and stay with me is what I'm talking about. I'll be all right."

"I'll feel much better if I know Drake is here. Let's not argue this one."

"Of course not. Let's just do it your way."

"Sure, because I'm right."

"Impossible man."

He rolled her over suddenly, moving above her. "This time with you has been the best ever."

"I think so, too," Laurie said solemnly, gazing up at him and wondering how difficult it had been for him to make that admission. "You know you could come to Kansas City later this year to see me."

"Yeah, I could," he said.

She smiled, knowing he hadn't finished his sentence, but certain he was thinking that he could, but he wasn't going to. She had known from the first that there was no future for them. He had made that abundantly clear, so she needed to let it go now and accept that soon she would tell him goodbye forever.

"You won't come, but you're going to miss me, cowboy," she said in a sultry voice, wrapping one arm around his neck while her other hand caressed him. "Let me show you why."

He lowered his head to kiss her and she felt on fire. Each time they loved, she wanted him more than the time before. He was becoming more important to her with each passing hour, and she knew she would leave Texas with a broken heart.

And then thoughts were gone, set adrift by passion as he stroked her and kissed her.

It was after two in the afternoon when he stepped outside to meet Drake. She watched the two men through the window. The afternoon was sunny, with deep blue skies. The land was green, wildflowers were beginning to dot hillsides, and she thought Josh was right—this was one of the most beautiful places she had ever seen. Or was she just seeing it through his eyes? So giddy and in love that the entire world looked beautiful to her?

Her smile faded. Their love idyll was over. She could feel that it wouldn't be much longer until something snapped—it couldn't be. Someone or something had to give. And then she would go home, back to her modeling life, and she wouldn't see Josh again. She was certain there wouldn't be lingering phone calls, visits to Kansas City or visits back to Texas. She knew he wanted to say goodbye, and it would be final with him.

She wasn't going to shed tears over him—at least not where he could see them. The tears would come, but hopefully later. She looked around. "Stop thinking about it," she said aloud to herself. Right now she was in his kitchen, and he would come home and make love to her tonight. She would probably be with him through most of the morning tomorrow.

She knew he had been neglecting his ranch, and he needed to get back to it and stop being a bodyguard for her. She could hire a bodyguard and let Josh get on with taking care of his ranch.

By suppertime her anticipation had grown, and she watched for him to return home. Finally she saw his pickup pull into the garage, and then he was striding toward the house. He wore his black hat, a T-shirt and jeans, and just the sight of him made her pulse race. She loved him and that was that. She shouldn't tell him—at least not yet. But she knew it was the real thing, and she wondered if she would love him the rest of her life.

Josh looked all around, turning his head slowly, and she knew he was looking for the killer.

She wanted to run meet him and throw herself into his arms, but it wasn't safe for her to step outside.

She waited until the door swung open, and then she did run—to wrap her arms around him.

Hours later she sat up in bed, pulling up the sheet and swinging her hair away from her face. "Tomorrow I'll know to eat while I'm here alone, because you're like a camel. You can go without eating for days."

"I think camels go without water. I hope I don't look like a camel."

She grinned and pushed away the sheet. "Let me look…. Oh, my! There goes eating for another hour."

"It's your fault," he said, pulling her down and rolling above her. "I'll feed you, hungry woman, and then it's back to bed."

"Sounds wonderful to me," she said, knowing each hour

just made her love him that much more, and bound her to him with even stronger bonds.

He framed her face with his hands. "Laurie—and you'll forever be Laurie to me—"

"That's fine."

"It's never been like this before for me. Not ever."

Her heart thudded, and she wondered if that was a monumental step for him in letting go.

She brushed locks of hair off his forehead. "I'm glad. I feel the same way, but I didn't know what you felt."

"You should know," he said gruffly. He kissed her throat. "Haven't I been showing you?"

"Yes," she said, winding her fingers in his hair.

His green eyes bored into her with an intensity that took her breath away. "I'll miss you like hell. I've always been able to say goodbye without hurting, but this time it's going to hurt."

"I love you, Josh," she whispered.

He closed his eyes and inhaled, and appeared to be in such pain that she hurt for both of them. "I didn't tell you that to hurt you more," she said.

"I know you didn't, but there's no future for us. We both know that. There's no point in talking about dates or you coming back to Texas or me going to Kansas City. You have your life and future there and I have mine right here."

She tried to stop the tears, but couldn't. He wiped them away with his thumbs and pulled her into his arms. "Don't cry."

"I can cry if I want to!" she cried. "At least I feel! You've got your feelings all bottled up and shut away. You're scared to let go and love."

"You're right, because I've lived through too many disasters because of love."

"Just try to forget me, Josh Kellogg!" she said, pushing him down on the bed and moving over him to kiss him.

* * *

Carter and Finn poured gasoline over a wide area and then tossed aside the gas cans. A sliver of moon left the world in shadows. Both men were dressed in black, with gloves covering their hands.

"Let's go," Carter ordered. "Start running. I'll toss the match."

Finn was gone swiftly, heading for the car. Carter struck a match and tossed it where he had deliberately poured a small circle of gasoline and then a trail to the large area they had doused.

It flared up instantly and Carter ran, knowing they were on to the next step of his plans now.

They drove to the entrance of the ranch, boldly taking the road until they'd almost reached the house. Then they turned off over rough ground, hiding the car beneath trees and getting out to walk into the woods. To Carter's satisfaction, he saw smoke spiraling up into the night sky in the distance.

As he watched, he heard the first shout of warning.

"Someone has spotted the fire," he said in satisfaction.

Finn turned to face him. "Then you better move damn fast. We're a hell of a way from the house right now."

"This will drag that cowboy out of the house and leave Ivy unprotected for me."

"I want my money now."

Carter raised the pistol he carried. He stood too close to miss. "Thanks, Finn. You won't be needing the money, and you're going to get that cowboy out here. Finding your body should keep them all busy."

Josh sat across from Laurie as they ate the first bites of warmed-over casserole. He wore jeans and nothing more, and he was in her silk robe. "You're a fabulous cook."

"All of my family could cook. My father was the real expert. A lot of the restaurant recipes were his."

The phone rang and Josh got up to answer it. He listened to Drake and then slammed down the receiver.

"Place is on fire. Rudy is coming up here to stay with you."

"Josh, you have alarms. You may need every hand. Shouldn't I go with you?"

"Nope. You stay here, and Rudy will be right outside." Josh left the room, and Laurie got up to follow him. In minutes he was dressed in jeans, T-shirt and boots.

"I have my cell phone. I'll call you after a while. The fire department is sending a pumper truck, and Drake will let neighbors know."

Just as he opened the back door, two shots echoed in the night.

Josh frowned. "Those were gunshots. The fire is in the far south pasture. Call Cordoba and tell him about the shots. He told me to let him know if anything happened and not go looking myself, so he can do it. And you stay in this house."

"Don't worry about me."

"You never do what I tell you."

She grabbed his shirt. "That works both ways. You take care of yourself! Don't run risks, and come back to me."

He kissed her lightly and left, and she watched him stride away. Closing and locking the door, she ran to call the sheriff.

She went upstairs to watch the fire from the window. Knowing the sheriff was on his way and would probably come to the house, she pulled on jeans and a T-shirt. When she saw the sheriff's car arrive, she went downstairs.

Will Cordoba crossed the porch, and she opened the door to talk to him. It took only seconds to tell him about the fire and the shots, and then he was gone and she locked up after him.

She paced the kitchen, switching off lights and staring out the window, wishing she could be out there with Josh, trying to fight the fire or be useful in some manner.

She went upstairs because she could get a better view of the ranch. She switched off lights there, moving to a bedroom window, and to the south she saw smoke and the red glow from the fire. The yard was filled with empty police cars. If Rudy was down there in the yard, she hadn't seen any sign of him.

As she watched, Laurie heard a scrape and bump in another part of the house, and frowned. She had been alone in the house enough now to have become familiar with noises. Neither of these sounds was anything she was accustomed to hearing when the house was empty.

Her eyes had adjusted to the dark, so she moved quietly across the bedroom and into the darkened hall, standing still to listen.

A board creaked. It came from the direction of a bedroom down the hall, a room between her and the stairs. If someone was in the house, she could phone for help or run outside. She went back into the bedroom, moving quickly to the phone. She picked up the receiver and heard only silence.

The phone wasn't working. She unplugged the table lamp and removed the shade, picking the lamp up to use as a weapon, and tiptoeing across the bedroom to open the door to the hall. She would try to get out of the house. Another bump sounded, louder this time, and she knew she wasn't alone in the house.

Cautiously, she slipped into the hall, staying close to the wall. She didn't see anyone, but bedroom doors stood open on dark rooms, and she would have to pass two of them to get to the stairs.

Her heart thudded and her palms were sweaty. She gripped the lamp base tightly, wrapping the cord around it.

Each open door was a hazard. She stood still and listened, scarcely daring to breathe. Another creak.

She couldn't tell which room it was from, but the noise was upstairs, not far from where she stood, between her and the head of the stairs.

She edged toward the stairwell, her gaze moving from one dark doorway to the next.

As flames danced through the trees and consumed underbrush and grass, men fought the fire. A pumper truck drove slowly along the edge of the raging inferno while firemen tried to douse the flames. More men arrived to help—Josh's neighbors—leaving their pickups on the road and running toward the blaze.

Needing more shovels, Josh climbed into his pickup, started the engine and swung in a circle. His headlights splashed over a stocky man climbing out of a truck. Josh slammed on his brakes and jumped out, leaving the motor running and the door open as he sprinted toward the man.

"Rudy! Why aren't you at the house?"

The man turned. "The detective from the Stallion Pass PD told me I wasn't needed. He's going to watch the house while the others are looking at the crime scene. He told me I could go help the firefighters—"

Josh was already gone, running for his pickup, his pulse racing. As he drove, he yanked up his cell phone to call Laurie.

When he couldn't get through, he called Will Cordoba. The minute the sheriff answered, Josh demanded, "Will, did you leave a detective at the house?"

"No. Want me to put someone up there? Laurie told me that you had one of your hands outside."

"Someone sent Rudy away and told him that he was a detective from the Stallion Pass PD. I'm on my way."

"We'll get up there. Josh, we found a body—a man shot and killed in the past hour, I would guess."

"She's alone, Will." Josh tossed down the phone to drive, pressing the accelerator to the floor and bouncing over rough ground as he cut across the fields.

Laurie passed an open door, feeling as if she were crossing a yawning abyss. The minute she was beyond the doorway, she paused, her heart pounding. One more to go.

A board creaked and something scraped against wood. She followed the sounds, which seemed to come from the bedroom across the hall.

Deciding to make a run for it, she dashed toward the stairs. A dark shadow emerged from the bedroom and lunged toward her. She grabbed the banister to go down, but rough hands locked on her arm and yanked her back.

Laurie screamed and swung the lamp with all her strength, smashing it against her attacker's head. He had his face covered with a mask and wore dark clothing. She couldn't see him, but she could detect aftershave, and she knew height and bulk. Carter Dahl.

"Bitch. Your luck has run out. You die tonight."

"Carter, let go of me," she said, swinging the lamp again and feeling it break over his head.

With a roar, he yanked her off her feet. She kicked and tried to bite. Howling in pain, he relaxed his hold and she pushed against him, throwing all her weight into shoving him off balance. His arms flailed and he toppled down the stairs, crashing against the banister and catching himself halfway down.

Laurie ran for the master bedroom, springing inside and locking the door. She could hear Carter pounding after her.

She raced to a window, trying to get it open. When it wouldn't budge, she moved to another one.

Carter rattled the doorknob and then kicked at the door.

She moved to the third window, yanking in vain.

The door splintered and Carter burst into the room, charging across the room to tackle her.

They both went down, Carter knocking the breath from her lungs. He pinned her to the floor, his hands locking on her throat. ''Now I'm finally rid of you.''

She struggled to break free. Lights swam before her eyes, and she knew in seconds she would lose consciousness.

Her head swam and all sounds receded.

Then Carter was gone. Dizzy, gasping for breath, she rolled away, dimly aware of other noises as she did so— sounds of two men fighting, crashing into furniture. Laurie looked for another weapon, snatching up a bronze statue and switching on a light.

Chapter 16

Josh and Carter were locked together, until Josh tossed Carter over his shoulder. Carter crashed into a table, but came up instantly, charging Josh, who slammed his fist into the other man's jaw.

Carter staggered back and Laurie dodged him, swinging the bronze statue of a cowboy and horse, smashing it against Carter's head.

He reeled and crumpled, sprawling across a chair and rolling to the floor.

Startled, she looked at Josh.

"Good hit," he said. "Get downstairs and let the sheriff in. He's on his way here. I'll take care of this guy."

She looked at the unconscious man on the floor. "He's Carter Dahl."

Josh yanked off his belt to bind Carter's wrists. She hurried downstairs to open the back door. Will Cordoba and another uniformed policeman were running toward the house. When they reached the door, Will asked, "Are you okay?"

"Yes," she answered as she pointed. "He's upstairs. Josh is with him."

She sagged against the door, looked at the bronze statue still in her hand and let it fall to the floor.

In minutes Josh came down. His hair was rumpled; his mouth and cheek were cut and bleeding. One eye was puffy and his shirt was ripped, but he looked wonderful to her and she rushed into his arms. He held her tightly.

"Thank heaven you're all right," he said. "I went through hell trying to get back here."

"How'd you know to come back?"

"I saw Rudy. Carter told him he wasn't needed here. Carter said he was a detective with the Stallion Pass police."

She nodded. They heard a commotion and watched as Will Cordoba headed toward them. Josh took Laurie's arm and stepped onto the porch, moving out of the way. In seconds Will came through the door and walked over to them, while the policeman with him led a handcuffed Carter away.

Carter glared at her, and Laurie stared back at him, lifting her chin defiantly.

Then he was gone, and she tried to turn her attention to what Will Cordoba was telling Josh.

"We've got an unidentified body. I'm guessing Dahl can give us answers. I'll let you know. Think they'll get the blaze under control tonight?"

Josh shook his head. "I don't know. I'm going back in a few minutes."

"I'll send someone out tomorrow to get your statements," Will said to both of them. "Want me to leave a man here at the house, just in case?"

"Thanks, Will. That would be much appreciated," Josh said.

"But I'm going with you to fight the fire," Laurie said. "I'm not staying here."

"We'll argue that one in a minute," he answered, and shook hands with the sheriff. "Thanks, Will."

"You better take care of your injuries before you tackle anything else. You, too, Laurie. See you both tomorrow."

He left and Josh led her inside, closing the kitchen door and then pulling her into his embrace to hug her tightly. "I just want to hold you and know for certain that you're all right," he rasped.

"I'm fine now, and I want you to hold me," she murmured.

They stood quietly a moment, and then Josh tilted her chin and leaned down to kiss her. When he pulled away, he gazed at her solemnly.

"Come in here and let me put some antiseptic on your cuts," she said, and took his hand.

"Sure."

They went to a downstairs bathroom, and Josh sat on the side of the tub. She tried to put a bandage on one of his cuts, but her hands shook badly. Josh took the bandage from her to stand and look in the mirror and do it himself. Then he turned to her and caught her hands in his. "You're shaking."

"I guess reaction is setting in."

Josh smiled at her. "You're a regular little alley cat. You decked him, all by yourself."

"Believe me, I needed you here."

He looked at the bruises appearing on her throat and swore softly. "I'm glad you hit him and I'm glad I hit him, and I'd like to hit him again."

She wrapped her arms around Josh and hugged him. "It's over. Really over. Carter is out of my life forever."

Josh held her close, knowing it was over. All of it—the good and the bad. Now she would go home and disappear from his life.

It took twenty more minutes for Josh to talk her into

staying at the house. Then he left to return to the fire. For the next few hours, as he worked putting out the blaze, all he could think about was Laurie's leaving.

She would walk out of his life forever, and there wasn't anything either one of them could do to change that. And he realized that, in spite of all his caution, all the years of guarding his heart, he was in love. For the first time in his life, he was deeply, truly in love. Hopelessly in love with a woman who was as impossible for him as reaching up and grasping a star.

He loved her! The realization shook him and hurt. How had she gotten so completely past his guard? Was he wrong, and mistaking lust for love? He knew he wasn't. He loved her and wanted her in his life forever.

She couldn't stay, and it would be easier for her to leave if he just kept quiet and said goodbye.

Josh fought the fire, his heart not in the battle, but struggling with another loss that was coming.

It was daylight before the fire was under control. He was bone weary, aching from the firefighting and from his fight with Carter, and hurting because he would have to tell Laurie goodbye. He didn't think she would linger. She had the world to go home to. A family, a fantastic job, friends.

He thanked neighbors and friends for helping, thanked the firemen, and finally headed for his pickup. Laurie sat on the fender, and his heart missed a beat.

"How'd you get out here?"

"I found one of the guys who had come back to the bunkhouse, and he gave me a ride. I haven't been here long or I would have helped battle the fire."

She looked as solemn as he felt, and they rode home together quietly. "You have broken furniture in your bedroom," she said at last. "I stacked it in the next room. You'll have to take care of it."

"Thank you. I'm going to shower."

She had showered and looked fresh and gorgeous in a red T-shirt and cutoffs. "Are you hungry? I can fix something for you to eat," she offered.

He agreed and left her, thinking about her all the time he showered and changed to a clean T-shirt and jeans. As he passed her open door, he spotted her suitcase on the bed. He stepped inside, and saw that it was partially packed.

The hurt he felt deepened even more. Parting had come too swiftly.

He went downstairs to find her in the kitchen, looking out the window. He crossed the room to put his hands on her shoulders and turn her to face him.

As she looked into Josh's deep green eyes, Laurie's pulse skipped. He looked solemn, almost angry, yet with all that had happened, she understood.

"It's beautiful here. You were right about that. I'll always remember it," she told him.

"Yeah," he said gruffly. "I ought to kiss you and let you go, because I know I'm going to have to, but I've been thinking about it all through the night and this morning. You were right. I want you to stay. I know you have to go back to your life. There's nothing here to compare to it, and I can't offer you half of what you already have at home. But I love you, Laurie."

Stunned, she gazed up at him. Her first reaction was joy, and she flung her arms around his neck, kissing him. He hugged her back, giving her one of those bone-melting, heart-stopping kisses that wiped every thought from her mind. Finally, when he released her, she looked up at him dazedly. And then reality set in and she thought about all her ties to Kansas City—her home, her future, her career.

Hurt swamped her and she touched his cheek, seeing the pain she felt reflected in his eyes. "I love you," she said solemnly. "But I don't know what we can do about it. Neither one of us can give up what we do. You have to live here and work on the ranch. I'm a model and it's all I know, plus I have the agency.''

He nodded and moved away, jamming his hands into his pockets. ''So what are your plans?''

''I've already made plane reservations for a flight at four this afternoon. I'll have to be at the airport two hours early. I called Emily to tell her that I'm coming home and Carter has been arrested. I figure Sheriff Cordoba will be out here this morning to take our statements.''

''I'm sure he will,'' Josh said solemnly, and she hurt, feeling something inside her breaking into a million pieces.

''I better go pack,'' Laura said, wanting to get away from him before she burst into tears. She hurried upstairs. *He loves me.* That was all she could think.

She finished packing and moved through the day, too aware of Josh, thinking only that he loved her.

Departure hour arrived, and Josh drove her solemnly to the San Antonio airport. Laurie checked her suitcases—her old one, plus a new one she had purchased to hold the clothes Becky had bought for her.

Finally Josh walked as far as nonpassengers were allowed to wait with her. They stood where they would be alone, and he leaned a shoulder against the wall, touching her collar. She had changed to a blue shirt and navy skirt, and her hair was fastened behind her head.

''You'll go home from here with scars.''

''We both have scars,'' she answered quietly.

''Now you won't have to sell your agency.''

She shrugged. ''I don't know. Emily said I had an eager buyer. It might be better to start over again without the taint of Carter. His presence was pervasive.''

They talked quietly until her flight was called. Then she studied Josh, looking into his green eyes and brushing dark

locks of his hair off his forehead. A knot hurt her throat.
''I don't want to go.''

''Then don't.''

She shook her head. ''I have to go and you have to stay.
Are we going to kiss goodbye?''

''It'll make things worse.''

''If you don't, I will.''

He wrapped his arms around her and pulled her to him
to kiss her long and hard, and she responded passionately.
Tears did fall and she could taste the salt, but she didn't
care. She loved him as she had never loved any man and
never would again.

He stepped back. ''You better go, Laurie,'' he said.
''You'll miss your plane.''

He looked angry and hurt. She wiped her eyes and turned
to hurry through security looking one more time at Josh.

Josh watched her, knowing he had done what he had
sworn never to do—lost his heart. He was in love and it
was forever. And she was breaking his heart into a million
pieces.

He watched her disappear down the hall. She was gone.
He straightened the hat on his head. There wasn't any point
in staying until the plane taxied down the runway. He turned
away, hating the burning knot in his throat. She was gone,
and he had known from the very first day that this time
would come.

He strode through the airport without conscious thought
of the people around him or where he was going. When he
stepped outside into sunshine, he paused, disoriented momentarily, trying to think where he had parked his pickup.
Remembering, he went striding away from the terminal.

''Josh! Josh!''

He whipped around and saw Laurie dashing after him.
For one stunned moment he blinked and couldn't believe
his eyes.

"Josh, wait!"

His heart thudded as he ran toward her, catching her up in his arms to kiss her hard.

He paused, holding her. "You missed your plane?"

"No!" She was crying and laughing at the same time. "I can do something here. I'm selling the agency. Why not open one in San Antonio? I don't care. I'm in love—what's there to go home to? This is home."

He was scared to breathe. "That's a snap decision. You better think it over."

"You think so?" she asked, tilting her head to give him one of her saucy looks.

"Oh, hell no! Will you marry me?" he asked, his heart pounding with joy.

"Of course I will! Didn't I warn you—"

He silenced her with another kiss, until a car honked and he realized they were standing in the street. "Come on. I'm taking you home. We've got a wedding to plan—and it's going to be soon!"

Epilogue

Josh stood impatiently in the shade of a tall oak. The day was what he and Laurie had hoped for, one with blue skies, bright sunshine and a warm spring breeze. The hillsides were blanketed in red Indian paintbrush, red lantana and yellow coreopsis, all dazzling against lush green fields. Every spring of his life Josh had looked at this land and thought the ranch was the most beautiful place on earth, but today he was only dimly aware of his surroundings or the people with him. He was barely conscious of Gabe Brant, his best man, standing beside him, because his attention was on the back door of the house. He was waiting for Laurie to appear.

Her uncle was giving her away, both sisters were maids of honor and Ben and Kevin were groomsmen. Josh's gaze roamed over the crowd, watching as each stepmother was seated. He felt a pang, wishing that his father were here. He reminded himself that he had the rest of his family, and now there would be Laurie.

He shifted impatiently. She should be coming out of the house. He was anxious to see her, anxious to say the vows that would bind them together.

Gabe jabbed him lightly in the arm with his elbow. "Check the guests."

Josh glanced at his best man, who was looking straight ahead. Josh's gaze shifted to the audience. He saw Ashley holding their little girl, Ella, with Julian, their son, dressed in his best. Ashley was smiling at her husband. Josh saw his stepmothers, all beautiful women, some remarried, some single. He scanned the other guests—ranchers, bankers, cowboys, cooks—and then his gaze went back to one and a shock jolted him. A broad-shouldered, black-haired man with a deep tan, mirrored sunglasses hiding his eyes, sat near the back row of chairs.

It looked like Wyatt Sawyer, yet it couldn't be! Wyatt— after all these years. Yet Gabe must have thought it was him or he wouldn't have told Josh to look at the guests. The man looked like Wyatt, yet didn't. And what would he be doing here?

Then Josh remembered the deaths of Wyatt's brother and sister-in-law. Had that brought his old friend home?

The music changed, and Josh forgot the guests, forgot Wyatt, forgot everything else as he watched Laurie's sisters emerge from the house. Emily was shorter than Laurie, with straight blond hair, but she was a beautiful woman with large blue eyes and peaches-and-cream skin. Talia was taller, equally lovely, with short, cropped, honey-blond hair. Then his bride appeared on the steps of the house, a breath-taking vision of beauty. Josh stared, his knees going weak. Tall, dressed in white, with her golden hair tumbling over her shoulders, Laurie was radiant. Smiling, she came toward him. Her long white dress showed her curves and tiny waist and slender arms. She looked gorgeous, and Josh was over-whelmed with love for her. Everything faded except Laurie's smile and then she was there, her uncle placing her hand in Josh's. He gazed down into her luminous brown eyes and he felt as if he would burst with happiness.

They repeated their vows, and as he said them, Josh meant them with all his heart. He wanted to love and cherish her forever, and intended to spend a lifetime showing her how he felt about her.

"You may kiss the bride."

He turned back her veil, smiling at her, feeling as if they were in their own world in spite of all the guests. He leaned down to kiss her lightly, a promise of deepest love.

And then they were hurrying past their guests, to the patio where the reception would begin. They posed for pictures and then joined the festivities.

Caroline was one of the first to speak to them, hugging Josh and then turning to hug Laurie. She leaned back to look at Laurie. "I am happy for both of you and I'm not surprised. After he brought you back to the ranch that Sunday morning, I think I expected this to happen."

Laurie laughed. "I didn't. Not at that time. But I hope you're all right with it. I love him."

"At the time, we were all worried about his safety, but I'm glad you came back. He needs you. I wish you both all the happiness in the world. Josh deserves a good marriage."

Laurie smiled at her, glad to find the family was accepting her.

Gabe and Ashley came to congratulate them. "I want you to meet Julian," Ashley said, looking around. "Right now he's playing with other children." She held a little black-haired girl. "This is Ella."

"Hi, Ella," Laurie said, smiling at the child, who smiled in return.

"You're a beautiful bride," Gabe said to Laurie. "And you've got one heck of a husband."

"Thank you. I think so," she exclaimed fervently.

He turned to Josh. "Congratulations! I'm glad for both of you." Gabe grinned. "Maybe that old legend about the white stallion is true. Look at us!"

"Baloney!" Josh said, smiling at Laurie. "That horse didn't have anything to do with this."

"Wyatt is here," Gabe said. "We just talked to him, and he met my family."

"I can't believe it," Josh said quietly, staring at the tall man approaching them. He looked faintly familiar, yet at the same time a stranger. Wyatt Sawyer was a man now, not a boy, as he had been the last time Josh had seen him. His wild black hair was cut shorter, yet still unruly. He was thicker through the shoulders, tanned. Josh clasped his extended hand and hugged him.

"I can't believe it," he repeated.

"I got here for your wedding," Wyatt stated huskily. Then he turned to smile at Laurie. "And I can't believe this gorgeous woman is marrying you."

Josh laughed and slipped an arm around Laurie's waist. "Laurie, meet my friend Wyatt Sawyer. My new bride, Mrs. Josh Kellogg."

"It's Laurie," she said, smiling.

"I was sorry to hear about Hank and Olivia," Josh said. "Is that why you're back?"

"Yes, it is."

Gabe's eyes twinkled. "He's been asking our advice. Guess why?"

Josh looked from Wyatt to Gabe. "Something's up. Advice on what—cows, horses, marriage?"

"Kids," Wyatt answered. "I've inherited my brother's baby. I'm the legal guardian for Megan."

"That he is," Gabe replied. "You're married—the impossible—and Wyatt is back, to be a father for a baby girl—even more impossible."

"No more impossible than a Ryder marrying a Brant,"

Wyatt retorted. "People are waiting to talk to you two," he said to Josh. "I'm here to stay, and we'll get together after the honeymoon. Congratulations!"

Wyatt, Gabe and Ashley moved away. Josh was filled with questions about his friend, but other guests came up to shake his hand and the afternoon passed in a joyful blur.

"Let's get out of here," he finally said to Laurie.

"It's fine with me. I've already told my family farewell, and your stepmothers, too."

"We're outta here." He took her arm and they went through the back door. Laurie hurried upstairs to change, slipping into a blue sheath dress and pumps and rushing back down to find Josh waiting. He took her arm and they went out the front of the house to his waiting car. Josh drove away swiftly.

In San Antonio they took a plane, and by late afternoon they were in their own villa with a private beach on Cozumel.

"So you do know how to get out of Texas," she said.

"Occasionally." Josh handed her a glass of champagne and raised his own.

"I'm causing you to drink?" she asked, arching a brow.

"This is a reason to really celebrate. To a long, long, happy married life, Mrs. Kellogg."

"I'll drink to that, Mr. Kellogg." Their arms entwined, each sipped from the other's glass, and then Josh took the glasses and set them aside.

"Now, come here and let me show you how much I love you," he said, pulling Laurie into his arms.

She wrapped her arms around his neck while he bent his head to kiss her. She felt his hands at the back of her dress as he pulled down the zipper.

Laurie kissed him back, holding him tightly, knowing she had made the right decision. And she intended that Josh would have the long, happy marriage he deserved.

* * * * *

And don't miss

THE RANCHER, THE BABY
& THE NANNY

the third Texas tale in Sara Orwig's
crossover miniseries
STALLION PASS
Rodeo rider and consummate bachelor
Wyatt Sawyer taking care of a baby?
This Texan hunk needs help—and fast.
Grace Talmadge is confident she can take
care of Wyatt's infant niece—but
can she handle her sexy new employer?

Coming to
Silhouette Desire
in January 2003

For a sneak preview, just turn the page.

One

"**O**h, no!" Holding a baby in his arms, Wyatt Sawyer stood at the window of his Texas ranch home and watched a woman get out of her car. As she approached the house, his practiced gaze ran over her and he immediately scratched her off his list of possibilities for nanny. She looked like a child herself. Naturally curly red hair was clipped behind her head with a few tendrils flying loose. Her lack of makeup and a nondescript gray jumper and white blouse made her appear to be sixteen years old.

"How many nannies will I have to interview for you?" he asked the sleeping baby and shifted her in his arms. Momentarily he gazed at his five-month-old niece and warmth filled him.

"Megan, darlin', we'll find the right nanny. I'm going to take the best care of you I can." He held her up and kissed her forehead lightly, then returned his attention to the woman approaching the door.

Bright May sunshine splashed over her, revealing a fresh scrubbed look that added to her youthful appearance. Wyatt wished he could inquire her age because it was difficult to imagine she was a day over eighteen, tops. Wyatt's gaze ran over her again, and dimly it registered with him that she had long legs. He thought about two of the women he had interviewed who had been beauties. Both times, when they had walked into the room, his heart had skipped a beat. Three minutes into the interview, he knew he could never leave Megan with either one of them.

He sighed. Why was it a monumental task to find good help? The pay he was offering was fabulous. But he knew the drawbacks—they'd have to live out on his ranch. Most women wouldn't accept a king's ransom to suffer such isolation. Those from ranching and farm backgrounds weren't any more interested than city women. Either that, or applicants were looking for a prospective husband, and Wyatt had no interest in matrimony.

The doorbell chimed, cutting into his thoughts, and he went to answer it. He swung open the door and stared down into wide, thickly lashed green eyes that stabbed through him with a startling sharpness. For seconds they were locked into a silent stare, a strange new experience for Wyatt. He blinked and studied her more closely. Faint freckles dotted her nose.

"Mr. Sawyer, I'm Grace Talmadge."

"Come in. Call me Wyatt," he said, feeling much older than his thirty-three years. How long would it take him to get rid of her? He had gotten the interviews down to twenty minutes per nanny, but this time he planned to give her ten. She could not possibly be over twenty-one.

"This is your little girl?" she asked.

"My niece, Megan. I'm her guardian."

Grace Talmadge looked at the sleeping baby in his arms. "She's a beautiful baby."

"Thanks, I think so. Come in," he repeated.

When Grace passed him, he caught a scent of lemony soap. He closed the door and led the way down a wide hallway, his boot heels scraping the hardwood floor. He paused and motioned her ahead into the family room, following her.

She stood looking around as if she had never been in a room like it.

Wyatt glanced around the room that he rarely gave much attention to. It was the one room in the house that had not been changed since his childhood; the familiar paneling, a mounted, stuffed bobcat, heads of deer and antelope that his father had killed. Shelves were lined with books, bear rugs were spread on the floor, an antique rifle hung over the mantel.

"Have a seat, please," he said, crossing the room, to sit in a rocker. He adjusted the baby in his arms and rocked slightly.

Grace Talmadge sat primly across from him in a dark blue wingback chair, her legs crossed at the ankles and her hands folded in her lap.

"So, Miss Talmadge, have you had any experience being a nanny?"

"No, I haven't," she replied. "I'm a bookkeeper for a San Antonio sign company. I've had my job for five years."

Five years surprised him. Wyatt decided she must have gone to work straight out of high school. "Then why do you want to be a nanny? You realize it means living out here on my ranch?"

"Yes, I understood that from the ad."

"If you've never been a nanny, what are your qualifications for this job? Have you been around children a lot?" Wyatt asked, leaning forward, about ready to escort her out of his house. She had no experience and that crossed her off his list of possibilities immediately.

"Actually, no, I haven't, but I think I can learn." Her voice was soft, soothing to listen to, but Wyatt's patience was frayed from too many interviews over the past few days.

Wyatt stood. "Thank you for driving out here. I know it's a long way, but I need someone with experience for this position."

She stood and faced him. "Have you had a lot of experience as a father?" she asked with a faint smile that revealed a dimple in her right cheek.

Startled, Wyatt focused more sharply on her. "No, I didn't have any choice in the matter, but I'm a blood—" He bit off his words, realizing what he had been about to say. Being a blood relative was no guarantee of love or care.

"At least give me a little chance here, please," she said.

"Why do you want this job if you have no experience? You might hate being a nanny."

She glanced at the baby in his arms. "Oh, no. I could never hate taking care of a little child."

He knew he was losing his tact, but he was worn-out with interviews. "You're not here, looking for a husband, are you? Because I'm not a marrying man."

Startling him, she laughed, revealing white, even teeth and getting a sparkle in her green eyes. "No! Hardly. I have a friend in Stallion Pass so I've heard a little about you. I suspect you and I do not have anything even remotely in common."

He could agree with her on that one. "Sorry, but some women I've interviewed do have marriage in mind, and they've been more than plain-spoken about it. So if you don't know anything about babies and you aren't interested in the possibilities of matrimony, why are you willing to live in isolation with only me and my niece? Why should I give you this job?"

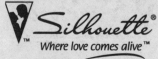

Silhouette® Desire®

**Meet three sexy-as-all-get-out cowboys
in Sara Orwig's new Texas crossline miniseries**

STALLION PASS

These rugged bachelors may have given up on
love…but love hasn't given up on them!

Don't miss this steamy roundup of Texan tales!

DO YOU TAKE THIS ENEMY?
November 2002 (SD #1476)

ONE TOUGH COWBOY
December 2002 (IM #1192)

THE RANCHER, THE BABY & THE NANNY
January 2003 (SD #1486)

Available at your favorite retail outlet.

Silhouette®
Where love comes alive™

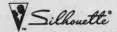

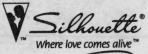

SPECIAL EDITION™

From *USA TODAY* bestselling author

SHERRYL WOODS

comes the continuation of the heartwarming series

Coming in January 2003

MICHAEL'S DISCOVERY

Silhouette Special Edition #1513

An injury received in the line of duty left ex-navy SEAL
Michael Devaney bitter and withdrawn. But Michael hadn't
counted on beautiful physical therapist Kelly Andrews's healing
powers. Kelly's gentle touch mended his wounds, warmed
his heart and rekindled his belief in the power of love.

Look for more Devaneys coming in July and August 2003,
only from Silhouette Special Edition.

Available at your favorite retail outlet.

Where love comes alive™

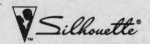

Silhouette®

COMING NEXT MONTH

#1195 WHAT A MAN'S GOTTA DO—Karen Templeton
Single mom Mala Koleski wasn't looking for a husband—especially one like Eddie King, the sexy bad-boy-next-door she'd grown up with. When he blew back into town, alluring as ever, she swore nothing would come of their fun-filled flirtation. But was this no-strings-attached former rebel about to sign up as a family man?

#1196 ALIAS SMITH AND JONES—Kylie Brant
The Tremaine Tradition

To find her missing brother, Analiese Tremaine became Ann Smith and traveled to the South Pacific, where he'd last been seen. Her only assistance came from a mysterious man who went by the name Jones. As they searched the jungle, their passion grew hotter than the island nights. And though they had to keep their identities secret, their attraction was impossible to hide!

#1197 ALL A MAN CAN ASK—Virginia Kantra
Trouble in Eden

Hotshot Chicago detective Aleksy Denko tracked his suspect to Eden, Illinois, where a convenient cabin made the perfect base—except for stubborn, fragile Faye Harper, who refused to leave. To preserve his cover, Aleksy found himself playing house with the shy art teacher—and liking it. Until his suspect cornered Faye. Then Aleksy realized he could handle danger, but how could he handle life without Faye?

#1198 UNDER SIEGE—Catherine Mann
Wingmen Warriors

He only meant to pay a courtesy call to military widow Julia Sinclair after her son's birth, but Lt. Col. Zach Dawson ended up making an unconventional proposal. A single father wary of women, Zach asked Julia to be his wife for one year. Soon their false marriage led to real emotions and had Zach wondering what it would take to win Julia's love for life.

#1199 A KISS IN THE DARK—Jenna Mills
Falsely accused of murder, Bethany St. Croix had one chance to save herself and her unborn child: Dylan St. Croix, her ex-husband's cousin. They had shared a powerful love but now were divided by painful differences. Drawn together again, could they put their past aside in time to save their future?

#1200 NORTHERN EXPOSURE—Debra Lee Brown
Searching for a new life, fashion photographer Wendy Walters fled the city streets for the Alaskan wilderness. There she met Joe Peterson, a rugged game warden set on keeping her off his land and out of his heart. But when Wendy was targeted by an assassin, Joe rushed to her rescue, and suddenly the heat burning between them was hot enough to melt any ice.

INTIMATE MOMENTS